Hate Lovers

Mandy,
There's a fine
line between
love and hate!

K WEBSTER
J.D. HOLLYFIELD

Hate 2 Lovers
Copyright © 2017 K Webster
Copyright © 2017 J.D. Hollyfield

ISBN-13: 978-1544804743
ISBN-10: 1544804741

Cover Design: All By Design
Photo: Adobe Stock
Editor: PREMA Editing
Formatting: Champagne Formats

This is a work of fiction. Names, characters, places, and incidents either are the product of the author's imagination or are used fictitiously, and any resemblance to actual persons, living or dead, business establishments, events, or locales is entirely coincidental.

Dedication

This book is dedicated to the two most amazing gals we know…*us.*

Dear Reader,

We hope you enjoy Andie and Roman's story! Writing together is an absolute joy for us and we hope that shows! As with Text 2 Lovers, one of us took the hero's POV and the other took the heroine's POV. If you read the first book, you'll remember! We'll also tell you at the end.

It is best if you've read Text 2 Lovers first though because you'll understand the dynamic of Andie and Roman better…plus, you don't want to miss out on all the laughs from book one!

Enjoy and we'll see you on the other side!
K Webster and J.D. Hollyfield

"I love you." – Princess Leia
"I know." – Han Solo

Star Wars: The Empire Strikes Back

Chapter One

Andie

Did the Whorehouse Lose a Whore?

WHEN SWEET LITTLE GIRLS GROW UP, THEY'RE taught manners. How to be polite. The whole sit-properly-with-your-back-straight and smile pleasantly thing. *Yes, please. No, thank you.* Fucking curtsey and all that shit.

Not me.

Unlike Dani, my best friend, I missed those lessons. I missed them all. When one parent decides he's not capable of being a parent, and the other one, who was supposed to teach you how to grow up into a lady, slowly dies in front of you, you have no one else to pick up where they left off. Those lessons are shelved for a later date called never because nobody else cared to teach them.

Having an absent dad from the time I was a child and losing my mom as a teenager set the mold for the person I became. I'm not a crier or a whiner. I don't need to be coddled, hugged, or fed fuzzy, bullshit lines to make myself feel better or wanted.

Because that's not who I, Andrea Grace Miller, am.

I am a driven, tough-as-nails, ball-busting woman. Andie.

A chick with a guy's nickname and the mouth of a sailor.

And a thirst for physical violence when I'm pissed.

I'm unbreakable.

At least that's what I keep telling myself while I snap and spit out the one thing I swore I wasn't going to tell him.

I'm pregnant.

The shock in his gaze was immediate. Any smart girl would equate that to an *Oh-I-am-so-fucked* look. I just told the successful Roman Holloway he's going to be a dad. And that asshole has the gall to look like *he's* the one who's fucked?

NEWSFLASH: I'M THE ONE WHO'S FUCKING PREGNANT!

I want to turn back around and take him out one shin at a time. It's his weak spot—I know this because he wears a permanent bruise on both. Because of me.

But sadly, this new side of me, which I'm battling with figuring out where it came from, overtakes my anger. This new side that causes me to cry at the drop of a hat is calling the shots. I snap at a simple glance and become insanely sad over normally lame Hallmark commercials that I once made fun of.

I am not only pregnant. I am possessed.

He possessed me.

Fucking Roman.

And he is more worried about himself.

I'm out of his office in a flash as I rush to the exit. But the problem is, my lower lip is out of control as it quivers with the threat of a good ol' freak show cry, and I'm seconds away from yacking up my breakfast. I make a beeline to the bathroom and slip into one of the stalls. The moment the door swings shut, I slide down the wall inside and burst into tears.

How did this happen?

Well, fuck. I know *how* it happened, but why me?

Surely, I could have handled breaking the news to him a little better.

I just stormed into his office demanding…*well nothing at first*. I'd wanted to punish him for knocking me up. To throttle him for giving me something I'm not sure I'm capable of handling. Then, the prick had the audacity to be gentle and kind. Friggin' offered me a job for Christ's sake! Still, I had to get all crazy and demand a bunch of dumb ass shit. And he said yes to every single silly request. I'd actually softened to him in that moment. Allowed a tiny prickle of hope to shine inside me.

But that look when I spilled the beans…

He doesn't want this.

An ache forms in my chest.

Oh my God, who would!?

I'm like a fucking hurricane. He probably only saw destruction in his future.

I begin to cry harder. Then even harder, if *that's* possible, because now I'm even more upset about crying in the first place.

Because I do. Not. Cry.

3

The door to the bathroom swings open with a loud creak and bangs against the wall.

"Someone's in here!" I yell.

I expect them to leave, but the door to the stall I'm in—which I apparently forgot to lock—is pushed open. When I lift my head, I see Roman standing above me.

Sexy god of a man. Motherfucker.

"Get out." I sniffle though my tears, trying to wipe the wetness from my cheeks.

He's giant and solid and too fucking big for this bathroom. "Not a chance," he tells me in that no-nonsense, low voice of his. "You just threw a bomb back there and you're going to explain." His eyes are narrowed as if they have the power to yank information from my head. "Now, Andie."

Nope.

Wrong move.

No one, and I mean no fucking one, tells me what to do.

I scramble to my feet and attempt to push him out of the way, but he's like a steel wall.

He growls, and I hate how it makes my body respond. Sometimes I provoke him on purpose just to hear that sexy, gravelly grumble. But today I'm upset, and I will *not* let my body call the shots.

His hand grips my elbow as he says, "I've allowed you to throw all your mood swings at me, and I take them. Every goddamned time. Hell only knows why. I allow you to have everything your way every time we're together. You storm in and out on me. But this time…" His gaze hardens. "Instead of just reacting, you're going to explain."

Fire builds up within me. My brain only knows one way to *react*. So that's why I do what I do…I *react* angrily.

And punch him.

"Jesus!"

"No," I spit out at him, trying to free myself from his iron grip. "Jesus has nothing to do with this. Damn you! I regret ever coming to this stupid place!" Despite my wriggling, he isn't giving in and grabs for my shoulders. With firm but gentle movements, he guides me so my back is now touching the wall.

"Baby…" he starts. I flinch at the endearment and he quickly continues, "I'm not playing games with you right now. Are you…are you really pregnant?"

God, even hearing him say it guts me. I start to cry again, my emotions out of control. He wraps his massive arms around me as if to console me, and my tears soak his fancy dress shirt. For a moment, I relax in his comforting grip. His scent calms me. His strength consumes me.

But it only takes a few more seconds for my brain to catch up and push my heart out of the fucking way. My mood flips on a dime and anger is again running the show.

"Yeah," I snap as I push away from him. This time, he allows me to break from his grasp, and I storm toward the door. Before opening it, I whip around and finish my thought. "But don't worry. I'm not keeping it."

Horror washes over his features.

His normally calm, smug face is pinched up in… *pain*?

That look shakes me to my core.

I know I'm keeping it, but he doesn't. Strangely, I already feel something fierce and protective over the little fucking thing that's inside me. But I won't drag Roman through this. Not if he doesn't want it. Before he can formulate a response, I turn back to the door and slip out so he can't stop me. The door swings open behind me, but he doesn't reach me before I run into Dani.

"Oh!" she says in surprise as I nearly run her over. "Sorry. Uh...Ram said he saw you two...um...well..." she stammers. "And he thought I should come back to... uh, get Andie." She darts her eyes up at me and then to Roman, who's breathing heavily behind me.

I suck in a deep breath, forcing myself to pull it together. "Great idea. I'm right here. Let's go," I reply quickly, but Roman is already on me.

"No," he growls, his warm hand gripping my shoulder possessively. "She's staying right here until we're done." His fingers send currents of awareness trickling through me. I count each digit as they rest on my skin. The same burn that I feel every damn time he touches me.

His voice is low and soft, his breath warm and I can smell a hint of coffee on him, as he pleads with me. "Baby, please. Don't leave like this. We need to talk. About everything."

His words are spoken with a vulnerability that I'm not used to hearing from Roman. It has me faltering for a moment. I want to let go and relax my body against his. Let him hold me like he does when he thinks I've fallen asleep, but in reality, I'm wide awake basking in the warmth of his masculinity.

I close my eyes to relish the moment, but then I'm replaying that look of shock on his face when I'd told him about the baby. Terror. Fear. Disappointment. Regret.

Popping my eyes back open to avoid that memory, I turn to him and stand my ground. "There's nothing to talk about," I tell him in a cold tone. "Your expression when I told you said enough." An ache forms in the pit of my belly.

"Roman," Dani says in a worried tone. "I think it's best if Andie comes with me right now."

I watch his eyes go lax, the way they become when I know he's about to go soft teddy bear on me. I can't stand his softness. I'm just not built to withstand it. His gaze never leaves mine as he ignores my best friend. "Tell Dani I'm not the asshole you claim me to always be," he murmurs, his fingers twisting around a strand of my hair. I'm seconds from leaning into his touch and forgetting everything if he'll simply hug away all of the stress. "Tell her that I'm not going to tie you up and beat you if she leaves you with me."

His words spark the memory of our last fight. When I mentioned getting kinky and wanting to do a little role-play. When he refused because he didn't want to hurt me. My anger spikes to dangerous levels. Is he seriously trying to throw that in my face now?

"Oh, you know what? Sorry, Charlie," I hiss. "No can do. Because you *are* an asshole." Dani gasps behind me, and his eyes flicker in surprise. As if I've struck him. The thought of actually doing so is tempting. But then he hardens his gaze as I continue. "And even if I did allow you to tie me up and spank me, you'd probably suck at it."

Roman's eyes blaze with anger. He knows I'm still mad about that. He silently gives me his *you-know-why-I-didn't-want-to* stare down, but I give him the same ol' *I-hate-you* glare.

Because I do.

I hate everything about that handsome oaf of a man. I swear it.

My bottom lip begins its stupid twitching routine again, and I know I need to get out of here before I break down in front of him once more. "Leave me alone, Roman," I tell him shakily. "I'm sorry I even told you." I actually shock myself when the words come out less harsh and more emotional. "Let's go," I whisper when I turn back to Dani.

Her arm wraps around me, and she pulls me to her tiny side. Together, we walk out of Holloway Advertising and Branding and I don't look back.

"Such a pretty day outside, don't you think?" Dani asks, trying to get me to talk as we drive to Bender's. She first suggested my place, but I can't go back there right now. For starters, my bathroom is littered with pregnancy tests. And when I say littered, I mean, I can build a fucking addition with how many I pissed on this morning only for them *all* to have the same fucking result. Two horrible, blue lines.

If maybe I would have just believed the first five I pissed on, all confirming the one thing I was praying to every single god out there to not be true, I wouldn't have been late to work. I wouldn't have told off my boss. And I certainly wouldn't have gotten fired. But I had to spend some time staring into space, wondering how in the hell I was going to get out of the mess I was in.

"Sure," I finally answer Dani, my voice but a whisper. "Nice day."

I'm gazing out the window, trying to decide if I should open the door and throw myself out when I realize my phone's been going off in my pocket. Pulling it out, I see a slew of text messages from Roman.

Roman: Please, don't do this. Talk to me.
Roman: This decision belongs to both of us. You're not alone.
Roman: Please don't do anything until we talk.
Roman: What if I told you I want this?

Reading the last message, my eyes begin to blur with tears. He doesn't even know what he's talking about. He can't *want* this. *We* are nothing. We're fuck buddies. I'm using him for his hot body and beautiful dick. And that thing he does with his tongue…

We're not supposed to have a baby together!

"Are you okay?" Dani questions, her eyes darting all over me in concern.

I'm crying. Again. "God, yeah, not sure what's wrong with me." I wipe at my wet cheeks with my jacket sleeve, taking in a deep breath.

Pull it together, idiot.

"Are you sure you want to go to Bender's?" she asks in a gentle tone, which normally soothes me. Today, nothing is soothing me. "We can go to my place if you don't want to go to yours."

"No," I snap a little too harshly. "Bender's. We need to drink. Lots of drinking. Day drinking for the win." Maybe if I pretend this isn't happening, it will all just go away. Seems like a good plan.

Dani flashes me a wary look, but I can't talk about it. Not right now, even with my best friend. There is still a chance that the entire aisle of pregnancy tests was from bad batches.

"Okay then…" Her shoulders shrug. She knows something's up but backs off. Dani knows me well enough to know when not to push. At least someone is smart enough.

We make it to Bender's and it's slow, being that it's just before the lunch rush. After spotting Brett at the bar flirting with a patron, we take our normal seats. I slam my hand on the bar to get his attention, causing Lunchtime Barbie to jump and Brett to turn.

"Well, well…" he says with an easy grin as he saunters over to us. "Did they let school out early today?"

"Did the whorehouse lose a whore?" I bite back, not in the mood to flirt. "Jesus, isn't it too early to be walking the streets?" I snap my gaze over to the bimbo down the bar. Brett laughs, while Dani shakes her head. "What? Seriously! That's not what the sign on the door meant, when it said '*It's a paying establishment*.'" I roll my eyes and grab for the menu. "Brett, buddy, get us a line of shots. And two cheeseburgers. Fries, too. Oh, and… and… a side of wings. Hmm…" I scan the menu. Everything sounds good now that my sickness seems to have left the building. "What else? Fuck it. Cheese sticks.

And whatever Dani wants." I throw the menu back on the bar, noticing two sets of eyes staring at me. "What?"

"Um… Nothing," Dani says with a chuckle. "You just ordered a lot of food."

I shrug my shoulders. "Pffft. Just snacks. But fine. Whatever. We'll share."

"Oh, that was all for you?" She gapes at me in shock. I realize I did just order a meal big enough for a family and even some leftovers for the dog.

Shit.

But I'm *so* hungry.

No I'm not.

Yes, actually, I am!

I can't help it, though. I fully understand the meaning of eating one's emotions right now. I just need to eat those two cheeseburgers, and then I feel like life will look better.

With a shake of his head, Brett keys in our order on the computer and returns, placing four shots on the bar. He fills each one to the brim. Dani is staring at me suspiciously, and I'm eyeing the shots. Not in a good way.

Guilt.

Disgust.

"Well, ready?" Dani asks, picking up a shot and handing it to me.

I accept it with hesitation, my heart rate thudding. She's waiting for me to go first. *Dammit.* A few seconds pass. Then some more.

With a sigh, I set the shot back on the bar. "I… I can't drink that."

Dani quickly plunks her own shot down on the

counter before turning to me. Stupid tears are already streaming down my face.

"And why can't you drink that?" she questions softly.

"Because I fucked up," I tell her with a sob. "And badly." I drop my head to the bar and proceed to gently bang my head on it over and over again. Dani starts rubbing my back, while Brett, the kind fucker he is, puts a towel between me and the bar to avoid injury.

"Honey, it's okay," she assures me. "I'm sure everything is going to be okay—"

I jerk my head up, my eyes wide with shock. "How are things going to be okay? Dani, I'm pregnant," I blurt out. "As in, with child. Knocked up. Carrying a bastard child inside of me! It's *not* going to be okay!"

"But it is," she kindly argues back, not at all surprised by my confession.

"Earth to Dani," I say, waving my hand in front of her face. "I just told you I was having a fucking baby. Me! Why are you not shocked or flipping the hell out with me? Why haven't you smacked me for being so careless or lectured me about the sanctity of marriage before children?" Where the fuck am I even going with this rant? I have completely lost my marbles. I pick up the water Brett graciously brought over and start chugging it, needing to just shut up for a damn second.

"Well…because I kind of already figured it out," she replies.

And…the water comes spitting back out. "You what?!"

Dani snorts her silly little laugh that I love—a laugh that possibly Ram loves more—then pats me on the

12

shoulder. "Honey, you have been"—she speaks slowly as to choose her words carefully—"let's just say, a little off lately. You get hormonal close to your period, but this is a"—her nose scrunches—"shall I say, brighter side of you?" Then she chuckles. "I mean, you cried when we watched *Dracula, Untold* last week and, well, that isn't exactly a movie one would cry at so, yeah."

Don't do it.

Don't do it.

Don't…

FUCK!

A loud, ugly sob escapes me. Why am I so broken? Are these, like, all the built-up tears I never shed? All coming out now to haunt me? Dani wraps me up in her tiny, but comforting, arms as tears of confusion leak from my eyes all over her puffy pink sweater.

"Dani, this is not good," I choke out. "This is me turning out to be just like my mom." Even though I swore I would make different choices—better choices—I still ended up following the same path.

An unplanned pregnancy. A rushed marriage. A father who vowed he would be there through it all. That he would love her. But then she got sick, and it was all too much for him to bear. Daddy Miller took off the moment things got tough. *I didn't sign up for this*, he'd said, and *I wasn't even meant to be a dad.*

And as I held my mother's hand as she took her last breath, she asked me—had the *nerve* to beg me to make peace with my dad. To fix things with the man who walked out on his dying wife and young daughter.

As if!

He left her to take care of me all alone, which really meant me taking care of her. She cried in her room every night when she thought I couldn't hear her. Never put his pictures away and always lit a candle on holidays for him. Through everything that he did to her, somehow she still loved him.

That man will never deserve my forgiveness.

"Andie, you are not like your mom and dad," Dani insists, her sweet voice dragging me from my inner hell. "Your mom loved you, and she made the best choice ever. To keep you and have you. And I wish I could thank her myself every day for my best friend." Her gaze is serious. "Listen. I'm going to assume it's Roman's, right?"

I give her the crazy eye. Does she really think I'm some hussy who's unsure who my baby daddy is? "Dude!" I snap.

"Well," she continues quickly. "You two feel the need to pretend no one around you has figured out you two are together but—"

"We are *NOT* together!" I screech. "I hate that fat oaf!" He's not fat but his head is.

Dani sighs next to me. "Okay, let's try this again. Let's just say, *hypothetically*, you and Roman may have had a thing. And he, *hypothetically*, may be the father of this baby. I think if you sat down and talked to him, you would be surprised by his reaction. I'm no love guru, but I think that man has it bad for you. I mean, Ram told me he made you his executive assistant. I agree, that's a bad idea right off the—"

Hold the phone. "Wait," I interrupt. "You think he has it bad for me, like *likes* me? As in more-than-just-fuck-buddies likes me?"

Another little sweet sigh. "Andie, open your eyes. That man has it *way* bad for you."

I take a moment to think about us and how it's been. Sex. Lots of hot fucking sex. All the touching and fighting to get at one another. The passion. The steam between us.

But then he always ruins it by opening his damn mouth. Trying to feed me lines, like I'm another one of the bimbos who he wines and dines. I won't fall for that. Roman is just like my father. A businessman who has it all. Looks, money, fancy car. My dad could have given our family the perfect life. But he chose to leave. He made a choice to abandon my mom. To abandon me. Because that's what asshole men do.

When I was younger, I read through the letters my dad used to write my mom. Sweet with those stupid trigger words that would make a girl's heart melt. You would have thought that at one point, he actually did love her. But not enough to stay. And in the end, my mom died, not only of sickness but from a broken heart.

I will *not* do the same.

I am not weak like her.

I shake my head and grumble. "Well, I don't care. He's not on my radar. Goddammit, Brett! Where is our food!?" I yell across the bar, causing a few lunch patrons to stare my way. "What!? Haven't you ever seen a hungry pregnant person before! Look away, you fucksticks!"

Thankfully for everyone else in the place, Brett begins placing baskets of food in front of me. I know it's because I have a demon inside of me. A curse, not the baby. So when I look down at the juicy burger, I swear it smiles back at me. I cradle the precious thing in my grip and bend down to lock my teeth around it when Dani speaks.

"Well, what are you going to do?" she implores. "You can't pretend this isn't happening."

Ugh, yes I can. I can sit here and eat this burger. Then, since I know Dani will take three bites and be full because she's like a mouse, I'm going to continue to sit here and eat hers, too. "For now," I tell her firmly, "we pretend it's not happening. I don't want to hear the name Roman, for the next twenty-four to forty-eight billion hours. Got it?" I bend back down, the perfect bite in view.

"But in forty-eight billion hours you will have a child. And you may want to have talked to him about it before then."

UGH! I love her, but she needs to shut up. I drop my burger and turn to face her. And because I love her so, I am not going to attack her with my vicious words and temperament. "Dani, let's put it this way right now. Roman and I are nothing. This *hiccup?* It's something I'll have to deal with, *after* I eat this burger, possibly *after* I eat those mozzarella sticks and wings. And most likely *waaaaay* after that. Let me pretend my life is normal. Just for a moment."

She looks at me with sadness in her eyes but nods. Smart girl. I finally get to dig into the burger and moan at the explosion of flavor in my mouth. I wish this juicy burger were my baby daddy because I seriously love it right now. I'm halfway through mine when I see Dani pick hers up to take a nibble. I squeeze mine harder, letting out a feral growl.

Dani notices and looks my way, then slowly puts her burger down. "What… Oh… Did you want this?"

My eyes light up and I take a large bite. "I mean if wour not going to weat it." I munch, a smile breaching my face, knowing I now have two yummy baby daddies to shovel down.

Chapter Two

Roman

I'm Playing for Fucking Keeps

FUCK.

Fuck.

Fuck.

I should chase her out into the parking lot and beg her to hear me out, but I get the sinking feeling she needs to calm down a bit first before I try again. With Andie, you have to go with the psychotic flow. Sometimes you ride the waves and it's bliss. Other times, she tries to drown you.

"Mr. Holloway," a cheerful redhead greets with a broad grin as I pass her desk outside of my sister Reagan's office. I frown for a moment as I try to remember her name.

"Susan—"

"Suzy actually," she interrupts with a high-pitched giggle as if I've just said the funniest damn thing. "Only my momma calls me Susan." Right. Her eyelashes are incredibly long and she keeps blinking them at me as if she has something in her eyes. She should really get that looked at.

I force a smile at her, wave at my sister through the glass, and then barge into Ram's office. He doesn't look away from his computer where he's clicking away in Photoshop.

"What's up?" he questions, his eyes flickering to mine briefly before returning to the screen. "Heard a bunch of yelling."

With a groan, I run my fingers through my hair in frustration. "Lunch. I need some. Now."

He gives me a mildly irritated look at the interruption before locking his computer and standing. "Since Dani stood me up for Andie, I guess I'll go with my big bro instead." He grabs his leather jacket from the back of his chair and regards me with a frown. "Jesus," he murmurs. "You look like shit."

Ignoring him, I stalk out of the building with him hot on my heels and take a moment to admire my car. My motherfucking dream car. The car I've salivated over for the past year, just waiting for the moment when I'd be running my own company and reach the much-anticipated success I've always strived for so I could afford such a thing.

And it happened.

Two months ago, my siblings and I became the proud owners of the biggest ad firm on the east coast. Our client list has grown quickly, and we're doing quite well for ourselves. Which is why last week when I purchased the Z4 Roadster BMW in a shiny black finish, I was fucking giddy. That car drives like a dream—a goddamned wet dream. A two-seater coupe with a sunroof.

Complete with every bell and whistle I could add on. The tan leather interior still smells new, and I have heart palpitations every time I climb inside.

"I love this damn car," Ram says with a whistle, mirroring my thoughts.

We climb in, and I zip through town to one of our favorite restaurants. It isn't until we're inside and we've ordered that I finally speak again.

"Shit's fucked up," I utter, mostly to myself.

Ram's brows pull together in concern. "With our company? A client? That asshole Reagan used to date didn't show up again, did he?"

Rage blooms in my chest at the thought of that prick waltzing into our building a few weeks ago and trying to play our sister again. For a second, I thought she was going to falter and take him back. I mean, he did travel across the country for her. But my sister found her Holloway balls and told him to go to hell. "Not Reagan. It's nothing you need to concern yourself with. I'm just fucked."

The black-haired waitress, Leah is her name, who always waits on us drops two beers down on the worn tabletop and angles her cleavage my way. Normally, I flirt it up with her because she has a nice rack and it's just what I do. But today, I'm not in the mood. Besides, her rack doesn't even begin to compare to a certain someone's…

Goddamn those tits.

"Andie." Ram's low voice jolts me from my thoughts when the waitress walks away.

I snap my eyes to his. "What?"

"It's about Andie. I can tell," he tells me and sips his

lager. "You get that same look in your eyes every time it's about her. What'd she do now? Kick you in the balls? Steal your wallet?" He snorts and amusement flickers in his eyes. "It's about her. Am I right?"

"Yeah…" I trail off and pinch the bridge of my nose. A baby. That crazy-ass woman is knocked up with my child. A flash of possessiveness filters through me, but I quickly chase it away by gulping down my beer. "Her."

Ram's eyebrow quirks up. "Want to talk about it?"

"No," I blurt out.

So we move on to safer topics. Football. His and Dani's wedding plans. Blah, blah, fucking blah. All I can think about is how upset she was. My fierce, strong, fiery woman was crying. The only other time I've seen her even close to being that upset was when we'd been in the throws of a *Your Mom Is So Stupid* insult game that resulted in a spaghetti fight.

Your mom is so stupid that she got hit by a parked car.

Something in my insult triggered an emotion, other than her usual anger, and she'd tearfully told me her mom was dead. I'd felt like such a fucking asshole—that is after she'd started throwing meat sauce at me and I'd finally managed to pin her down. My thoughts drift to that night.

"PUT ME DOWN, YOU BIG OAF!"

I ignore her beating my kidneys to a pulp as I stalk down the hallway with her skinny ass slung over my shoulder. "STOP SQUIRMING, GODDAMMIT. YOU'RE GOING TO GET SAUCE ALL OVER THE WALLS."

She's pissed but still emotional. "I WANT TO GO HOME!"

"NOT UNTIL I CLEAN YOUR ASS!" I swat her round bottom as I push through my bedroom door. She's still wriggling in my arms as I kick the door shut and head straight for the bathroom. I twist the water on and dump her under the icy spray.

"IT'S FUCKING FREEZING, YOU DAMN LUNATIC!" she screeches, killing my eardrums.

"You're the damn lunatic," I growl as I push into the shower with her, also fully dressed. The water is already warming when I begin peeling away my soiled clothes. Her eyes are bloodshot and her plump bottom lip is quivering. Andie is always so strong. Seeing her upset makes my chest ache. The moment I push down my boxers, she holds her hand up.

"OH NO, BUDDY! PUT THAT THING AWAY! YOU ARE NOT GOING TO DISTRACT ME WITH THAT!"

Ignoring her hollering, I get naked and prowl over to her. She doesn't put up much of a fight when I begin slowly unbuttoning her blouse. Her shoulders sag as she gives in to tears. I strip her out of the rest of her clothes before pulling her against my solid chest. Andie is tall but still stands below my chin. Her perfect tits are sandwiched between us, and I ignore the hard-on they're creating. Instead, I stroke her hair and kiss the top of her head.

"I'm sorry."

She lets out a ragged sigh. Seeing her vulnerable like this is rare. I want to cradle her weakness and protect it. To let her know she can show me more of it and that I'll protect that part of her, too. It doesn't always have to be rage and bravery and no fucks given with her. Sometimes, it can be simple and easy. Nice. All she has to do is give me that piece of her.

But, as per usual, she snaps out of her daze. Her soft hands slide up my pectoral muscles and curl around the back of my neck. When I tilt my head down to look into her bright blue eyes, her sadness melts away as desire fights its way front and center. I let out a groan when her lips part. Fuck me, I can never tell that pretty mouth no.

I smash my lips to hers, and so begins a hungry kiss that tastes faintly like spaghetti and longing. I'm sure it's me who's wishing she would give me more. I am definitely the only one doing all the longing around here. Just once I'd love for her to let her guard down and leave it down. Let me in so I can show her what kind of man I can be for her.

My hands find her ass, and I lift her up. Her long legs encircle my waist. Our lips never break apart as I enter her with a hard thrust that has her digging her claws into my neck and releasing a long moan.

I buck into her but break from our kiss. I need to see that look in her eyes again. The soft, broken one. I need that scared person inside of her who hides behind the vicious outer layer to see I can fix things. That I'll make it all better.

"I hate you," she whispers, her lips full and succulent and fucking bitable.

"I know, baby."

Her blue eyes shimmer with tears once more as I make promises to her with my gaze. This seems to spark her orgasm because a moment later, her eyelids flutter as she comes hard around my dick. I grunt out my own release before stealing a long, sweet kiss.

And just like that, it's over again.

"So help me, if that shirt stains, I'm going to stain your backside with Andie-sized footprints," she threatens as she slides her legs back down and pushes me away. Sadness lingers in her eyes, but she quickly replaces it with one of her signature bitch glares. She shoves a bar of soap against my chest. "Wash my back, oaf."

"Roman."

I blink away the memory and give my brother a nod that I'm still here. He launches into a story about one of our new clients he's working on a design for as Leah drops our fish and chips baskets in front of us. But my mind is still on Andie. That night in the shower was probably when our baby was conceived. I'm pretty sure I used a rubber every other time.

Except that one other time, in the bathroom of the outdoor mall where I'd found Andie ice skating. She'd looked like a fucking fairy, and I couldn't even get her out to the parking lot before I was shoving her inside a bathroom stall to fuck her. Hell, what am I saying? Any time we've been in a bathroom together, we haven't used a condom. Just too fucking eager, the both of us.

Jesus Christ.

That woman.

She's so damn difficult.

And perfect.

"Let's go," I bark out as I shove the rest of my food into my mouth and slam down a hundred-dollar bill. "We have shit to do."

Ram doesn't argue and chugs the rest of his beer before following me. Wisely, my brother is quiet and only blabs about Dani on the way to our next destination. Eventually, he goes back to gushing over my car.

"You know," he teases. "This car is almost as sweet as the 'Stang. I mean, I love my car, but I bet the trunk works on this one. Too bad it isn't a little bigger. The girls would love to cruise with us in this thing." He drums the dash with his fists along with the song playing on the radio.

I mash the button to turn off the music as I roll into the parking lot. "It's too small."

His eyes are wide once he realizes where we're at. "Okay then."

One painful hour later, we're halfway to Ikea driving my new wheels. A used Range Rover. Still nice but not custom anything. Practical. The seat warmers are better than the Z4, so I guess that's something.

"I know we didn't just trade in that bad ass fucking car you've wanted for what seems like forever to get something big enough to haul furniture around," Ram says thoughtfully when we finally pull into Ikea.

"I need more space," I tell him with a growl.

Space for a car seat. Space for Andie. Space for baby shit. I don't know what the fuck babies need, but I know they need room, that's for damn sure.

"Okaaaaay," he drawls out as we head inside the store.

Another hour later and I have everything I need. A desk. A fucking cool-ass ergonomic chair that I'm jealous of. And loads of organizational office crap. I'm not even sure any of it is useful.

But it will be useful to her.

It will make her happy.

The thought, though a pleasant one, is fleeting. I'm not sure she'll even show up in the morning for work. And that thought is frustrating as hell.

I want her.

Whether she wants to believe it or not, I want her.

All of her.

Even that little bean we created in the heat of the moment growing inside her belly.

That's mine too.

"You going to tell me what's going on?" Ram questions. "I mean, I'm assuming that once we get back, I'll have to help you put all this shit together. That means I'll be late going home to my girl. If I'm going to be late to help my brother who is going through some crap, then I expect you to at least tell me what the hell it is I'm missing out on dinner and a blowjob for." He smirks. "This better be good."

"Andie's pregnant."

His head snaps to face me from the passenger side. "No shit. Who's the father?" he jokes.

I glare at him. "Fuck you."

"Calm down," he utters. "I'm just kidding. Of course the kid is yours. Wow. Pregnant. You think I'll be a good uncle?"

My nostrils flare with anger. "Uncle? You think I give a rat's ass about whether or not you'll be a great uncle right now? I'm the father of the devil woman's baby. She fucking hates me. What am I going to do about this?"

He's quiet for a minute. "Is she keeping it?"

"I'm not giving her a choice," I seethe. "That baby is

mine too."

Ram chuckles and it unnerves me. "Well, considering how fucking crazy you are over this kid and you've barely just found out, I think everything will be just fine. I already feel sorry for her future boyfriends. Need help cleaning your shotguns?"

Grumbling at him, I gas it down the highway back to the office. The very idea of having to run off future boyfriends for an Andie lookalike has me seeing red. "I don't own a shotgun." That's the only thing I have to say about that right now.

"Not yet," he says with a laugh. "Seriously, though. Calm the hell down. I honestly don't see what the big problem is. You like Andie. Andie tolerates you. You guys made a baby. You're mostly responsible adults. I think you've got this covered."

I pull into the parking lot at the office and shut off the car. Scrubbing at my face with my palms, I try to tamp down the fear hiding deep down inside me. What if this is really all a game to her? What if she doesn't want to try and do right by this kid with me? What if she was fucking serious about not keeping it?

I'm pissed and confused and stressed the fuck out.

All I keep seeing are those sad tears streaming down her puffy red cheeks. I'd wanted to cradle her pretty face and kiss her until all our problems seemed like distant memories.

But. She. Won't. Fucking. Let. Me.

"Andie doesn't want to be a team," I grumble. "She doesn't want to be anything. I wish I could get inside her thick skull and see what makes her tick."

"You could always call in reinforcements…" Ram trails off, a mischievous glint in his eyes.

"Reinforcements?"

He doesn't have to answer because I know. Ram climbs out and leaves me to my thoughts. With a sigh, I dig my phone out of my pocket. I'd expected a response back from Andie when I texted her in the middle of signing paperwork at the dealership, but she never texted back. My brother was right. It's time to pull out the big guns. I mash the number and wait for a sweet voice to answer.

"Roman?"

"Momma," I choke out. "I fucked up and I need your help."

Her voice is soothing—aside from the "*Oh my God I'm going to be a grandma!*" squeal—as I tell her the entire story from top to bottom without missing a single twisted detail. I may not be able to get Andie to talk to me, but nobody can tell my lovely, petite mother no. She's too cute and too sweet and you'd have to be an asshole to be mean to her.

A smile creeps up my lips.

Sorry, Andie, but when it comes to having you, I'm no longer playing fair. I'm playing for fucking keeps.

Chapter Three

Andie

Big Stupid Oaf

"**O**H MY GOD! YOU HAVE TO WAIT LONGER than ten seconds before you come back over here, otherwise it just follows you!" Dani squeals, covering her nose.

"I'm so sorry," I tell her with a laugh, but I can't be holed up in the corner every time I have to fart. Eating two cheeseburgers, cheese sticks, wings, and then spending the night at Dani's eating taffy gave me the worst gas. Add in my amazing new bodily hormones and, holy cow, I am smoking us both out.

"Seriously, at least one minute. You can't do that to me again." She has her hand over her nose and mouth now and is using a magazine to fan the area.

"Dude! I said sorry. But I can't hold it in! What if this speck of life inside me smells it instead?"

Halfway back to the kitchen, I feel my stomach contract again. Shit! I debate on letting it go while I walk back, but last time I did that Dani about drowned me in Febreeze. I turn around to go back to the corner as she busts out laughing.

"This isn't funny. This gas is no joke." I go back and stick my butt in the corner and let another one rip. Dani, who is bent over trying to catch her breath, is now using her sweater as a mask. I catch her fiddling with her phone and panic.

"Who are you calling?" I demand. "You better not Snapchat this! Or text your man! I'll murder you. I don't care how sweet you are!" I stalk over to her, knowing I have an entourage of stank following me.

"I'm not. I'm googling how to get rid of gas. You're in serious need of a remedy."

Oh, okay. I can work with that.

I let her do her thing, while I attempt to drink some juice. I wanted to drink coffee, but Dani told me that caffeine was a no-no while pregnant. I told her that it was a myth, because I hoped it was, and to give me back my mug. She just smiled sweetly and handed me the stupid juice. It made me feel bad for poor Ram. He will never win with her. It's that damn cute fucking smile that will win every time. Nobody is immune.

I spent the night laying on Dani's couch, and we stayed up late watching *Sens8* on Netflix while eating the entire stock of taffy Ram gave her for Christmas. It took me some time to find my sane spot, but once I did, I was able to have that heart to heart Dani was so patiently waiting to have.

The typical questions were asked.

Will I keep the baby? The answer is yes. There's no doubt.

Would I allow Roman to be a part of the experience?

Next question.

If it was a girl, would I name it Danielle? We'll see.

Dani was beyond excited to, as she put it, become an aunt. That made me excited because she was going to be an aunt to *my* kid. *I* was having a kid! Holy fuck! It was crazy. And scary and confusing. I laughed, cried, and swore—no emotion was safe from me. The biggest one was fear. I was worried I'd turn out to be a horrible mother.

Because what do I know about having a baby?

Absolutely nothing.

I know that way too many people bring them to restaurants and ruin my meal with their crying misfits. And would Roman be a part of this? I sat for a long time, trying to imagine him holding a baby. Tenderness was ingrained in him. The softness and possessiveness. He would make a great parent. A great dad. But would *we* make a great anything?

I won't lie. Beneath all the hard exterior, there have been those late nights alone when Dani was busy with Ram that left me to myself, a box of wine, and *Full House* reruns—*Have mercy*—long nights when I imagined Roman and I together. Not fighting. Well, still play fighting in the bedroom, because if that ever went away, so would he. That's a given. But us together. Truly together. And it felt…good. Safe. I remember just wanting to know how it would feel to be in a relationship. To wake up to the feel of a man, who is so deeply in love with you, cradled around you, that your heart and soul ache at having to get up and leave the perfect little mold you've made beneath him. Meals that are shared with laughter

31

and quick, flirty glances. Love making that continues into the night and early morning. Pathetic ol' Andrea Grace Miller wanted that. The whole dang package.

I remember testing out the waters one night and trying to show Roman a side of me people rarely saw. A kinder side. I made dinner and sent him a text to come over. I waited for over three hours, and by the time he finally made it over, claiming an issue with a client kept him away, it was way past dinner, and my nice side had long since expired. The meat was dry and the food cold. I had also drank close to two bottles of the wine I had bought for us to share. I was in no mood to play nice or test out any more waters. I was angry. And in the end, he got the Andie he always got. The angry, pissed off one. We had the best sex that night. It was hot and intense. I think we both walked away with bruises, but hot damn, did I get a workout. My legs were stiff for almost a week and my pelvis was bruised from how hard he crashed into me. It was what we did best. And so, at the end of the day, I realized what we had just worked, and that we didn't and shouldn't try to be anything more than fuck buddies.

As for yesterday, a lot of shit went down. Finding out I was about to form a life, telling off my boss and getting fired, telling off my baby daddy, then having my baby daddy offer me a job. *Then* telling off my baby daddy *again*… It was all too much. Too much madness for one day.

Dani asked what my plans were with work. I clearly needed to grovel and apologize to someone. My old boss or my new one. Either way, I needed a job. Desperately. I was a mom now. I had a fetus to feed.

The best option was to apologize to my new boss/ soon-to-be baby daddy. It was mainly because the big idiot had offered me a salary way past my potential and experience. So, Dani and I shut off the TV, and like a good little girl, I went to bed early because I would start the brand new job in the morning.

Mothers have responsibilities.

And I'm a responsible mother.

But now, as I stand in the corner of Dani's living room in a black pencil skirt and red blouse, releasing toxic gases out of my ass, I don't feel so responsible. I feel out of my element, and the only thing I'm pondering is how many sick days I'll have because I may need to take one today.

What a way to start off my first day…

"Got it!" Dani yelps from the kitchen and begins digging in her cabinets.

What exactly are you looking for? I wonder as I walk away from the toxic corner. Seriously, I'm going to pass out if I have to stand there any longer.

"Well, it says the easiest way is to just let them rip, which we obviously know isn't working. An option is to chew on some ginger, which sounds kind of gross, or eat pumpkin, which is totally out of season, but I do have peppermint tea. So we're gonna test this out." She sets to making me some tea, which she also tells me I cannot drink a lot. Pregnancy and all. But we're making an exception today.

The good thing is that the tea runs right through me, and I have to hit the bathroom right after I drink it, preventing any future gas from forming. *Yuck.* Moving on. The bad news is that I'm now late to work. On my first day. Awesome.

Walking into Holloway Advertising, way calmer than I did yesterday, my nerves are still slightly out of control. I don't know why I'm so nervous. Is it because I'm starting a new job? Because my boss is Roman? Because I'll be working in the same room as him all. Day. Long?

I plead the fifth on the last two and chalk it up to first day nerves. I already have my argument down pat if he even thinks about grilling me for being late. *How dare he raise his voice at the mother of his child?* As I walk into his office, I notice Roman is absent. His large mahogany desk is missing his large frame, even though I can still smell the lingering scent of his cologne. The scent that he leaves on my pillow every time he's in my bed. The scent that has always been a trigger for me. Would I sound like a psycho if I admitted that when he leaves, I sleep with that pillow tucked between my legs?

I toss my purse and jacket on the couch to the left, wondering what the hell I'm supposed to do. Wait for him? Leave and go grab breakfast? I'm sure Dani could take an early lunch… "What the…" My eyes stop surveying the room when they land on the area that held a large conference table just yesterday. I gape in shock and my fingers cover my parted lips as a tiny gasp escapes from my throat.

Yesterday's table has been replaced by a brand-new, quaint desk covered in supplies. And not just any supplies, a fabulous desk filled with a colorful array of pretty office supplies that Rainbow Brite would be jealous of.

He bought me my desk.

And everything I asked for.

Taking a few steps closer, I spot it. He even got me that stupid paper holder thing I demanded. *This is why he's going to be a great dad,* a voice inside my head says. I remove the space between me and my new desk, brushing my fingers along the top of it. It's so pretty and perfect. Even the chair screams girly and comfortable and perfect.

I bring my hands to my chest, cupping them over my heart. My eyes blink rapidly, fighting off the tears that are forming as I inhale deep breaths.

Please don't cry.

Please don't cry.

Shit.

I swipe the tear away. But this time it's different. It's the product of an emotion that sits heavy on my heart. He did this for me. Even after the spectacle I made yesterday. A small part of me prepared for the speech, the one where he'd tell me it was a mistake offering me a job, and that it would be best for me to look for one elsewhere. I would have agreed. Inside my head, of course, because I'm not sure this arrangement is a wise choice either. But the tough Andie argued back and said he did this to me. He has to pay. And pay the piper he shall.

But the kindness that he's shown, even after my meltdown, it does something to me. Fills my angry heart with happiness. Dulls the pain of the never-ending lonely ache. He is willing to try. He said he wants this. Maybe he is telling me the truth. Maybe this *can* work. A small smile creeps onto my face, knowing when he walks through that door, I'm going to be a new me. No more outbursts. He deserves the same kindness he continues to offer me.

It's then when I hear his deep voice outside. He's coming. *Oh shit!* I throw my hands into my hair, trying to smooth it out. It is super windy today, taking my normally sleek blonde hair and turning it into an eighties tease, bouffant mess. I turn to face the door, hoping he'll like my outfit. *Like my outfit? Jesus.* Let's not turn *that* soft. Brushing my hands down my skirt, I take a deep breath as he walks through the door.

With a beautiful redhead on his tail.

"You were just wonderful, Roman," she chirps in a sweet voice. Too sweet. Like nasty off-brand syrup. "I love watching you work with clients." Her arm lifts and she daintily brushes his shoulder with her fingertips. And it's not a friendly sort of pat either. It's a whoreish cat pet. Like given the time, she'd rub a lot more body parts all over him.

What the fuck?

"I'm free for dinner tonight if you want to celebrate," she adds as Roman storms through his office, not even noticing me. It's when I vocally snarl at her suggestion of dinner that he whips his head in my direction, acknowledging my presence.

"You came," he says, seemingly surprised to find me here.

"Well, not exactly, but it sure looks like your

girlfriend wants to," I snap in response. Gone is any hope of being nice, and in its place is the temperamental girl who just caught her baby daddy being propositioned by a redheaded skank.

"What? What are you talking about?" He still doesn't acknowledge the redhead and takes two large steps toward me. He places his warm hand on my shoulder. "Is everything okay? Are you feeling okay?" He scans my face and then my body, concern in his eyes. What is *wrong* is that Jessica Rabbit over there is still too close for my liking, and her hand is slowly starting to raise to rest on Roman's shoulder.

"Hi, I'm Suzy," she greets with a plastered-on smile that barely hides her irritation at seeing me. "Roman's executive assistant."

My eyes bulge and there's possibly a wee bit of steam billowing from my nostrils.

Roman's executive assistant?

Oh, hell no.

I shove Roman's hand off my shoulder so I can sidestep him to glare at the woman. "That's interesting," I grit out. "Because *I'm* his executive assistant." I'm ready for this battle. No one touches what's mine.

Note to self: Remember to deny I said that later.

Suzy's smile falters, and the phoniness behind it becomes much more noticeable. She may as well have the word "take" smeared across her fugly, over-bronzed face. "That's funny. But I am his—"

"Get out." Roman's low, demanding growl startles us both.

"Excuse me?" Suzy replies. "I thought we were going

to go over—"

"You *are* excused." He turns to her, his power like a red glow, radiating off him. "First off, you are Reagan's assistant. You helped me while they were hiring someone to replace Beth. She has now been replaced. Ms. Miller is my new executive assistant, and if you need anything from me, you will go through her first. Is that understood?"

Suzy's eyes are wide with shock. Her smile fighting not to turn upside down. Good. Cunt. Beat it.

"Yes, sure Roman, anything—"

"And for Christ's sake, it's Mr. Holloway," he snaps. "We have a level of professionalism here."

She quickly nods and pivots before scurrying out the door. I wave at her stiff back as she retreats. Roman's attention is on me as he places his two giant hands on my shoulders.

"Now, let's try this again," he says in a soft voice, which works its way straight to my core. "How are you? Do you feel okay? When you weren't here this morning, I was worried." His hand raises to cup my cheek, and I lean into his touch. The scent of his cologne is overwhelming, and coupled with the way he just told that sleaze to beat it, my heart and libido react. I swear, ever since he knocked me up, my sexual appetite is out of control. Starved and unsatisfied. Trying to play hard to get when all you think about day and night is sex is impossible.

I grab for his head, plunging my fingers into his perfectly styled mane, and pull his lips down to mine. The instant groan rolling off his lips is euphoria to my ears, and I just want to crawl up his strong body. I lift on my toes, giving him the silent instruction to lift me up so I can straddle my legs around his waist.

But instead he clutches my hips and urges me back down while trying to break our kiss.

"Andie, we can't do this here," he murmurs, his voice hoarse with barely contained need. "Yes, we can," I argue and try to stick my tongue back down his throat.

He pulls away, but I grab his hair and pull. Hard. I press my mouth back to his, parting my lips, and our tongues collide in a feverish kiss. He is *not* going to say no to me.

Okay, so maybe he is.

Another tug and he plucks me off him. His fingers curl around my shoulders, holding me at arm's length. "Andie. No. This is my office. We *can't* do this here."

My mood plummets.

With a huff, I throw his hands off me and storm toward the door.

Roman sighs loudly. "Now where are you going?"

Gripping the doorknob, I whip around to face him. "You know," I say with a slight shake to my voice. "I don't understand you. You want me, but then you don't."

Roman throws his hands up. "What on earth are you talking about? When did I ever make you feel like I didn't want you?"

"Right now."

"We're at work, Andie!"

"Well, it didn't stop you and your girlfriend. Did I ruin your morning plans by actually showing up and—"

"Oh, just fucking stop already."

"No. You stop. I see why this is a bad idea now.

Because I'm going to ruin all your hook ups!" I finish on a yell.

Roman snaps his head up and whispers something that could be a prayer or a string of curse words up to the ceiling. Bringing his eyes back to me, he says, "Andie, I do not have hookups at work. This is a business."

"Liar." My voice sounds less angry, more emotional.

I watch his eyes soften. "I'm not lying. How can I prove it to you?" He takes a step toward me.

"Have sex with me. Here. Now."

He groans, spearing his fingers into his now messy hair. "Andie," he warns.

"You know what? Don't you *Andie* me! I am all hot and horny and I need some fucking sex. This thing inside me is producing way too much of *something,* and now I have needs that aren't getting fulfilled. If you aren't willing to help me out, I'll just find it elsewhere. I saw a cute guy in the mail—"

"Shut the door."

"Wait. What?"

Roman starts pulling at his tie. "I said shut the damn door."

My eyes light up.

Yes!

Winner.

My vagina claps together, thanking me for going the distance and not giving up. I don't take my eyes off him as my hand fidgets with the door. With the lock in place, I watch as Roman removes his tie and begins unbuttoning his crisp white dress shirt. His white shirts are my favorite. They cling to his muscled torso and showcase his ridiculously defined body. I like the way his shoulders are broad but his body narrows down to a fit waist. He's bulky but not meathead bulky. Just enough muscles to make a girl like me go wild with the need to lick every one of them.

"Get over here. Now."

This is the side of him I crave. The man who demands. Takes and devours.

I release the handle and my thighs are already clenching together. The moment I make it to Roman, he grabs for me, lifting me up and placing my ass on my new desk. "Is this what you want, baby?" His voice a low grumble. His hands roam up my thighs painfully slow, while his lips brush against my earlobe. "Tell me what you want, Andie." He sucks my earlobe into his mouth, and I let out a groan at the soft pressure of his teeth against my skin.

"I was hoping for less fucking *talking* and more actual *fucking*," I whisper, desperately trying not to lose control, an impossible task. With his hands on me, his bare chest peeking through the undone buttons of his shirt, I finally snap, letting the animalistic need for him out.

His hands push my skirt up, hiking it way above my waist. When my black-laced thong is exposed, a soft growl leaves his perfect lips, and with no care, he rips the material.

"No fucking screaming," he threatens in such a vicious voice, I nearly come right then. "Do you hear me? You want this so bad? Then you'll stay quiet." His gaze darkens. "Or I'll gag you."

Fuck, my clit pulsates at his threat. There is nothing

I want more than for him to tie me up and fuck me hard against this brand-spanking-new desk.

"Why are you still fucking talking?" I ask, taking my hands and going for his belt. It's off in a flash, and I'm unzipping his pants, pulling out his already hard cock.

God, he has the most beautiful cock I have ever seen.

Not that cocks are really supposed to be good looking, but damn, his…

Just fucking perfect.

Roman causes me to squeal when his hands grip my bare ass, pulling me to the edge of the desk. He aligns himself at the opening of my sopping wet sex. His eyes lock with mine and he utters, "Not a peep." And before I can even respond, he slams into me.

My head instantly falls back. "God yes," I moan as he pulls out and shoves himself deeper inside me.

"I said no talking," he grunts as he thrusts in and out. He removes a hand from my ass cheek, plunging it into my hair. He pulls hard, causing my neck to stretch. His lips are on me instantly as he sucks on my sensitive skin.

"Fuck, yes, harder. Fuck me harder," I demand, meeting him thrust for thrust. He crushes his lips to mine as he fucks me hard.

This is what I needed.

His thick cock inside me.

His sexy, plump lips on mine.

The scent of him and our arousal surrounding us.

"No…fucking…talking," he growls against my lips as he pulls out and then slams back home. His movements are becoming aggressive and hard. Just how I like it. I'm starting to moan louder, like a cat in heat. This feels so…

It's then that he makes good on his word. He grabs for his tie, bundling it up in his hand, and shoves it into my mouth. My eyes widen, but his are black with lust. He takes control, grabbing my hips, and thrusts, faster and faster, until I am gone. Lost. Overboard. Throwing myself off the highest orgasmic mountain. I moan loudly, even with the barrier as I break, coming all over his dick. Roman is right behind me and groans out as his release blasts through him.

Our breathing is labored. He pulls the tie out of my mouth. I allow my head to rest against his sweaty chest until I'm able to feel safe that my heart won't give out.

"That was just what the doctor ordered," I mumble into his chest.

I feel his lips kiss the top of my scalp. I want to sigh, but brush off the urge.

"This was a one-time-only thing," he tells me in a firm tone. "Understand?"

Bullshit it was. I give in to the sigh I held in moments ago, and I snap back into action. I push him off me. We forgot to use a condom, but I guess now it's a moot point. I grab a few Kleenexes from the floral tissue holder and wipe myself up. Tossing the saturated tissue in the trash, I jump off the desk and pull down my skirt.

I watch as Roman goes to his closet and discards his shirt, along with his tie for a new one. I stand there adjusting my blouse while I admire the flexing muscles in his back as he throws the new shirt over his shoulders. He turns to me and I smile. We share a moment, both of us sated and in a good place.

Sadly, he speaks and ruins everything.

"So we need to talk about yesterday."

Ugh. Not a chance. "No, we don't." I push away from the desk and head toward the door.

"Andie, yes," he bites back, irritation in his voice. "We do. I want this. I should have a say." His voice softens. "I want you to keep this baby."

I whip around to face him as he buttons up his shirt. "And why? Give me one good reason? We don't even like each other!"

He winces at my words. "What? How can you say that? I like you just fine. It's you who has this vendetta against me, for some reason. If you would just let me—"

I pick up a stupid book off his shelf and whip it at him. It doesn't hit him, unfortunately, but he gets the point.

"That was a first edition of *Christine* by Stephen King!" he barks at me, the muscles in his neck tense with fury.

"Oh, was it now?" I turn and grab the book next to it.

And toss it.

"What edition was that one?"

His eyes are now matching mine. Pure anger. "Knock it off, Andie."

Wow.

Newsflash.

Telling me what to do? Big no-no.

Telling me while pregnant what to do? Huge mistake.

I raise my hand, ready to swipe all the books off the shelf, when his voice booms through the office. "Don't you dare," he warns me, taking a threatening step toward me.

"Don't tell me what to do," I hiss.

"Then stop acting so goddamned crazy." The words fall from his lips, and the second they're out, I notice the regret lacing his features. "Andie, I didn't mean that."

Yes, he did. I bite my stupid lower lip, which has a mind of its own.

"Shit," he groans. "Baby, I'm sorry I didn't mean—"

"I hate you," I say, my voice quivering.

He stops his attempt to comfort me. "I know you do," he replies, sounding defeated.

"It's fine," I choke out, trying desperately to not cry. "Because I'm here to work. I need the money because *you* knocked me up. Can't have our child starve because you don't know how to wrap it up."

At that he smiles.

It both irritates me and sends a rush of damn butter-flies fluttering around inside me.

"What the fuck are you smiling at?"

Big, stupid, handsome oaf.

He's calling me crazy and he's the one having mood swings over there.

"You said *our* child."

Shit.

Oops.

"I meant whoever's child. I'm not even sure it's yours," I lie.

His eyes darken again, and it makes my skin tingle with need. "Andie, it's mine and you know it."

"Nope," I argue, hoping to poke the bear some more.

"Could be anyone's."

He takes another menacing step closer to me. "Knock it off. You know—"

"What I *know*, Mr. Holloway, is that I need to get to work. Harassment is taken very seriously here, and I won't hesitate to speak to HR about what just happened here today."

His mouth parts in shock for a brief moment.

That's right. I win. "Oh, and you might want to spray something in here. It smells like sex!" I fan my nose. "Phew."

He glares at me as he makes a show of stalking over to the back credenza and plugging in a Scentsy warmer. Then he smirks, and says, "There. Crisis averted."

"Fuck off." I roll my eyes at him and head toward the door.

Idiot.

Leaving the smug bastard so he can assist his own goddamn self, I open the door to leave.

Before I succeed in exiting stage left, I run head-on into an older woman.

Chapter Four

Roman

Mine. Mine. Mine.

"H EY, MOM," I GREET WITH GRITTED TEETH. When I meant I needed help, I didn't mean the very next morning, or for her to show up at my office. "What are you doing here?"

Mom's eyes twinkle in a knowing way. "I just wanted to come bring my kiddos some treats. That's not a crime, is it?" She turns her sweet smile on Andie next. "My, my. And who is this stunning woman? I didn't know you guys were hiring models."

Jesus. Laying it on thick much?

Andie darts an unreadable look my way. If I didn't know any better, I'd say Andie looks petrified. Not my fiery, fierce girl. She's not afraid of jack shit…certainly not my dainty mother.

"Andie, this is my mother, Virginia Holloway. Mom, this is Andie Miller my—"

"Executive assistant," Andie blurts out and offers a shaking hand to my mom.

I was going to say…

My assistant.

My girlfriend.

My baby momma.

Mine. Mine. Mine.

"Oh," Mom says with a wide grin. "*The* Andie." Instead of taking Andie's offered hand, she pounces on my girl and wraps her up in one of those hugs no one can deny. Andie is stiff for a moment but relaxes in her arms. Something like pride beats around in my chest at seeing the two of them. Mom eventually releases her but then takes Andie's hands. "I've heard so much about you, sweetheart. Not just from Dani either. Roman just goes on and on about how wonderful—"

"He talks about me?" Andie questions, shock in her voice. Her eyes dart to mine in confusion. Unlike Stalker Suzy out in the hall, Andie's eyelashes are sexy as hell as she bats them over and over again as if to try and make sense of the encounter.

"Of course he does. Smart, blonde, beautiful," Mom chirps and then leans in, lowering her voice. "Worthy of a chase. Way to make him work for it, angel." She then makes a clucking sound with her tongue. "I'm still upset you haven't come for dinner, though. Surely he's told you I'm a great cook."

Andie's cheeks are bright red, and she's back to staring down at my meddling mother. "I, uh, I…" she stammers in response before shooting me a *help-me* glare.

"She's been busy," I offer as I come around my desk and pull Mom against me for a hug. "Andie was in between jobs but now that she's here, everything should be smooth sailing." I make sure to give her a pointed stare to let her know the double meaning.

Andie swallows but seems to get ahold of herself. "I'm so sorry. Perhaps another time soon?"

"How about tonight?" Mom quips as she beams at my girl.

"I don't know—" Andie starts but is interrupted.

"Meatloaf. Green beans. Homemade mashed potatoes." Mom looks up at me and smiles. "It's my big boy's favorite meal. I even have some made-from-scratch yeast rolls rising in the kitchen. I'd love to have you over. I won't take no for an answer."

"We'll be there," I tell my mother. "What did you bring me?"

She swats me but grins. "Not just for you. I brought enough for the whole office. Cookies. Lemon bars. A key lime pie. I even brought one of those brownie truffles your sister loves so much."

"Yum," Andie groans. "That sounds amazing." Her initial shock and fear seem to have worn off. I make a mental note to woo this woman with food. It's her weakness.

"Let's go have a taste then," I agree and place my palm on the small of Andie's back.

"Darling, what's that smell?" Mom questions as we head for the door.

Andie chokes and starts coughing. I simply shrug "The Scentsy warmer."

Mom furrows her gaze and sniffs the air. "I don't suppose I know the scent. What is it?"

"Sweet cherry pie, I think is the name," I lie and then let out a chuckle when Andie nudges me. She's pinning me with a glare that says: *Don't embarrass me.* I wink at her.

"Well then." Mom doesn't seem convinced, but she lets it go.

The office *does* smell like sex. And ever since Mom left, my dick's been at half-mast. With our scent still lingering in the air and Andie as my eye candy, I can't seem to focus on one single damn work-related task. Thankfully, Andie has taken it upon herself to label all of her hanging folders. She's quiet as she focuses and shovels in cookie after cookie. *Thanks, Mom, for taming the dragon.* With her blonde eyebrows furrowed together in concentration and a strand of blonde hair hanging in her face, she almost looks innocent. Childlike. Vulnerable.

I stealthily take out my camera and snap a picture. Once I've saved it as the wallpaper on my phone, I begrudgingly get back to work. I'm buried in contracts when I become vaguely aware of Andie removing piles of paperwork from my desk. Normally, I'm average when it comes to neatness. Around the loft, Ram is the one who cleans all the time. I tend to keep my space clutter free, but I don't even know where we keep the duster. Fuck, I don't even know what a duster is. So compared to my brother's office, mine is a little on the unorganized side. My defense is that I have a shitload more to keep track of. He gets to play in Photoshop all day.

I haven't been able to speak to Andie much since we came back to work. She's been unusually reserved since Mom showed up. And if I weren't so busy, I'd ask her what's up. But apparently, every damn person on the planet has felt the need to call me today. Just when I end a call, Andie sticks a new pink Post-it on my computer monitor with someone else I need to call back. While I attempt to listen properly, I can't help but notice how neat her handwriting is. Ram hunts for hours for fonts that look as perfect as her writing.

I'm hashing out an error on a contract from one of our newer clients when I finally look away from the computer. My desk is completely cleaned off. I stare at it in shock, absolutely mystified at how that happened. When I dart my gaze over to Andie, I can see she's been hard at work creating color-coded files. I'm so fucking proud of her, I could shout it—that is if I didn't have this wiseass griping at me on the other end of the line. Her tired gaze meets mine for a brief moment, and I flash her a wide smile followed by a wink. I want to stare at the way her smooth cheeks turn slightly pink, but this prick on the phone wants me to look at the goddamned contract again.

Half an hour later, I finally hang up with that fucker. When I glance back over at Andie, her cheek is on her desk. She's completely passed out. Leaning back in my chair, I take a moment to stare at her without her noticing or getting angry. Andie doesn't like when I peel back her outer layers and peek at her soft center. She likes her hardened edges to always be on display. Problem is I want all parts of her. I crave to dig deep inside her and find that person who she so often hides. After I snap another picture of her looking so innocent, I tuck my phone away and rise from my chair. My back aches, and

I take a moment to stretch.

I can't believe she cleaned my desk off. It's like a damn miracle. I haven't seen the surface since the moment I sat down behind it for the first time. When my siblings and I bought out Tucker, I just moved all my shit into old man Tucker's previous office. Stacks of paperwork and all. Now, I look professional. Like the real CEO of a legitimate company.

Thanks to my girl.

I walk over to my closet and root around for my coat. Once I find it, I drape it over the back of Andie's shoulders. She can't possibly be comfortable, but something tells me growing a tiny human inside of you will tire you out. I stroke her hair before striding back over to my desk. Now that I've caught up on voicemails and shit, I'm going to read up on this whole pregnancy situation. I want to help her, and I don't even know how.

An hour and an entire notebook filled with notes later, I scratch my jaw as I realize just how unprepared we are for this kid. I make a necessary phone call and am just hanging up when I hear a groan from the corner.

"Oh my God."

I lift my gaze to see Andie swiping drool from her face. There's an imprint of her keyboard on her cheek from where she rested her face on her keypad. She looks so fucking cute all disheveled.

"Morning, sunshine," I tease.

Her eyes dart to mine, guilt shining in them. "I can't believe I fell asleep. How long was I out for?"

At least an hour.

"Not long. How are you feeling?" I keep my voice

calm. I've been dying to talk to her, but she keeps getting pissed off. We've run in circle after circle.

"Fine. I don't think that Chinese food we ordered for lunch is agreeing with me, though," she tells me, her face paling.

I jolt up and remember what I read on the pregnancy website. "Stay put. I'll get you something to help with that."

When I return, she's a little more put together but still looking green around the gills. Her eyes widen in surprise when I set down a can of ginger ale and a sleeve of crackers I'd stolen from the break room cabinet.

"This should make you feel better," I assure her. And before I can stop myself, I stroke an errant strand of blonde hair out of her eyes.

She offers me a sweet, thankful smile that does amazing things to my ego. My heart thumps with pride. I put that look on her face.

Food is definitely the key to her heart.

"Thank you," I tell her as I walk around her desk and thumb through the hanging files on top. "You did a great job of organizing all this stuff."

Her gaze snaps to mine, a defensive look in her eyes. But once she senses I'm being genuine, she relaxes. "It was a mess. Your loft is always so neat. Who knew you were such a slob, Mr. Holloway."

My dick twitches at the way she says my name. *Mr. Holloway.* I clear my throat and hope my hard-on will go the fuck away before I do something stupid, like take her again in my office. That was terribly unprofessional, and yet, I can't stop thinking about it.

"I like your handwriting," I blurt out, ignoring the widening of her eyes. "It's pretty. Like you."

She smirks. "What do you want?"

"You."

Her smile falls and her brows scrunch together. "Is this us 'talking'?"

I let out a sigh and kneel next to her chair. "This is us 'trying.'" When I place my palms on her thighs, she lets out a gasp. "All we can do is try, right?"

She nods and leans slightly forward. Goddamn, those tits are within biting distance. I refrain from mauling her. Instead, I do what I came over here to do. I talk.

"Nothing about this is going to be easy, Andie," I tell her, my thumbs rubbing circles on her legs through her skirt. "But nothing worth having ever is. I've never backed down from a challenge. You're the most challenging damn woman I've ever met, and if anything, it makes me want you even more."

Her hand tentatively covers mine. "You're pretty difficult yourself."

I laugh, and it makes her laugh, too. But then I grow serious as I draw the back of her hand to my lips. "We were careless and wild. But we had fun. We *still* have fun."

"This morning was definitely fun," she agrees with a naughty grin. "You owe me a new pair of panties, though."

I kiss her hand before placing it back in her lap. Our eyes meet once again. Tender Andie is so fucking rare that I want to prolong this moment for as long as I can. "I'll buy you plenty more, baby. Don't you worry." I grin, but then it falls away when I take a moment to realize how fucking beautiful she is. Her normally blazing blue eyes are wide and shimmering. Fucking hope glitters in them. A girl like Andie looks like she eats hope for breakfast. But not today. Today, she looks as though she wants to wrap herself up inside hope as if it were a warm, fuzzy blanket. I continue, "I want to do this together. I want to try for us and…" I trail off and drop my gaze to her flat stomach. "I want to try for this little one too."

Her breath hitches when my palm splays on her belly. Then, her fingers slip into my hair and she pulls me against her. I slide my arms around her waist to hug her. We stay locked in the intimate embrace in utter silence for a long while. It's fucking bliss. Her walls are down and I'm inside. She's never getting rid of me now.

"Roman," she chokes out, her voice wobbling with emotion, "I'm scared."

The vulnerable side of her shines brilliantly like a million rays from the sun. Beautiful and blinding.

"I know," I mutter and kiss her breast through her clothes. "I know, but I'm not going to let anything happen. You just have to fucking trust me."

She starts to cry. Hot tears splash the side of my neck. I don't dare let her go. Not when she has a death grip on my hair and is holding on to me as if she never wants me to leave.

I'm not going anywhere.

Eventually, she composes herself and lets out a ragged sigh. "I don't know a thing about being pregnant. All I've learned so far is that I'm gassy, emotional, and sick."

I pull away to smile at her. "Which is why tomorrow

afternoon, we're going to see Dr. Patterson. I set up the appointment and—"

"You set up the appointment?" she hisses, all sweetness chased away by her venom. "What are you? My dad?" Her foot kicks out and she narrowly misses my shin with her pointy heels.

Put the claws away, beautiful.

"You were so tired," I tell her in a calm tone. "Did I mention Dr. Patterson's office is next door to one of the best Italian restaurants in the city? *Mmmm,* breadsticks. We could have lunch after the appointment. My treat."

Food.

Food.

Woo her with food.

My new mantra.

Her anger melts away and she laughs. Fucking laughs. Goddamn she's so pretty when she does that. "You've really upped your game, Roman Holloway."

I stand up and then bend over to plant a kiss on her forehead. "The stakes just got a little bit higher, Andie Miller. And I don't lose."

Chapter Five

Andie

What to Expect When You're Expecting

"**N**O… NO… FUCK NO… AND NO!" GOD, HOW does nothing I own say, *Wear me to dinner with your baby daddy's mother*!? I mean, not that sitting and eating goodies while making small talk with no panties on is any more appropriate than what I'm nixing.

Why didn't I just say no to this? Um, because his mom is like super tiny and the cutest damn thing I have ever seen. She smelled like vanilla and she gave really good hugs.

UGH!

I try on my third pair of jeans and these, just like the other two pairs, are too snug. How is this possible? I stand in front of my full-length mirror while I watch the impossible. Wrestling with the button, I realize there is no way it's latching. I suck in a deep breath and bounce up and down, wiggling my ass, but nope. "FUCK!" I yell, ripping the jeans off me, catching one leg in the process, causing me to trip and fall. Thankfully, I land in my man-made pile of *can't-wear-these-to-Momma's-house* reject outfits.

With a loud huff, I give up, lie on the floor, stare at the ceiling and let my thoughts drift back to earlier.

Virginia Holloway.

The nicest person on this planet.

Besides Dani… And my mom.

It's been so long that I almost forgot how it felt to receive a real motherly hug. Complete with the tenderness moms are built with. It reminded me of my own mother. When I was young, she would chase me around the house, telling me she needed a hug or the world was going to explode. I would laugh so hard, squealing as I ducked under chairs or ran up and down the hallway. She would quickly run out of steam, her legs giving out on her. I would always come back, pretending she caught me, and fall into her lap. The quiet moments we would share as I let her cradle me, whispering sweet things to me, her love, her promise to always watch over me. Because one day, she said, she would have to go away. It was a few years before I finally understood what she meant. It made me wish I'd known then what I know now. I would have run straight to her, instead of away, every single time.

Virginia stated that Ram was busy taking Dani to lunch, and Reagan was stuck on a call. She invited me to sit with her while she chatted with her eldest. I wanted to object, but she was holding a really tempting bag of sweets, and I really needed in that bag.

It turned out to be amazing. She hadn't been telling

a lie when she'd said she was a great cook. She went into detail about how she got into cooking, and I pretended I was having allergy issues when my eyes started to water. I felt so horrible for her. For Roman. It also made me think of some moments—ones buried in my past—of my mom before she died.

Virginia saw the sadness building in my eyes and laid her small hand over mine. She quickly changed the subject after that, for which I was thankful. She went on to explain that all the ingredients in her treats were organic, with no caffeine or synthetic sugars. Safe for all kinds of tummies. I silently thanked her, not needing a replay of this morning.

The more I sat and listened, the more I fell in love with her. I think it was because she reminded me so much of Mom. Her cheeriness, her love for her children. She told a story of when Roman was just a little kid, being fascinated with all things little. The neighbor boy's family had just had a baby, so the boy spent a lot of time over at the Holloway's to give the parents a breather. Since Roman was barely four years old and didn't understand what the big fuss was, he insisted his mom take him over there so he could find out why his friend William couldn't go home. Roman didn't understand that William's parents weren't kicking him out. But, as Virginia explained, he was a kid and this was how he understood things at the time.

So Roman stomped over next door with Virginia behind him, wanting answers, only to have Carolyn, the mother, answer the door holding a three-week-old baby. Roman was in awe. He didn't quite understand where the little girl came from, just that she was super tiny. He had asked to pet her, which made Carolyn laugh, and she allowed. He asked its name, which was Violet, and what it ate. The mother said *she* ate formula right now because she was so small, but as she grew up she would eat vegetables, just like he did. Roman, of course, gagged saying he didn't eat vegetables. They "*were stinky.*" He went on, asking the million other questions a four-year-old could come up with and finally, after answering all of them as best as she could, she invited little Roman in and asked him if he would like to hold Violet. And he did.

Virginia explained that it took Roman a good ten minutes to get comfortable enough to hold her, but when he finally did, he was absolutely fascinated. He asked more questions and received more answers. Close to two hours had passed before they returned home. Roman came home with a mind full of knowledge, and the first thing he wanted to know was if he could have a baby brother or sister for his birthday, if he was a good boy.

Virginia went on to say that she took Roman over to the neighbors' house almost every day to visit. He was always asking to hold Violet and wanted to help feed her. He even changed a few diapers. Little did Roman know that Virginia and Jacob were already pregnant with their second child, Ramsey.

And when Ram came along, Roman immediately began his big-brother training on his little brother and spent less time with Violet. But, to this day, they all still keep in touch. And continue to tease Roman about his parental urges, even at age four.

The story was sweet and touching. I kept stealing glances at Roman while his mother spoke. His small nods and chuckles as he, too, recalled the memory. I wondered about the irony of the story. Thirty years later, and he's about to have a Violet of his own.

Or a mini Roman.

Our chat wrapped up quickly after that when Roman's phone began buzzing with alerts of an upcoming conference call. Virginia and I hugged goodbye, and Roman had to all but peel me off her. Then she left, telling us she would see us for dinner.

Which leads me to my current situation, in a pile of clothes I need to burn, and me debating on cancelling. The sound of banging on my door has my eyes darting to the clock to see it's already six.

"Fuck. Shit, fuck." I stand, looking around my room. What a disaster. The knocking on the door starts again, and I yell, "I'll be right there. Calm your tits," and groan, knowing I can't go in my underwear and bra.

Then it hits me.

"God, I can't believe this."

I go to Dani's drawer, which I gave her to put anything she wants to leave here.

And I grab for a pair of her goddamn leggings.

"Here, let me get that for you," Roman says as he steps in front of me to open the car door.

Curious, I ask, "Whose car is this?" I know it's not his, since I remember the day he bought his fancy Beamer. He came over shortly after, happy as a kid in a candy store with his recent purchase. He smiled broadly as he dangled the keys in front of me, telling me that he was going to fuck me senseless, then take me for the smoothest ride of my life. Of course we never made it past the fuck-me-senseless part.

"It's mine. Watch your step."

I would have if he hadn't thrown me off with his reply. I turn, confusion surely etched across my face. "What do you mean it's yours? You own two cars now?"

"Just one. I traded in the Z4."

I falter as he takes my hand and helps me into the Range Rover. I turn again. "What? Why? You loved that car? This is a downgrade. A…a…"

"A family car?" Roman finishes my sentence on a smile.

My mouth parts in shock. The meaning behind his smile slowly hits me. Heavy inside my heart. "Family?" I draw a deep breath. "Roman, you loved that car." My voice is just above a whisper.

He leans in, dropping a gentle kiss to the top of my nose.

"And I believe I will love this family more."

Jesus, they live in a fucking mansion! I gape at the beautiful house coming into view as we pull up the long driveway. Virginia is already waiting for us, waving as she sees the Range Rover pull in front.

Roman helps me out but is pushed out of the way so Virginia can offer me a hug. She grabs my hand and guides me into the house, Roman chuckling as he trails behind us.

"Dear, I hope you're hungry. I made a feast."

Just then my stomach grumbles. Embarrassed, I throw my hands over my belly. "Wow, I guess I am," I softly chuckle.

Virginia leads us inside—the house resembles a Holloway Family museum. The walls are bright and filled with family photos and crafts. I slow my pace to take a look at some drawings by Reagan and Ram and even some football photos of Roman.

"Wow, you had longer hair?" I ask Roman, who's standing next to me observing the wall as well.

"Let's just say it was a phase," he says with a laugh, pulling me away so that I'm unable to get a better look at the rest.

"Hey, I was looking at those!" I whine as he tucks me into his side, bending to drop a kiss to the top of my head.

"Yes, that's what I was afraid of. I need to get you to *like* me first. Having collateral against me, such as those awful photos, isn't safe when I'm not fully on your good side."

I elbow him in the ribs, and he chuckles.

We make our way through the largest kitchen ever and into the dining room, where I see so much food, I swear to God, I think drool immediately drips from my mouth.

"Wow, who else is coming?" I ask, staring at an amount of food that's fit for an army.

"I told you she likes to cook."

Virginia just sighs, pulling her seat out as we all sit.

"You can never be too sure how hungry your guests will be. Especially my baby boy. He can eat." She turns to me and winks.

The entire dinner is filled with more stories and laughter. However, there is a lot of silence from me, since I'm too busy stuffing my face. Holy cow, they weren't lying when they said she could cook. I want to stuff food in my purse to take home, but then I snap out of my insane plan because I'm pretty sure she would just offer me a goodie bag to go.

After dinner, as Roman cleans up—which, I might add, is a really sexy look on him, with his shirtsleeves rolled up as he washes dishes—Virginia and I sit in the library as she pulls out photo album after photo album.

"Roman was such a cute baby," I tell her, using my thumb to brush over an old photograph. Even back then he had that charming smile and his big, shining pale brown eyes.

"He was the best baby. Still is a big baby at times," she replies. For some odd reason, my mood flips. The continuous mention of the word *baby* has me all sorts of messed up.

I use my palms to cover my face as I begin to cry.

"Oh dear, I'm sorry. I didn't mean to upset you." Her small hand pats my shoulder.

I want to tell her it wasn't her. But I can't seem to stop the waves of tears from falling.

"It's not you. It's me. My emotions are a mess." I give her a wobbly frown. "I… I have something to tell you." I wipe my cheeks, trying to control my hiccupping.

"All right, sweetie. What is it?" She smiles that

honest, kind, motherly smile that I miss from my own mom so much. I begin to cry again, because I wish my mom were here. I wish she were holding my hand, telling me it's going to be okay.

Virginia moves in and wraps me in her tiny frame. I accept her embrace and melt into her as I cry. When the tears begin to settle, I pull away.

"I'm sorry," I choke out. "I'm not normally like this. I promise."

She grabs my hand, offering me a reassuring squeeze. "There is no judgment here, sweetheart."

I don't know why it's so hard to say it. The words begin to work their way up my throat, but I fail every time they threaten to fall from my lips.

"Virginia…"

I'm suddenly nervous.

How will she take the news?

Will she think ill of me for getting pregnant before marriage?

Will she want someone better for her son?

I'm spiraling into a panic attack, my eyes squeezing shut, when the two words vomit out of my mouth.

"I'm pregnant." *Oh God, that felt like a million bricks off my shoulders.*

I open my eyes to see what kind of woman I'm now dealing with.

But her smile is just the same.

"Did you hear me?" I question, because she doesn't look fazed at all. "I said I was pregnant. With your son's baby."

Why isn't she mad or trying to drag me by my hair

out of her perfect home? Maybe she's in shock. I would be too. Having to deal with a bastard baby probably doesn't sit—

"I know, dear."

And what?

"Wait, you knew?" I ask stunned. "How?"

Virginia grabs the photo albums sitting in my lap and sets them on the end table. Turning back to me, she says, "A mother knows things like that. If my son hadn't already confided in me, I would have figured it out during our talk today. You remind me a lot of myself when I was pregnant with my first."

My eyes mist over. Roman told his mom.

"I'm very close with my children. I raised them to know they could always come to me. No judgment. Roman confessed you were with child yesterday. He was filled with so many emotions. Nervous you would turn him down. Scared he would fail you as a co-parent. Fail the child as a father. He confessed that as strange and unexpected as it is, he's excited. He feels something fierce for you and that growing child."

I don't know how to respond. It's just too much to take in. I'm throwing myself back into her embrace when heavy footsteps enter the room. "Am I interrupting something here, ladies?" Roman's voice breaks us apart, both of us wiping the freshly shed tears.

"Yeah, I was just telling your mom what we did."

"What we did?" Roman laughs.

"That you and this amazing woman are having my grandbaby," Virginia replies with a grin from ear to ear.

Roman smiles, his eyes soft and tender as he regards

me. He walks over and kneels in front of me. Taking my hands into his, he lifts them, placing a gentle kiss to the top of my knuckles.

"*We* sure are."

Walking up to the doorway of my apartment, I feel lighter on my feet. My mood is up, and I have a smile on my face. I haven't stopped babbling to Roman about every random, nonsense thought I've had since we got back into his car.

"And then the photos. Just think, if we had a boy, he would have the same mop of hair!" I push my key into the lock and swing the door open. As I make my way into my apartment, I'm feeling extra frisky. I toss my keys on the table and begin undressing. "I swear all this talk is making me seriously fucking horny." I pull my shirt off and turn, only to realize Roman is still standing in the doorway with his hands in his coat pockets. "What are you doing? Get in here. Clothes off," I instruct. "Hurry."

He still doesn't budge, which causes me to worry.

"Roman. I'm talking to you. Get in here." But he doesn't make a move to enter my apartment.

My stomach knots as I fret that maybe this is too much for him. Maybe I said too much. Put too much pressure on him.

"I'm not coming in tonight."

"Why?" I ask, my voice shaking.

"Because I want more than just our passion. I want you. All of you. And if it takes having to start from the beginning, then that's what I plan on doing."

I don't understand.

"I want us to start over, Andie," he explains, his tone firm. "I don't want you to hate me."

My heart squeezes so tight I fear my legs will buckle. "I get it," I say just above a whisper. I struggle to maintain eye contact, so I break the hold and grab my shirt, throwing it back over my head. "It's fine. I've been a bitch. I'd probably want to take it slow, too. I'll see you tomorrow." I offer him a wave, turning to walk to my room.

"Wait." His voice is strained. "Give me an hour. I'll be back."

I nod and watch him shut my door.

Just as promised, an hour later, Roman is knocking on my door.

I open the door to see his hands are filled with plastic bags.

"What…"

He doesn't ease my curiosity but walks past me and drops the bags on the kitchen counter. Shuffling through them, he begins pulling out books.

"*What to Expect When You're Expecting… Birthing from Within….*" He pulls out another one, waving it around. "*The Expectant Father.*" He offers me the most handsome wink.

"Since I won't be letting you rip my clothes off, I figured we could catch up on some reading material."

If I didn't think he was perfect before this moment, when he pulls out two tubs of ice cream, it's definitely confirmed. He *is* perfect now.

"Roman?" I say as I grip at the front of his coat and pull him to me.

"Yes, babe?"

I stand on my toes and brush my lips against his. "I don't hate you."

"I know." And he presses his lips back to mine.

Chapter Six

Roman

Sometimes a Man Just Knows These Things

"Ew! So did you know that your body creates mucus during pregnancy and right before you give birth, there's this thing called a plug that falls out of you?!"

I look up from one of the books to see Andie's upper lip curled in horror. She shudders before shoving another bite of ice cream into her mouth.

Chuckling, I point at the book in my lap. "Did you know that it is very common for the father to become the stay-at-home parent?"

She stretches her legs over my thighs and brushes against my cock. We're supposed to be trying something new here. Partners. Friends. Parents. But right now, I'm barely holding back from dragging her all the way into my lap and sucking ice cream off her tits.

"Did you know that my vag is going to expand to ten centimeters so a human head can squeeze through it?"

Annnnnd my boner is gone.

"That's disturbing," I tell her with a grunt and change that terrifying subject. "This book says we should keep a journal of all your appointments and measurements in order to be cognizant of the changes."

She's already shaking her head. "No way. You are *not* measuring me, Mr. Holloway. If I get fat, you better deal with it, because this child is going to be a big oaf like you. Your fault, not mine. But, dear God, I hope this kid doesn't have your big head." Despite her tough girl act, she's fighting a smile.

That smile is going to be the death of me.

Boner back on track.

With a growl, I toss away our books—which makes her giggle—and steal her tub of ice cream—which makes her growl. Once our hands are free from distractions, I pull her into my lap where she belongs. Her long legs straddle my hips, and she gazes down at me with an un-guarded expression. I could get used to this side of her.

"You're beautiful," I tell her, my gaze boring into her eyes. "Now. Two months from now. Big and fat and swollen with my kid inside of you. And after that too."

Her palms find my cheeks, and she drops a soft kiss on my lips. "We're really doing this?"

I smile against her lips and clutch her ass. "You bet-ter fucking believe it."

We kiss slowly. Usually, we're all but devouring one another. But I promised her things were going to change between us, and I'll be damned if I let us go back down that same road again. My cock aches, especially now that she's slightly rocking against it, but I refuse to strip her down and fuck her.

"Let's go to bed," I murmur against her mouth.

She nods and reluctantly climbs off my lap. Her cute ass jiggles when she bends to steal one last bite of ice cream before putting it away in the freezer. Once the apartment is all locked up and the lights are out, I lead her to her bedroom. We've fucked more times than I can count in both of our beds. And a few times we accidentally slept as well. This is the first time we've made a conscious decision to spend the night with each other.

"I don't think I've ever seen you looking so casual," she muses as she fusses with turning down the sheets on the bed.

I smirk as I tug my T-shirt off my body and toss it at her. "You've seen me naked but seeing me in sweatpants is suddenly alarming."

She sticks her tongue out at me. "You know what I mean."

When I push down my sweatpants and saunter past her into the bathroom, wearing nothing but black boxers, I don't miss the hiss of air that leaves her throat. Andie can be downright crude, but tonight she's prim as she brushes her teeth beside me at the sink and side eyes me. She's still fully clothed, but I see her wiggling in the mirrored reflection.

"What?" she grumbles as foam from the toothpaste dribbles down her chin. "I have to pee."

"So pee," I challenge with a lifted brow.

She spits and shakes her head at me. "No way. Not in front of you."

At this, I laugh. "So I can have my tongue between the lips of your pussy and my finger up your ass, but I can't watch you take a piss?"

Her elbow in my ribs knocks the breath out of me. "No! Now get out!"

I barely get to spit and rinse before she's shoving me out of the bathroom. With a chuckle, I turn off the bedroom light and crawl into her small bed. My bed is larger and more ideal, but I'd rather be here with her than alone anywhere else.

Maybe one day we'll have a bed together.

The thought warms me as I stare up at the dark ceiling. Once Andie finishes peeing *in private*, she climbs into bed with me. She also lies on her back and doesn't touch me.

"Roman?"

I roll over onto my side to face her. My palm rubs her stomach. "Mmm-hmm?"

"I like your mom."

Grinning, I lean forward and plant a kiss somewhere on her face, although I can't tell exactly where because it's dark. "I like her too."

She's quiet for a minute but then exhales and it sounds sad. "She reminds me of mine."

An ache forms in my chest. We lost Dad over a decade ago. I couldn't imagine what it would feel like not to have Mom in our lives.

"I'm sorry." My voice is husky, and I press another kiss to her face.

"I miss her. She would have…" she trails off. In the darkness, she sniffles.

I wrap my arms around her and roll onto my back, bringing her to rest against my chest. While stroking her hair, I tell her, "She would be proud of you."

Silent tears stream from her and soak my bare chest. "I don't know how…to be whatever it is you want us to be…" Then she lifts up from our embrace and breaks down in sobs.

"Shhh," I coo and cradle her face with my palms. I urge her to me and start kissing her wet cheeks. Her legs are bare now, and I'm thankful she's no longer wearing yoga pants. I kiss her plump lips softly at first. And then I kiss her with more need than I mean to exhibit.

"Roman," she whimpers against my mouth. "I need…"

I find the hem of her shirt and tug it away from her. Once she's naked up top, she finds my hands and draws them to her chest. Goddamn those tits.

"You're beautiful," I murmur as I pinch her nipples. "So beautiful and mine."

She lets out a shocked gasp when I roll her onto her back. I peel away her panties and push down my boxers. My intention was to take things slow, but the fire burning inside of me will only be quelled when I am deep inside this woman. I'm about to ram inside her, but something makes me stop short.

This time feels different.

There's more substance.

Emotion.

More than desire and excitement.

A need that goes beyond the surface—straight to the heart.

"Spread your legs," I instruct in a hoarse voice. "I'm going to taste you now."

She obeys—which is really fucking surprising because she usually hates when I demand things of her. I nuzzle her clit with my nose before running my tongue up the seam of her perfect cunt.

"Yesssss," she cries out, her fingers spearing into my hair.

I've tasted many women in my life, but never have I tasted one I wanted to completely devour down to her soul. I'm strangely possessive over Andie and it only seems to worsen by the minute. When I nip at her clit, she yelps and pops me upside the head. I can't help but chuckle as I massage away the pain with my tongue until she's squirming with need.

"I need you," she tells me, her voice breathless. "Now."

Since she's right on the edge, all it takes is my sucking on her clit and pushing one finger inside her slippery pussy for her to lose control. She all but rips the hair straight from my scalp. Sometimes Andie's mean and violent and physical—and that really gets my dick hard.

As soon as she stops shuddering so wildly, I climb over her perfect body and search for her sweet mouth in the darkness. Her lips are greedy as she kisses me hard. I let out a groan when she digs her fingers into my ass cheek and growls at me. "Inside, Roman."

Her cunt is hot and welcoming as I push into her tight opening. My cock fits perfectly inside her. Just snug enough to strangle me with bliss. Just deep enough to send her hurtling toward the edge with every thrust.

"You're mine," I murmur against her lips as I buck into her harder and harder. Her fingers gouge into my flesh, and I like that this woman bruises me all the god-damned time. It's like I wear the proof of her everywhere I go. Carry her with me even when she's not around. She certainly has already colored herself all over my heart. "You're mine," I say again, because I don't want her to ever forget.

"I know," she utters.

As soon as her body shudders beneath me and her pussy clenches with her orgasm, I have no shot in holding out. My dick spurts its heat deep inside her. If she wasn't already pregnant, I'd have knocked her up with the amount of sperm that seemed to gush into her.

This need to mark her is so feral. So goddamn animalistic. So overwhelming that I can hardly see straight. And I feel like it's only going to grow wild as time goes on.

I'm fucking obsessed with her.

And I hope to God the feeling is mutual.

"That's the heartbeat," Dr. Patterson says with a smile on his face. "Do you hear it?"

Thump, thump, thump, thump, thump.

Steady. Strong. Our child.

Andie's grip tightens around my hand, and her eyes are leaking tears. She's so fucking beautiful in nothing but a paper gown and a smile that could blind those who aren't ready for it.

I've never been more ready.

"Our baby," I tell her proudly, my own grin matching hers.

Hate 2 Love

"Everything appears to be healthy," Dr. Patterson tells us. "Ms. Miller, you're measuring about nine weeks along."

I try not to think about ten minutes earlier when he had a wand pushed inside my woman's vagina. Dr. Patterson is probably in his late forties and looks good for his age. The thought of him touching what's mine was infuriating, but it all faded away the moment I saw the tiny blob on the monitor.

"I'm going to prescribe you some prenatal vitamins. I also want you to make sure you're getting plenty of folic acid and drinking lots of water. Exercise is crucial too. You're carrying a human inside of you, so you're going to need to take extra care of both yourself and your baby," he tells her and pats her knee.

Andie and I are both in a daze as we leave the clinic. It isn't until we're seated next door in the Italian restaurant that it really sinks in.

"It's real," she murmurs as she absently tears off the end of her breadstick. "I heard it. It's alive in there." She shoves the bite of bread in her mouth and pats her belly. "Food's on the way kiddo," she garbles out between chews.

I simply stare at her in awe. Over the next several months, her stomach will swell with the growth of our child. Our child. Intense pride courses through me. She's mine. This baby is mine. We're a…family.

My mind whirs with a thousand thoughts. I'm a planner by nature. I've already begun to create mental checklists of things that need to be done or bought before the birth of the baby. I'm about to open my mouth

77

to start belting off the list when Andie lets out a big yawn and shoves more bread in. She's texting someone—who I assume is Dani—as fast as she can one-handed, because God forbid she let that bread go. My smile widens.

She's so fucking pretty when her guard is down. When she lets happiness shine through. But she's also tired. Dark circles paint the flesh below her eyes. Her normally shiny hair is slightly duller today. And her shoulders are hunched. This kid has barely begun to grow, and she's already fatigued. My gut tells me to demand she stay at home to take care of herself during her pregnancy. But my mind knows she'd castrate me if I put her on an extended leave. I'll just have to be more aware of how she's doing.

"I think something's wrong with Dani," she says suddenly and looks up. Her blue eyes are strained. Those two women are as close as can be—it's written all over her face. I've seen the torment in my own eyes when Ram's not been himself, flirting with depression. It's the worry of one sibling over the other. I'm happy Andie has Dani to lean on as if she were a sister. Unlike myself who has a brother and a sister, Andie has no one.

"Why do you say that?"

She frowns and looks down at her phone before showing it to me.

Dani: 9 weeks...awesome.

Arching an eyebrow, I give her a look of confusion. "Why do you think something's wrong with her?"

Andie huffs. "Because she's Miss Explanation Point always. This is a big deal for me. Normal Dani would be squealing or sending me a thousand exclamation points or sending me a bunch of those heart-eyed emojis."

"Okay," I say slowly. "Maybe she's distracted at work?"

Guilt causes her lips to tug into a frown. "I miss working side by side with her."

I reach across the table and take her hand. "I'm sure she's just having a bad day. Maybe," I tease, "her finger slipped and she hit the period by mistake."

Unconvinced, she tugs her hand away and starts rapid-fire texting. When she finishes, she shows me.

Andie: Everything okay? I'm worried about you. I can tell you're upset. Tell me what's wrong. Who do I have to kill? I can kick Ram's ass if necessary. Is it Frank from work? Tell that cocksucker to go find some other poor sap to do his errand running! Seriously. Who do I have to kill? It's not Daryl bothering you, is it? Because if it's him...Ram will kill him for you. Babe...tell me what's wrong. Are you mad I'll be a fat heifer standing next to you at your wedding? Cows can be cute, though... don't hate. I love you to the *mooooooo*n and back.

While she's holding her phone out for me to read, Dani replies.

Dani: I'm fine. So happy for you.

When Andie brings her phone back to her eyes to read the text, she bursts into tears. "S-S-Something is wrong," she sobs. "She's upset."

Ignoring the irritated scowls from a couple of old ladies at a nearby table, I climb out of my seat, walk around the booth and slide in next to her. I pull her against me and kiss her head. "We'll make it a quick lunch and then give her a call on the way back to the office. She's excited for you. You know this. Maybe she's just busy. Think about all those times you would get slammed at the bank and ignore my texts."

She snorts. "I ignored your texts because you were an asshole."

I wrap my finger around a lock of her hair and give it a playful tug. "I'm *still* an asshole. And you *still* like me."

Her chin lifts, and she turns her head to look up at me. "Nah, I hate you." The amusement twinkling in her teary eyes has me chuckling.

"No you don't. You've fallen in love with my massive baby-making cock."

She giggles. "I *do* hate you. And I do *not* love your cock. It's okay. Like, you know how donuts taste so good straight from the bakery? But the next day, they're just like sort of okay, but you eat them anyway. Your cock is a day-old donut."

"More like a thick, cream-filled éclair," I retort. "Super long too. You can't deny it."

"Ew," she says, pretending to shove a finger in her throat. "Stale, more like it."

Smirking, I give her tit a playful pinch through her shirt. "It's hard. I'll give you that."

"You're disgusting, Roman," she hisses and sends a punch to my ribs.

I grab her by the wrist before she can exact any more damage and bring her knuckles to my lips. "You like it."

Her eyes are all soft and dreamy despite the hard

words she likes to spit out. I love that her wall is no longer erect—that it's a pile of rubble at my feet. *Good fucking riddance, wall.*

"I hate you," she tells me with absolutely no venom in her voice. "I really do."

I kiss her ring finger and make a silent promise with my eyes to mark her here too. "I know and frankly, my dear Andie," I tell her with a growl. "I don't give a rat's ass."

My lips smash to hers, and I kiss her like we're the only two people in the restaurant. I ignore the gasps of the offended old ladies nearby and even the throat clearing of our server as he sets the plates down on our table.

I simply kiss her until her lips are swollen and raw. I kiss her until we're both hungry for more than the food on this table.

"Eat up, baby momma," I order and give her a wink. "My son is hungry."

The flash of pleasure that glimmers in her eyes at my words is enough to start working on my mental checklist. I will make sure Andie hurts for nothing. I will make sure she doesn't lift a damn finger. I will make sure she and this baby feel every bit of the love I know I can give them.

"We don't know the sex," she argues, her lips turning up in a full grin.

I puff out my chest and give her a smoldering stare. "It's a boy. Sometimes a man just knows these things."

She rolls her eyes as she drags her gigantic bowl of fettuccini toward her. "And sometimes a man knows nothing. Especially you. It's a girl."

I smirk as she slurps up a long noodle and lets out a moan of pleasure. With my thumb, I swipe away some sauce at the corner of her mouth.

"Want to make a bet?" I challenge.

She narrows her eyes at me. "Game on. If I win, you're changing diapers for a straight week."

"And if I win?"

"You get whatever you want." Her smug tone indicates she thinks she's already won the bet.

"Deal," I tell her as we shake on it. "I'll start thinking about what I want."

What I don't tell her is that I already have everything I want. And she's sitting right beside me.

Chapter Seven

Andie

That Big Headed Asshole

One week later…

"I SWEAR, YOU JUST LOVE GETTING A GOOD LAUGH at my expense," Dani huffs, sipping on her glass of merlot.

I, on the other hand, can't catch my breath long enough to respond. "I'm… I… Shit." I break down into another fit of laughs. We're currently at Bender's after Dani called me and told me I needed to meet her there ASAP for some heavy day drinking and celebrating. Roman's busy anyway, so he won't miss me if I take a longer lunch. My initial thought about Dani's excitement was that Ram knocked her up and we get to have babies together. I wouldn't have to do this all alone. But when she went into her story, I realized that not only was she not pregnant, but she's been using her set of steel balls too.

"*Now* what's her problem?"

I lift my head to see Brett standing across the bar,

tossing that damn towel over his shoulder and wearing that dumb smirk on his face.

"Excuse me? What's *that* supposed to mean," I snap, my laughter instantly dying. "And why are you looking at me like that again?"

"It means you're an unpredictable bet," he tells me simply. "Not sure what I'm gonna get with you."

I sit up straighter, absolutely no humor showing. "And exactly what does *that* mean?"

"Babe, last time you were in here, you started throwing silverware at me because you thought I gypped you on fries. And then, you cried because I put a drink in front of your friend here, and not you." He shrugs his shoulders, wiping his hands on his towel. "You're unpredictable. Crazy. You kind of fucking scare me actually."

Now it's Dani's turn to bend over laughing.

"Stop laughing!" I yell as I kick her stool.

"No can do." She giggles, lifting her head and giving Brett a high five.

"Hey, stop that! You're supposed to be on my side, not his!" I bark, getting mad because he *did* gyp me on fries. I finished them in, like, three seconds. There was no way I could have done that if he'd given me a full plate.

"Well you did gyp me. And I still think you owe me an extra side next time." I cross my arms over my ridiculously growing chest.

"But," he says with narrowed eyes, "how about the other day when you tried to bite me when I went to remove your empty plate?" He stares me down as if he has made some sort of point or something.

"What about it? You stuck your hand out aggressively. I was trying to protect myself. You're huge and beefy. A girl's gotta be on watch," I say, returning his shoulder shrug.

"So then telling me you still had crumbs and to fuck off was just a ploy to protect your female rights?"

I mean, I would go with that. "Yep."

Brett's stupid grin starts breaching his tough features as he slowly leans over the bar.

"All right, then. How about I make it up to you? Ice cream with double hot fudge and a cherry on top?" he rumbles, his voice low and seductive.

My lips part, my mouth watering at the thought of cold ice cream under layers of silky hot fudge.

"Would you like that?" he asks, beginning to tap his fingers on top of the bar.

My head slowly nods. Not only do I want that, but I am seconds away from grabbing him by his thick neck and threatening his life if it's not in front of me in the next two seconds.

"Then how about you finally spill who the baby daddy is, and it's all yours, darlin'."

I go to smack him while Dani begins another cackle of laughter. Ever since last week, when I blurted out that I was pregnant, Brett has been all up in my business with his curiosity about who the father is. He's also jokingly trying to convince me it could be his.

Speaking of this past week, minus my insane mood swings and hormonal imbalance, it's been awesome. Roman has been perfect. Patient. He hasn't once commented on my sudden need to eat, cry, or sleep. If

85

anyone asked my opinion, I wouldn't recommend ever intentionally getting pregnant. They definitely make it seem a lot easier on TV. They never mention the crabbiness or bloating. The unstable mood swings and the quick wardrobe changes. I mean, I can't fit into shit! But for some reason, Roman must be just as crazy as I am, because he's put up with me. We haven't been able to spend our lunches together, like we did the first week, since he's been so busy, but we spend our nights together. We match one another on gross baby facts, which I wish were never spoken, or promises that if I get fat, he will along with me. I mean, who says that!? My guy does.

"Dude, not telling you. And for the last time, it's not you. Stop asking."

"You sure? That one night you and I…?" he kids with a boyish smirk.

"Ugh! There *is* no us! I wasn't that drunk that night. I know you're fucking with me. Plus, I wouldn't touch your nasty ass with a ten-foot pole after you let that hooker whore suck on your nob."

Brett belts out laughing. "Well speaking of—"

"Oh my God! Stop, you two," Dani interrupts. "I was trying to explain my day before Andie kept rudely laughing."

With a shrug, Brett turns to Dani, all ears open.

"Thank you. So obviously, as you guys know, this past week has been hell." Which it was. My poor girl is getting a beating ever since my departure from the bank. When we left lunch last week, I couldn't let the text message lie. I made Roman drive me to the bank to see what was up with my girl. And, low and behold, the normal cocksuckers were being cocksuckers. Poor Dani was slammed to the wall with bank customers while stupid Frank had his Next Window sign in his window.

"So all week I tried to keep my mouth shut. Be the nice, polite Dani I always am. But today I had it. I snapped. I *never* snap." She pauses to take a healthy gulp of wine, then continues, "And well, Ram has been telling me to leave that place forever. To just tell them to, excuse my French, go fuck themselves and do what makes me happy. He tells me all the time that I don't have to work. He can support me. But that's just silly. I want us both to care for one another." She pauses again, her cheeks becoming flushed.

"Ew! Please do not share what you're thinking," I interject.

"Ew, what?"

"You have that daydream look. Let me guess, it went like this, '*Oh Ram, thank you for being my knight in shining armor. Now let's do nasty things to one another*'."

Dani begins to giggle, knowing I'm fucking right. Ew. Those two are so perfect, it's sick. And cute. And fucking perfect.

"Are you going to let me finish telling my story to Brett or what?" She offers me her cute little pouty look. I nod, placing my hands in my lap like an obedient friend.

"Okay! So, as I was saying, today I had it Ram's advice weighed heavily on my mind all day. My manager was being a jerk to no end. And all I could think about was how I could be somewhere I loved instead of there. I was wasting my life being miserable, when I could be happy some. Place. Else! So, I told Mr. Sphincterson he was a no good, fat, bad breathed, sloppy, poor excuse for a boss. And then I quit. When Frank started griping about being shorthanded, I stuck my tongue out at him. Ha! Then I walked over to JC Penney's and applied for a job. And I GOT IT!" She finishes on a squeal as she picks up her wine, gulping down the rest of the glass.

I'm still laughing about the part where she called Harold a fat fucker, which he his, so it takes a minute for the rest of her story to register. As she exclaims that she got a job at a department store, like it's the best thing on earth, I proceed to choke on the sip of water I am taking and spit it out, hitting Brett in the chest.

"You what?"

"I got a job at JC Penney's. I told them I am a pro at folding towels and the hiring manager was just so pleased. I even offered to demonstrate, which they allowed!" She smiles so big while I stare at her as if she's turned into an alien.

"You're serious right now? I thought that was just like a weird thing you enjoyed. I didn't know it was a career goal," I tell her, super confused right now.

"Well, now it's my job. So you can congratulate me, and we can celebrate over a hot fudge sundae or you can eat it all alone while I sit here and drink more."

My expression hardens immediately.

I clearly have no intentions of sharing that sundae.

"Oh goodness, I don't want the sundae. I just want wine. Today, wine is good," Dani says as she taps her glass at Brett.

Brett fills her glass to the brim. "Proud of ya, darlin'. This one's on me, since crazy over there doesn't look like she's going to share or admit that it's my baby."

Dani laughs and takes a sip of wine while I lift my water, ready to toss it at him. He's lucky a waitress comes over and places a large sundae in front of me, avoiding future head trauma from my glass. He seems completely unfazed, too, as he simply laughs at me.

"Don't worry, babe, it wouldn't be the first time this week someone threw a glass at me. Your bestie was here the other day trying to hook up. Asked her if she wanted my dick again. Didn't appreciate me saying it in front of her date. Threw her glass right at me. Bitch has good aim."

Since my bestie is right next to me, I lift a brow in question. "And who the fuck is my bestie?" I ask, shoveling ice cream into my mouth.

"Your girl you set up. The one who fucked with your man," he says as he points to Dani.

My eyes go wide, and I choke on my full spoon.

"Chelsea was in here?" Dani asks.

"Yeah. Real bitch. Seems like my bar is a new stomping ground for your whole gang now."

Seriously, what the fuck is he talking about?

"Dude, I don't speak in bro code. Get to the point. Who else did you see?"

"The other guy you two were with. The big dude. He was here with a chick on Wednesday for lunch."

The words leave his mouth, but it takes a second for my brain to catch up. Big dude… The other guy we were with… Fucking Roman.

"He…he was here with Chelsea?" I'm confused. He wouldn't do that to me. He's committed to me. To us.

He's done nothing but work to convince me, since the moment I broke down a piece of my wall, that he is willing to fight for us. Brett has to be wrong.

"No, Chelsea came by, but not with him. The other guy was with some blonde chick. Fuckin smokin'. They ordered burgers and drinks but barely touched them, then left together. Jealous. Man, that bitch had a set of tits on her."

Tits.

Roman's MO.

He apparently *would* do this to me.

"Honey, I'm sure he has a good reason." Dani tries to pat my shoulder. More like *pet* it since she is on her third glass. *No* good reason amounts to justifying a lie. And no matter what he says to me, he lied. He said he was swamped with lunch meetings all week. *Especially* on Wednesday when Suzy, the tramp home wrecker, came in to give him a message which came through on Reagan's line.

I asked him if I needed to schedule anything, and he said he would take care of it. Because *he* didn't want me to see it.

That fucking lying, cheating…

"Oh no, you're turning red. You need to calm down," Dani pleads.

Calming down is far from what's on my agenda. That bigheaded asshole. I grab for my phone and pull it out. I'm going to set him up. Give him the opportunity to tell me the truth.

If he does, then I will allow him to grovel until our baby turns five and then think about forgiving him.

If he lies…

I'm going to murder him.

"Andie, don't call. It's probably not a good idea."

Fuck calling.

Me: How are your "meetings"? Want me to bring you a burger from Bender's?

Roman: I'm deep in contracts. No thanks, baby. I already ate.

Me: What else are you "deep" into?

Roman: Hoping to be deep into you later.

Me: Wow…figured your appetite would be full from Wednesday.

Roman: I can never get enough of you.

Me: I know, right? Between me and the big tits bimbo you had lunch with on Wednesday, you're barely sated.

Fuck giving him the opportunity to tell me the truth.

Roman: What are you talking about?

Dani: I love you.

Me: Oh, you know! Too full from staring at her big tits to eat? Had to leave and get a taste?!?!?!?!

Dani: You're pretty

I look up to see Dani smiling at me, her eyes glossed over. "What? You look angry. I wanted to cheer you up."

My phone dings again, and I pull my eyes away from her.

Roman: What are you talking about? Are you feeling okay today?

Me: Fuck you…I feel fine. I'm not a cheating asshole!

Linc: Hey, I need to talk to you.

Jesus! I'm being blasted by everyone I know.

Roman: How am I cheating? What's your problem?

Dani: Your ice cream is melting.

Me: Don't act like you don't know. I know you were at Bender's on Wednesday!

Linc: Can I come by?

Just what I need right now. I have bigger fish to fry than having to deal with Linc, too. He always seems to show up at the worst times, but I can never tell him no.

Roman: She was a client, Andie.

Me: Fuck you. I hate you.

Linc: Why? What did I do to you? You know you love me.

Me: Oops! Sorry, wrong person. Yeah, let's meet up later. I miss you.

This time I make sure to send my message to Roman.

Me: Fuck you. I hate you.

Roman: You don't hate me.

Dani: You don't hate him.

I lift my head up to see Dani hovering over my phone. "Oh, I hate him," I assure her.

Me: I do. Don't come over tonight. I'm sick and won't be back in the office today.

Roman: Don't be ridiculous! Come back to work...you're not calling in sick.

Anger floods through me. I'll be damned if I'm going to let him boss me around—even if he is technically my boss. This has nothing to do with work and everything to do with him being a liar!

Me: I'm inviting Brett to my place. He's a tit man like you. But I'm sure he will appreciate them more.

Ha! Take that, asshole.

Roman: Of course I appreciate your goddamned tits!

Roman: Andie, you fucking stay away from him.

Roman: I'm coming over.

Roman: Answer me dammit! I swear to God if he touches you, I'll kill him!

Linc: Perfect. I'll find you. I have an idea where you're at.

I roll my eyes at the last text and reply back to Linc.

Me: Been stalking my Facebook again I see…

Dani: I'm sorry I just took a bite of your ice cream. It was yummy.

My eyes flit up from my screen to see Dani giving me puppy dog eyes. Damn girl gets away with everything with that look. I stick my tongue out at her before turning my attention back to my phone.

Me: Fine, I'll go to his place. I hate you.

Roman: Andie! You have the wrong idea here.

Me: That's a shame because that's the idea I'm sticking with. <middle finger emoji>

I slam my phone down, not needing any more of his bullshit. I should have figured. A fucking hot, successful guy like him could never be faithful. He wouldn't want to stick it out with a moody, fat, pregnant grump like me. I should have never dropped my guard with him.

But we had something. I know I didn't dream that up.

Had.

A grumble leaves my throat, and I bang my fist on the bar.

"Brett, I'm gonna need a bigger bowl of ice cream."

Chapter Eight

Roman

Fuck Professionalism

SCRUB MY FACE WITH MY PALM AND LET OUT A GRUNT of frustration. That woman makes me batshit crazy sometimes. It's just the hormones, though. Has to be it.

Guilt sits heavily in my chest. She knows I went to lunch with Diane on Wednesday. That fucker at Bender's must have told her. And now, apparently, she has quite a few ideas about Diane and I—all of them the worst possible scenarios, no doubt.

Why can't she just leave well enough alone?

Because she's motherfucking Andie Miller.

Drama queen to the nth degree.

Her fiery passion and sailor mouth are normally what I enjoy most about her. But when they're turned against me, things get tricky. I like her wrath when I'm buried deep inside her. All other times, though, are more complicated.

Despite Diane and I accomplishing what we've been working together on all week, I am frustrated. This is supposed to be a happy day for me. One that I'd hoped to share with Andie soon. I'll have to do some smooth talking to calm her down. It's not what she thinks.

I mean, yes, I've met up with Diane every day this week.

Yes, Diane and I have had lunch together.

And yes, Diane is doing her damnedest to help me.

But I'm not a pig, like Andie is so quick to assume. Goddammit, she pisses me off sometimes. I'm about to fire off a text, asking her to stay at Bender's until I get there—because that's obviously where she is and learned of Diane from—when my office door swings open. I expect to see one of my siblings or even Reagan's assistant Suzy. A part of me had even hoped it was Andie, ready to rumble. I'd have yanked her clothes off, bent her over her desk, and fucked the fire right out of her until she listened to every damn thing I had to say.

But it's not Andie.

It's some crazy-eyed looking motherfucker with a chiseled jaw.

"Can I help you?" I snap, my voice a little too harsh for my visitor. I mean, he could be a client, but based on his thuggish appearance and the disdainful look on his face at my appearance, I highly doubt that.

The man's gaze skips over me and darts right over to Andie's desk. That simple action—as if this stranger knows my woman and where she sits—has me rising to my feet and my fists clenching. The man is bulky with a thick neck that's sporting some colorful ink, snaking its way up his throat toward his jawline. His black T-shirt has the word "SWAT" emblazoned across the front and is stretched to the limit over his solid frame. I may have an inch or two on him, but he's bigger than me. Hell, he's even bigger than Ram.

"Where's Andrea?" he questions as he saunters over and picks up a sleeve of crackers on her desk. He tears it open and shoves a cracker in his mouth.

I crack my neck and wonder who the fuck this guy thinks he is waltzing in here like he owns the place. "Lunch. May I help you?" It takes everything in me to maintain a decent level of professionalism when I'm getting bad vibes from this prick and am dying to tear his throat out with my teeth. Something about him rubs me the wrong way.

He turns and sits his ass on the edge of her desk. It's just a desk from IKEA, and if he keeps swinging his legs like a goddamned kid, the entire thing is going to implode from beneath him. The thought has me smirking. I'll buy her a new desk, but seeing that shit would be worth it.

"Just looking for Andrea," he tells me in a cheery voice that grates on my nerves. He tugs a grey beanie off his head and scratches his dark buzzed scalp, before putting it back on and crossing his arms over his chest. His black eyebrows lift up in question. "How'd she get a job like this, anyway?"

The asshole steals another one of her crackers and chomps away.

"She applied and she got it. Andie is an excellent assistant and more than capable. How do you know her?" I demand, my voice faltering and allowing some anger to seep in. Fuck professionalism. I'm three seconds from pummeling this asshole.

His mischievous green eyes narrow as he sizes me up. I don't like being under this loser's scrutiny. "She and I go way back." He winks at me, and I suppress a growl.

"She's not here. I have work to do but I'll tell her you stopped by..."

"Linc," he finishes with a grin that produces a dimple on his left cheek, giving him a playful, innocent look despite his hardened exterior. I'm not some pretty girl who will fall for this asshole's charms, though.

"Get out of my office, Linc."

His dark eyebrows rise almost to the edge of his beanie. He must sense my barely contained rage, but instead of shrinking away like he should, it seems to provoke him. I can tell he's the antagonistic type. "We all know Andie isn't qualified for a job like this. Who'd she have to blow—"

"Don't fucking finish whatever is about to come out of your mouth," I snarl, all sense of decorum gone.

He smirks at me and shoves his hand into his back pocket to produce his wallet. Then, he flips it open to a picture. When he holds it up for me to see, fury bubbles inside of me.

Andie is young in the picture. Maybe eighteen or so. Her bright blue eyes are heavy-lidded as though she's stoned or something. Her normally long blonde hair is cropped short and curves just under her chin. She's fucking adorable in the photo. What isn't so fucking adorable is this asshole in front of me sitting beside her in the picture. His much skinnier arm is draped around her shoulder. He's smiling as he seems to be speaking something into her ear.

They look happy.

Too happy.

Why is her motherfucking ex-boyfriend in my goddamned office?

"Get out!"

He laughs—fucking laughs—in my face as he snaps the wallet closed. "Nah, I'll wait right here. Does she still smell like that lavender shampoo she always used?" he taunts.

I know he's poking at me, and it pisses me off.

"She smells like *me* because she's *my* girlfriend. Now get the fuck out before I knock your pretty teeth out," I roar, my chest trembling with rage.

He edges closer to me until his chest bumps mine. All joking has left his demeanor as he glares at me. "Your *girlfriend*, huh?" he snaps. "That's not what I heard."

I shove him hard away from me. "I warned you. Get out before I make you," I seethe.

The brave punk stalks back over to me and gets right back in my face. "Is Andrea really with an overbearing dick like you? I swear to God if you hurt my—"

"She's mine!" I bellow as I grab a handful of his stupid shirt. "If you so much as touch her ever again I'll kill—"

"I'll touch her whenever I want because she's my—"

"SHE'S NOTHING TO YOU!" I scream and shove him harder this time. "SHE'S HAVING *MY* BABY!" He stumbles against the wall and a picture crashes to the floor.

"You knocked her up?! And I'm just now finding out

about this?" he yells back, hurt lacing his tone.

I hope his heart is fucking broken to bits.

"It's not your place to know about—"

"ROMAN!"

Linc and I both jerk our gazes to the woman in the doorway. My little sister Reagan is glaring at me in horror. I shake away the rage and take a few steps back, so I don't knock this asshole's head right off his shoulders. She waltzes into the room, looking too pretty and petite to be in his presence. Reagan is innocent and this *thing* in my office has *future carnie* written all over him with his stupid neck tattoos and fake-ass "SWAT" T-shirt. I don't want that fucker near Andie *or* Reagan.

"What the hell is going on in here?" she demands, her small hands going to her hips.

Linc's anger melts away as he regards her with his dumbass dimpled grin. "Just having a talk with Andrea's psychotic 'boyfriend.'" He steps closer to my sister. "But I'd much rather talk to you."

Reagan's firm stare lingers on him for a second before darting to mine. She's a great CFO because numbers are her thing. My sister analyzes data faster than anyone I've ever known and interprets it in a way that makes sense. She has solutions to problems. My sister is a fixer.

Which is exactly why I don't like the way she's now regarding Linc, as if he needs a little fixing. I'll fix his face with my fist. Problem solved.

"You know Andie?" she questions him.

He nods. "I do. And I love her." With that comment, he looks over his shoulder and gives me a smug stare.

Red.

Motherfucking red.

I charge with my fist ready to slam across his jaw when Reagan steps between us. She jumped in the middle of her fair share of fights between Ram and I back in the day. My sister is fearless when it comes to furious big boys swinging fists.

"Move," I seethe.

She shakes her head. "You move your ass right back over to your chair." Her small hand gestures with exaggeration to my seat.

I growl but force myself to step away before I whip this fucker's ass and get myself involved in a lawsuit. I drop into my chair so forcefully, I'm surprised it doesn't collapse beneath me.

Reagan turns to look at Linc once more, and I hate how close he stands to her. The way he seems to sniff her perfume. The goddamned way he licks his bottom lip as if he'd like a taste—

"SIT DOWN, ROMAN!" she screeches.

I realize I'm back on my feet ready to climb over my desk to beat the shit out of him. With a huff, I obey my feisty sister.

"Everyone is going to calm down," she says in a soft tone. "Now who are you?"

"Lincoln Carter," he replies and extends his massive hand out to shake hers. "You can call me Linc, angel." His smile broadens at her as he lays his flirt on thick. It only makes me want to choke the look right off his face.

She simply chuckles at him and shakes his hand. I hate how small she seems next to this giant fucker. "Reagan Holloway. Nice to meet you." I grit my teeth when she leans in to him. "And I'm immune to," she says and waves at him, "whatever this is."

I bite back a laugh. She's had a little more bark to her ever since her man troubles in California sent her back home to us. Now, she has some bite to go with it.

"This is the beginning of something beautiful," he assures her with a smoldering grin. "Anyone ever tell you that your hair is smooth. Like unnaturally smooth. Like fucking Disney-princess smooth?" He lifts a hand and tugs at a strand. "I like it."

"Enough," I snap, ending his shameless flirting. I'm about to call Ram in here, so we can tag team this idiot. "He needs to go."

"Roman," Reagan huffs. "Chill. If he's a friend of Andie's, he's a friend of ours."

Linc chuckles and shoots a dark look my way. "Oh, we're a *whole lot* fucking more than friends."

"You asshole!" I spit as I stand so fast the chair goes sailing behind me and crashes against my credenza. "Come say that shit to my face!"

I ignore Reagan's protests and all fear of a potential lawsuit as I stalk over to Linc and send a splintering punch right across his jaw. He stumbles away, shaking away the blow to his head for a brief second, before he charges back at me. His massive hand clutches my throat as he tackles me. We both hit the ground hard. I haven't gotten into many fights in my life, but all of them were with Ram. It's hard to hurt someone you love. But this asshole, I could hurt him all damn day. I land a few punches to his ribs, but his grip on my throat has me seeing stars. Luckily, I manage to roll him over onto his back where I have the advantage. There's commotion all around us, and soon I'm physically torn from him by my younger, but stronger, brother.

"What the fuck?!" I roar in protest as he drags me away.

"Everybody just calm the hell down!" Reagan screams.

Ram's grip tightens on my biceps. "Dude, stop whatever the hell you're doing right now."

I'm about to open my mouth when Andie comes storming into the office with a stumbling Dani on her heels. Is she drunk in the middle of the day?

"I forgot my vitamins in my desk drawer, but don't worry," Andie snaps, her fiery eyes on mine. "I'm going home sick. *You* make me sick."

Linc starts laughing hysterically, and I fight against Ram to let me go at him. "S-She doesn't even like you," he chokes out between breaths.

As if just realizing there are others in the room, Andie tears her gaze from me and it lands on her ex-boyfriend. When she sees him, standing there all disheveled with blood trickling down his bottom lip, she loses all anger with one ragged breath.

"Oh my God! Linc! What happened to you?" she demands as she all but runs over to him.

I watch with crushing devastation as she throws her arms around his neck. He watches me over her shoulder and winks. The hug he gives her is full of warmth and love.

"Stop," Ram growls in my ear.

"He," Linc tells her in a fake-ass shaky voice,

"punched me. Your boyfriend hates me."

She jerks away from him and glares at me. "He's *not* my boyfriend anymore," she answers him in a cool tone. "And *I* hate *him*."

This makes him laugh more, but all of her focus is back on me. How can she even like this guy? I thought what we had was unbreakable, goddammit!

"You," she snarls as she stomps over to me. "I can't believe you have the audacity to hurt him when you're over there breaking my heart, you cheating asshole!"

There are two shocked gasps that I recognize as belonging to my siblings. I reach for her, but she bats my hand away. "Andie, it's not what you think—"

"Isn't that what all cheaters say?" Linc questions, adding in his unwanted two cents.

Ram growls behind me. "Dani. Reagan. Get him out of here. Please."

Our sister nods and she ushers Linc toward the door, her small hand gripping his elbow. He goes all too fucking willingly, which causes more rage to surge through my veins. Dani stumbles over her feet and lets out a hiccup before closing the door behind them. Finally, Ram releases me.

Andie remains glaring at me. "I trusted you."

Running my fingers through my hair, I let out a sigh of frustration. "That trust hasn't been broken. What you think is some torrid affair is just business, baby."

Her eyes are bright blue with fury but sadness flickers deep within them. "Brett said she was pretty."

Ram, realizing we need our privacy, leaves silently.

"Brett thinks everyone is pretty. He let Chelsea, of

all people, suck his dick, and we both know she looks like she's one Botox injection away from becoming a Kardashian. Since when do you listen to or care what Brett thinks, anyway?" I question, tentatively reaching my hand up to swipe a strand of hair from her face. This time, she doesn't bat me away, so I let my palm slide to the back of her neck and draw her closer to me.

"Do you like her?" Her chin slightly quivers. "Better than me?"

At this, I laugh because it's the most insane thing I've ever heard. "First of all," I tell her in a low voice as my other hand grips her hip. I pull her the rest of the way to me until our chests touch. "Nobody, and I mean nobody, is as pretty as you are. You're so fucking beautiful it hurts to look at you sometimes."

Her cheeks turn pink. "Lies."

I smile. "Truth. And second of all, there's nobody I like as much as you. Sure, you're mean as hell sometimes but you're mine. I don't share. Not with Brett and not with that fucker Linc." All smiles are gone as I grit my teeth just thinking about the way she hugged him.

Love.

I felt it. Saw it with my very own eyes.

The pain it causes is nearly crippling, but I won't let it win. She'll love me too, eventually. I don't care if I have to murder all of the competition just to make that happen.

My lips brush against hers, and she lets out a small sigh. It makes me starved for her.

"You have to believe me when I say that I've been dealing with Diane in a strictly professional manner. Please just trust me," I murmur against her plump lips.

She doesn't promise me, so I decide I'll convince her in other ways. I slide my palm from her hip to the front of the cute leggings she's taken to wearing lately. When I touch her between her thighs, her knees buckle. Her hands find my neck as she holds on. We kiss hungrily as I massage her clit through her clothes. Before long, she's whimpering into my mouth as her orgasm slices through her. Once she's calm from head to heart to toe, I remove my hand and regard her with a serious stare.

"We need to talk about Linc."

Her blonde eyebrow lifts in challenge. "Talk about what exactly?" she demands, a hint of defiance in her words. "Are you going to tell me I can't see him ever again?"

"That's exactly what I'm going to tell you," I snap back.

She shoves me away from her, but I grab her elbow before she can get away. Her attempts to shake me off are weak, but the tongue lashing she gives me is not. "I'll get right on that, *Dad*."

She fucking hates her dad.

Her barb stings more than I want to admit.

"You're mine. You and this baby are mine. Not his!"

Her blue eyes blink at me, at first in a furious way, but soon she starts giggling. My crazy Andie has actually lost her mind. Fucking pregnancy hormones.

"Oh!" she cries out, clutching her stomach.

"Is the baby okay?" I demand, all anger dissipating as I pull her against me.

She keeps laughing, though. "The baby is fine. It's you that is so very confused. I should have known he'd stir up shit. He didn't tell you?"

"So help me, if he's this child's father, I'm going to lose my fucking head," I bite out.

Her fingers grip my chin and she draws my face down. Tears of laughter stream down her cheeks. I love how pretty her lips look when they're curled into an amused smile. "Roman. You're the father. Don't even insult me. I haven't been with anyone else since that night we first hooked up after the snowball fight."

Relief floods through me. "I've only been with you, too." She needs to hear those words from me. I love how her body melts against mine in relief. Apparently we're both afraid as hell of losing the other to the point we're borderline self-destructive to our relationship.

"Linc is my brother. Step brother to be precise."

I stare at her.

Brother.

"That motherfucker," I growl. "He made me think..."

"I know," she says with a sigh. "It's a problem of his. He likes to cause trouble wherever he goes. But I *do* love him."

I stiffen at her words, although they don't hold the same meaning anymore. She loves him because he's family. Like I love Ram or Reagan. "He's still an asshole."

Her eyes twinkle with delight. "For sure. The biggest asshole. He's a good guy, though, once you get to know him. If it weren't for him, I wouldn't have made it through life very easily after my mom's death. Linc kind of dragged me along after that."

"I didn't know you had a brother," I tell her, hurt lacing my voice.

"I've honestly been so focused on us and the baby, I didn't really think to tell you. You know how my past is. Ugly and sad. And I still cannot stand my dad, even though by marrying Lana he gave me a brother when I needed one most."

I slide my palms to her ass, which feels all too delicious in her thin leggings, and pull her tighter against me. "From now on, I want to hear all the details about your life. The ugly and sad ones too. And Linc really is an *ugly* part of that past," I grumble.

Her eyes light up. "You were jealous. You fought my brother because you thought he was my secret lover?" At this she cackles and then snorts. "So damn funny!"

"I don't share," I growl and grip her ass hard. "Just ask Mom. She used to beat me all the time for going off on Ram when he'd try to play with my toys."

"Your mom did not beat you," she argues and slaps at my chest.

"She so did. That wooden spoon went everywhere with her. We'd get out of line, and she'd start digging in her purse. We'd get right back in line before she even pulled it out." I smirk at the memory.

"I think it's hot when you get possessive. Jealous Roman is a turn on," she teases.

I drag her with me over to the door so I can lock it first before hauling her over to my desk. She squeals the entire way with laughter. When I get her over to the clean surface—thanks to her surprising organizational skills—I bend her over it. Her elbows rest on the wood and she eyes me over her shoulder. "What are you going to do? Spank me? You're the one who needs the spanking, Mr. I Don't Share," she taunts and wiggles her ass at me.

I narrow my gaze as I undo my belt. "You can spank me later. But for now," I tell her softly, "I'm going to punish you for being such a bad girl and keeping your brother a secret from me." She doesn't fight me when I drag her leggings and panties down to her knees. "I'll punish your pretty white ass for jumping to fucking conclusions because Brett is a tattling bitch who doesn't know what he's talking about." Playfully at first, I whap her ass.

Her blue eyes darken with lust, and she licks her lips. "I thought you didn't like hurting me. What about all those times I begged you to get kinky with me?"

I smirk and hit her ass harder this time. It makes her squeak and it makes my already hardened dick jump in my slacks. "Apparently I have no self-control with you. You push and fucking push until I'm hurtling over the edge."

"I like when you lose control," she tells me with a wicked grin.

I pop her ass again. Three red welts color her creamy flesh. "I guess you got what you wanted then, huh?"

She bites on her bottom lip and nods—the evil look she gives me is at war with her angelic blonde hair and innocent, plump lips. God she fucks with my head.

I slap her ass a few more times with the belt until she's squirming and begging for my cock. Ever since I started sleeping over at her house each night, we've yet to fuck in my office again. She'd respected the professionalism I was striving for. But now?

Fuck my stupid rules.

K WEBSTER AND J.D. HOLLYFIELD

With one hand, I jerk my pants and boxers down and toss away the belt with the other. My dick slides against her wet pussy in a teasing way, but I don't enter her just yet. She whimpers and shoves her ass toward me. I grip her silky blonde hair, tugging it to me, so that she lets out a gasp.

"I'm going to fuck you right now," I say and barely push the head of my swollen cock into her hot cunt. "And you're going to love it."

She moans and nods but can't move much with the death grip I have on her hair. "But they'll hear," she murmurs. She doesn't care, that much I know. She knows I care, though, and it warms me.

I thrust so hard into her that my balls slap against her clit with an obscene sound that is overshadowed by a scream of pleasure. "Let them fucking hear."

Chapter Nine

Andie

He Gave Me Crabs

DON'T DO IT… DON'T DO IT…

"Hey, what about this one?"

Dammit.

"Um, yeah. It's really…sparkly," I comment, which is an understatement. I respect Dani's love for Christmas and all, but dressing her bridesmaids up as shiny Christmas ornaments is where I have to draw the line.

"It sure is, isn't it? You all will glimmer on the dance floor! So pretty." She claps her hands together in excitement.

I guess it beats the green dresses she originally picked out, making us all look like a standing line of Christmas trees.

"I think it's the one. Will you try it on?"

Please no.

"Anything for you," I say with a smile, grabbing the disco ball off the rack and walking back to the dressing room.

The things you do for friends. I swear.

"So how did the appointment go today? Everything look good?" Dani asks through the dressing room door.

I'm tugging my leggings down and fighting with the ankles as I respond. "Yeah, everything looked good. Doctor said the heartbeat was strong as a bull. I swear I thought Roman was going to start fucking weeping."

I hear Dani laughing, then giving me a good ol' sigh. "I think that's so sweet. He's so in love with that baby, it's just so precious. Did you know he gave us a speech on babies the other day, on when they begin to hear? He told us at nine weeks, their ears begin to grow and at eighteen weeks, they can hear. This all sparked when we asked what all the packages at the door were. You know what he told us?" She sighs again. "He went off naming every single device capable of playing music. Prenatal sound wave machine, Bellybuds headphones, womb music. He just went on and on. Ram ruined it by laughing, but I was practically in tears with how touched I was."

I've since stopped fighting with my leggings, now sitting on the ground listening to the story. A smile tugs at my lips as I lift my hands to rub at my still, kinda sorta flat belly while remembering that night when he came over.

"God, you're sexy." He walks in, and before dropping all the bags he's holding, leans down and offers me the best Roman Holloway kiss ever. When we finally break away, my eyes veer toward the excessive amount of bags he's carrying, piquing my curiosity.

"More ice cream?" I ask in a hopeful tone.

"Even better. I wanted to keep it a surprise, but I couldn't wait any longer. Sit." He guides me to the couch, throws off his suit coat, and starts pulling items out of bags.

"What is all this?"

"This, my sweet girl, is a prenatal sound machine. It's a band that you strap around your belly, so you can play music to the baby." He drops it and grabs for another box, "And this? It's called a BellyBud. It's so you and the baby can listen to the same thing. Did you know that his ears are already growing? In seven more weeks, he will be able to hear sounds. I want him to hear us all the time." He drops it and picks up one last smaller box. "This one records voices. So you can record whatever you want and play it for him. He will know our voices." He drops the box, bending down to take my lips. I wrap my hands around his neck as he lifts me up, bringing me over his lap.

"Thank you," he whispers so softly, I almost miss it.

"For what?" I ask.

"For giving me this child. He'll be just as amazing as you are."

My lower lip begins to tremble. The tenderness he shows is something I might never get used to. I bring my hands to his cheeks, our eyes locking. "Again, what makes you think it's a he? It could be a she, you know."

"God help me if it is. Good thing for these sound machines, because if we find out it's a girl, my recording to her will be on repeat for the rest of your pregnancy."

I giggle placing a peck to his lips. "And what would it say?"

"Stay away from boys till you're forty."

My chest is tight as I blink away the memory. Since I'm not good at sharing my own emotions, I ended up crushing my lips to his that night, hoping he could feel what I was trying to silently tell him. This new thing between us has been more tame. Patient. The way he slowly devours me. Far from our usual rough, wild sex. It's been like this ever since finding out about the baby. Roman knows my little needs, but he also wants to show me how it's not just about raw, wild pleasure with us anymore. There's more emotion and meaning. There's an unspoken promise that what we are doing is going to be something more powerful than just passion. He is committing to me.

I wipe the single tear that glides down my cheek, and stand, pulling my shirt over my head. "Well, that big oaf has my apartment filled with books, devices, and all sorts of random baby crap. We don't even need to bother registering because he's bought the whole damn store already," I grumble, unzipping the dress and stepping into it.

"Oh, no way, José. We're registering. I'm helping pick out those cute baby socks—"

"Have 'em."

"Okay, well then I've seen the cutest little bathtubs—"

"Have one already."

"Stuffed animals?"

"I have a stuffed animal zoo currently in my living room."

"Baby blankets?"

"Have have have! I'm telling you, I'm only twelve

weeks in. Can you even imagine what we will own by the time we hit nine months? I can barely walk around my apartment now with all this crap!"

Dani starts laughing, and eventually I join in. I guess it does make it real when you walk out of your bedroom every morning to find your man reading a baby book, while trying to operate some sort of new monitor, swing, or watching a video on how to swaddle an infant. I can take a guess at what I'm going to walk out to tomorrow, since he has already texted me three different kinds of homemade baby food machines.

"Do you have it on yet? You have me biting my nails off out here."

I finish adjusting it under my gigantic breasts and turn to look in the mirror.

"Jesus," I grumble. Thankfully, the material billows out around me, so as my stomach grows, I'll most likely still be able to wear it.

"What? Let's see!" Dani starts jiggling the door handle. One deep breath and I slap a smile on my face and open the door.

"Oh, I LOVE IT!"

I was afraid of that.

"Yeah me too. Very…"

"Shiny…wow." We both turn to see Reagan, out of breath, entering the dressing room. "Sorry I'm late, guys. My lunch plans ran over." She glances at me quickly, but pulls her eyes away to Dani, then to the dress in question. "So. Wow. Very festive. Where are the other options?" She looks around as if hoping to find other racks of dresses.

"You're looking at it," I chime in. "Isn't it so pretty? We're gonna just shine on the dance floor." Reagan offers me a *no-we're-not* look until she sees my *yes-we-are* look in return.

"Oh! Oh, yes. It's perfect." She smiles and turns to Dani, taking her in her arms. "I couldn't ask for a better sister-in-law. This wedding is going to be perfect."

They hug it out while I stand there feeling like chopped liver. "Um hello?" I pout.

They pull apart laughing. Reagan comes at me, almost knocking me over and throwing her arms around my neck. "And you and Roman are going to be the best parents ever to my little niece or nephew." I pull her off me because she's starting to choke me.

"Thanks, wow. For a second there, I thought that was a ploy to get close enough to kill me." I rub at my neck.

Reagan responds with a laugh, waiving me off. "Sorry, I'm just so happy. And one day, when you become a Holloway, we'll all be sisters."

My smile falters, while Dani's smile turns more empathetic. She knows my feelings about marriage—how it is something I never see myself doing. My mom gave her life to a man who left her. I swore to myself I would never do the same.

"What?" Reagan questions, her dark eyebrows knitting together in confusion. "What did I say?"

"Nothing. It's fine," I lie. "I just don't see myself getting married."

With a gasp leaving her lips, Reagan steps closer. "Why? Roman loves you. You two are perfect together."

Okay. I still don't plan on getting married, but *what*?

"He what?"

Reagan's expression falls. "Oh. Oops. I... I mean... He...he hasn't told you?"

"Told me what exactly?" *Say it again. Say it again.*

"That he loves you. It's clearly obvious. He talks to my mom nonstop about you. He's like a freaking chick!"

We all, in unison, start to laugh.

She thinks Roman loves me.

I think Roman has tried to show me that he loves me.

But can I let him?

I'm so afraid. I've always been one to guard myself, so that if and when I'm let down, the fall won't hurt as bad. To let myself entertain the notion that Roman and I could be a forever thing scares me. Because what if we're not? What if one day, he realizes this isn't what he wants?

I always think back to the pain in my mom's eyes when my dad left. The broken heart she endured during the last few years of her life. At the time, these were the thoughts that plagued me daily. She wasn't afraid of dying. I think a part of her embraced it. She knew that when she left this world, she would finally stop hurting.

I shake off Reagan's silly words, not allowing them to sink too deeply. "Well, he loves a lot of things. So let's not get carried away. What we should focus on is our girl, who just picked out the prettiest bridesmaids' dresses, and go out to lunch to celebrate!" I exclaim, changing the topic and mood.

"We had lunch right before we came here," Dani reminds me.

I shrug her off, head into the dressing room and shut

the door.

"Snack then. Celebration snack." In the form of cheeseburgers.

After getting both of us measured and the dresses ordered, we made our way over to Benji's Café, where we all settled with lattes and tarts—a hot chocolate and two cherry Danishes for me.

"Andie, do you mind me asking a personal question?" Reagan starts in soon after we sit down.

"As long as it doesn't come between me and this Danish, have at it." I shove a huge bite in my mouth needing to make it to the center where all the gooey cherries are.

"How did your mom die?"

Dani chokes on her coffee while I pause mid bite. My tongue was *just* at the center.

"I'm sorry. I just… Linc talks about it. He's just not really good with details…"

Dani turns to her and asks, "Wait, you talk to Linc?" I just stare her down and nod because my mouth is full.

"Well, kind of. I mean we have lunch sometimes… Or dinner…or both. I mean…"

"Dude," I mumble, trying to get my bite down. "Your brother is going to kill you. Shit, or kill him if he finds out you're hanging out with my brother. And wait, *why* are you hanging out with my brother?"

"Better question is *how*?" Dani chimes in.

Reagan looks nervous. A trait you don't see on her often.

"I'm not really sure how we started. I, well, I met him that day when he showed up at the office and Roman tried to kill him."

That he sure did, big idiot.

"So yeah, doesn't explain how you two are like, hanging out," I state, taking another bite. God this is so delicious. I should have ordered four.

"Well, when you two wanted to be alone, he left with me. And he said he wanted to wait. And well, you two… were kinda busy." She blushes, admitting she knew, or heard, for that matter, how our fight ended.

"Any who. He just looked like he needed a friend. So I offered. I gave him my number. Told him if he needed a familiar face around town he could call."

My damn brother. I should have known he would spot Reagan in a heartbeat. The cute innocent type that he can't help but challenge himself with. I need to make sure to have a talk with him about staying clear of her. I really don't want my baby daddy killing the only living relative I actually care for.

"Great, but you know Roman's going to flip if he finds out."

"Ram may not be so happy either. No offense," Dani says as she turns to me.

"Well, they aren't going to find out," Reagan replies, sipping on her latte. "Listen, I just want to be there for him. He needs a friend. We're just pals."

I want to argue and tell her it's not fine and to stay clear. I love my brother, but he isn't the most stand up guy and trouble seems to follow him. I just don't want to hear *I told you so* from the Holloways as they stone me out of the family because my brother fucked with their baby sister.

But then there's a side of me that also feels grateful to Reagan. Aside from his faults, he *does* need a friend. He didn't have any better of a childhood than I did. We might not be related by blood, but we do share a past.

When my mom died, I was still a minor. And the shitty thing is that no matter how long you've been taking care of yourself and playing the adult, to the child welfare system, you're still a kid. My dad was nowhere to be found, regardless of all the attempts my mom made to write or search. In the end, I was forced to live with the only living aunt who would take me in. She'd never been married and was a huge bitch. She hated kids, which meant she hated me. I was pulled out of the only town I knew, away from my school, my friends. Dani's parents, the saints they were, offered to take me, but my aunt fought, wanting the insurance money my mother had set up.

I lived with her for almost a year before my dad knocked on her door.

He looked older. Aged. He and my aunt fought, and then he told me he was taking me home with him.

He'd explained to me that a few weeks before that time, he had received an abundance of letters that had been lost in the mail. The letters my mother had sent.

Almost a year it took for him to receive them.

To find out my mother had died and left me with no one.

It made me hate him more.

He didn't care enough to find me before.

I cried. Yelling at him for being such a horrible husband. A horrible dad. Screw those letters. Why didn't he come when he heard she had died?

He admitted to being a coward. I agreed.

He was exactly that.

The last place I wanted to go was with my father, back to his new home, with his new family. I wasn't going to be the red-headed step child. The damper in their probably perfect life. But my options were either that or stay with Aunt Edith. So I went with him.

That's when I'd met Lincoln. Linc to everyone else. He swears if I give away his full name, he's going to find a way to make me pay. Linc was Lana's—my dad's new wife—son from a previous marriage. Linc, being just as rebellious, was never in favor of their marriage. He'd started acting out when his parents got divorced. From the stories, it sounded like my dad faced the brunt of his outbursts, which made me happy. He deserved it.

For the couple of years I lived with them, Linc and I became really close. We leaned on one another when it got to be too much for my dad and his mom to carry the weight of two out-of-control kids. I'm pretty sure the only reason their marriage was saved is because both of us finally left home.

Linc just disappeared.

I finally accepted the offer from Dani and her family and stayed with them.

"I'm sorry if I overstepped," Reagan says, breaking my inner thoughts.

"Oh no. It's fine actually. My mom died of multiple sclerosis. She was diagnosed when I was really young.

Hers was considered mild, so she lived for many years with it. It wasn't until I was about twelve that it kicked into high gear. Her body gave in three years later. She died when I was fifteen."

Reagan's eyes become sad. It's the reason why I never tell anyone about my mom. I don't want sympathy. The time I had with my mom was nothing but the best. She made sure to be both parents, even if one was completely absent. She tried to hide her guilt for what I was enduring through her sickness. She didn't want her child having to take care of her. She wanted me to go out with my friends and enjoy my life.

I just wanted to be with my mom.

"Seriously if you look at me all sad like that any longer, you're going to owe me a Danish. For real. It's fine. Change of subject, though?" I throw out there because I'm over tarnishing this day with my past.

"Yes! Okay, so I wanted to tell you guys," Dani says with a squeal, "Ram and I picked a venue!"

The rest of the second lunch, as I'll call it, since I definitely ate three Danishes, was full of *awws* while listening to Dani's excitement for her wedding, a little baby talk, and laughs, because apparently hot chocolate can be added to the list of gas triggers. And then we talked about all the things Ram and Roman are going to do to their little sister if and when they find out she's hanging around my brother.

Finally, leaving the café, we all go in for a three-way hug.

"Oh my God, I'm so glad I came home. This has been the best year. Dani, I love the dress, and thank you guys for the pep talk. I'll make sure to wear a hard helmet, just in case the cat gets out of the bag." Reagan winks and takes off in the opposite direction to her car.

Dani and I drove together since she picked me up from work. I grab her hand as we walk down the busy street, the sun feeling great on my face. I squeeze her hand, as a silent thank you for just being a good friend.

"What the fuck are you all smiles about?"

Since I'm not paying attention, and the guy comes out of nowhere, I trip and fall into a solid frame. Somehow releasing my hand from Dani's during the fall, I lift my palms to the man's chest, and before I even put a name to the voice, I stare into the eyes of Frank Gillson.

"*Frank*?"

"Yeah, me, the one you called in a complaint on, and got fired from the goddamned bank." His eyes seem darker than normal and his face is unshaven. I give him a quick once over. He doesn't look as put together and douchey as he normally did at the bank.

"Dude." I try and push off him, but his hands are now squeezing my shoulders, making it impossible to escape his grip. "Fucking let me go, douchebag."

"Not until you admit you were the one who made the anonymous call. You got me fucking fired!"

His voice raises to an uncomfortable volume. Dani is now next to me, trying to pull his hands away from me.

"Frank, let her go," she pleads. "You're hurting her."

"Good," he snarls. "You listen up, you little bitch. You fucked with the wrong person." He doesn't say any more and releases me with a hard shove, almost knocking me backward. Thankfully, Dani grabs for me, and I end up falling into a couple behind me.

Frank takes off through the street and disappears while we stand there, in shock, staring at where he faded into traffic.

"Oh my God, Andie, are you okay?" Dani grabs me.

"Yeah, shit. I'm fine." Kinda fine. My heart is racing out of my chest, and I'm still trying to catch my breath. I'm no sissy, but that freaked me out a little. Frank wasn't looking too hot and angry certainly doesn't look good on him.

"What the heck was that all about?"

"No idea." But my expression must not be convincing because she gapes at me.

"Oh no," she whispers, her fingers going to her lips. "What did you do?"

I huff, shrugging my shoulders. "What? You were so upset! And I knew just telling Harold off wasn't good enough. Let's just say I avenged you."

"By?" she pushes, her brows tugging together in concern.

"I may have called in an anonymous complaint that Frank harassed me into doing things in the back room—on company pay—and that he gave me crabs."

"ANDIE!" she squeals, stopping a few people walking.

"I may have also called three separate times," I admit. "But he was hateful to you!"

And nobody is mean to my friend without consequence.

Chapter Ten

Roman

Technically It's Not a Lie...Right?

"I DIDN'T KNOW THIS WAS GOING TO BE A WORK party," I grumble as I put some snacks on a plate for Andie.

Reagan crosses her arms over her chest and frowns. "They're my friends. Why are you so grumpy today?"

I set the plate down and let my gaze wander to Andie, who is sitting on the couch next to Dani and Ram. Earlier today, we'd gone to lunch at a restaurant across the street from Babies R Us, and we ran into an old co-worker of hers. She'd been laughing and jabbering on until he said hello to her. When she dropped her shopping bags, and I stopped to help her pick them up, the guy left without even a goodbye. The whole encounter unnerved me, but she blew it off and changed the subject. A twinge of jealousy has settled in my belly ever since. I wonder if they'd fucked before. I quickly run that thought out of my head. I don't want to think about Andie fucking anyone but me.

"Sorry," I tell my sister. "Andie has just been oddly reserved today."

"Maybe she's having second thoughts," she teases with a grin.

I glower at her and she giggles.

"Lighten up! I was just kidding. But, since you're in a sour mood anyway, I guess now's the time to tell you," she says with a sigh. "I'm seeing someone. Someone you know."

My eyes dart all over the living room looking for Linc's sorry ass. She'd invited him for some goddamned stupid reason—claiming she wanted Andie to be happy—and I've been annoyed ever since. He and I haven't exchanged words since we tried to kill each other in my office. I don't plan on ever speaking to the motherfucker again.

But so help me, if he's banging my sister…

"Hey," Chase Douglas chirps as he enters the kitchen. Our HR manager is casual since it's a Saturday and dons a Carolina Tar Heels hoodie. "What do we have to eat? I'm starving." Despite his casual outfit, his shoulders are tense. Chase is never tense. "What's up, Roman?"

I give him a shrug of my shoulders. "My sister here was just explaining that I was going to have to kick her new boyfriend's ass. Want to help?"

His eyes widen in horror, and Reagan curses at me. "Dammit, Roman," she huffs. "You're a prick."

My eyes flit to the living room where Linc sits sprawled out in my sister's recliner like he owns the damn thing. It rubs me the wrong way.

"Please don't kick my ass," Chase says with a nervous

chuckle. "You're like twice my size, and I really like your sister."

I snap my attention back to my friend. Ex-friend now. "Wait? You're fucking my sister?"

"ROMAN!" This time Reagan slaps her hand towel at me. "You're an animal!"

Glaring at Chase, I ignore her. "Isn't this against some HR policy?"

"I, uh, come on, man—"

I stalk over to him and stare down at him. The poor guy looks positively petrified. I guess between Chase Douglas and Linc Carter, I'd rather have this guy dating my sister. At least Chase is the type to be faithful to her, put a ring on her finger, and make a good husband one day. Linc, on the other hand, looks like he'd fuck her every time they are alone and would end up stupidly knocking her up by accident.

Like you knocked up his *sister.*

I shake away the thought and force a grin at Chase. "Congrats, you two. Hurt Reagan, though, and I'll hurt you." My voice is playful but my threat is serious. Chase swallows and nods, the threat felt by him.

Snatching up a plate piled high with snacks that I know Andie will want, I saunter into the living room. I'm a little more relaxed now that I realize Reagan isn't dating that fuckwit. Ram pulls Dani into his lap to make room for me on the sofa. Once I sit, I set the plate on Andie's lap, she lets out an appreciative groan.

"Oh my God, I love y—" she starts but quickly shoves a pinwheel in her mouth. "Mmmm, so good."

Dani snorts at her. "Didn't you just finish telling me

how stuffed you were from dinner? I thought you two had steaks before you came over."

"Shush," Andie grumbles as she downs another pinwheel.

I slide my arm around her and lean back on the sofa. When I lift my gaze, her brother is glaring at me. I smirk at him.

"What are your intentions with my sister, anyway?" Linc questions with a growl. "I mean, she's pregnant with your kid. Will you pay child support? She already has one deadbeat dad in her life."

Andie stiffens at the sudden outburst, but I'm infuriated.

"Fuck you, loser," I snap. "I'm taking care of her, and it's none of your goddamned business."

Linc rises to his feet but Reagan and Chase are both at his side before he can jump over the coffee table to attack me.

"Come help me set up my new DVD player in my room," Reagan clips out at him. "You need to step away and calm down." She grabs him by the elbow and leads him from the living room. Chase follows behind them like a lost fucking puppy. When they're gone, I ignore the whispering between Dani and Ram beside me and look over at Andie.

"I'm sorry," I murmur and press a chaste kiss to her cheek. "He just pisses me off."

She swipes at a tear with the back of her hand but continues to shovel in 'lil smokies and cheese cubes like someone might snatch them right off her plate at any moment.

"Babe…"

"So!" Dani chirps, from beside me. "How did that new client meeting go? Ram was telling me you met with that construction company that is in dire need of rebranding. Was it a win?"

I give Andie's shoulder a comforting squeeze before chatting to my future sister-in-law about stuff she doesn't understand or care about. I suppose we all could use the subject change. When she gets on the subject of a new line of soft towels at JC Penney's, I let my thoughts wander.

I'm not like Andie's father. Late at night, when the lights are all off and we're cuddled naked together, she tells me stories of her past. The ones of her mother make her cry. The ones of her father make her scream. The very idea that Linc compared me to him makes me sick.

I'd been thinking hard lately about our future. There's no future for me without her. One day, when she fully warms to the idea of us, I'm going to put a ring on her finger. I'll spend my days making her heart happy and my nights making her body happy. We have this beautiful child on the way. I'd thought we had plenty of time to plan and settle into a life that would be ours together. But fucking Linc makes me feel like I'm doing a disservice to her. Should I be ring shopping? Picking out fucking venues like Ram and Dani. Suddenly, I feel pretty awful about everything.

I *did* knock her up.

I should be giving her a shiny rock and an expensive wedding with all the bells and whistles. I should be giving her much, much more.

But Andie's different. Despite Linc's venom-filled words, I know her better than anyone. I'm one of the few people she drops her guard for. Rushing certain things with Andie can only mean disaster. She comes around to ideas on her own time. When you tell her how it will be, she usually turns and hightails it in the opposite direction. Hell, it's one of the reasons I haven't come right out and told her I love her yet. I *do* fucking love her. I love that little bean in her stomach too. But I'm afraid if I tell her too soon, she'll panic like she tends to do. That she won't be ready to say the words back, and it'll be a catalyst for disaster.

So I wait.

I keep those words tucked carefully away in my heart until the right time. Until a time I know she'll hear them.

After a little bit of chatting, Andie calms and settles against my side. I'm stroking her hair when Reagan and Chase come back in. Chase sits in the recliner and she plops down in his lap. His hand rests on her hip while she absently pats his arm. They seem comfortable with each other. If anything, Reagan looks content. I only want my sister to be happy. I'm warming a lot quicker to the idea of these two than I originally thought. Mom would love Chase, so that's also a win in my book.

"So when do you find out the sex?" Chase questions.

I slide my palm to Andie's swollen belly and rub it. "We already know it's a boy."

Andie laughs and playfully slaps my thigh. "It's a girl actually."

My siblings and Dani all laugh, but it's Chase, Mr. Serious, who frowns at us. "I thought that ultrasound didn't happen until like five months."

"They don't go for another month," Dani answers for us. "They just like to argue for the sake of arguing. Don't you?" She nudges me with her foot.

I shrug and hug Andie to me. "Arguing is our foreplay, isn't it, babe?"

She sits up and lifts a brow at me. "I hardly call it arguing when we all know *I* have the best insults. You just stand there with your big mouth hanging open catching flies while I whip you with mean shit. You like it." A playful grin tugs at her lips.

"If I recall," I tease. "It's you with the big mouth. Huge mouth. I mean for it to fit my thick—"

"Yuck!" Reagan bellows. "Enough of that!"

Everyone chuckles, and I start in on Andie again. "I say mean stuff too. My *Your Mom* jokes are better, and you know it."

Andie scoffs. "They're terrible and stupid. Like you." Her nose scrunches. "In fact, you're so stupid, you thought Boyz II Men was a day care center. Our kid will not go there…because he's a she."

Linc snorts from behind us as he saunters into the living room and plops down on the floor beside the recliner. Ignoring him, I pretend to glare at Andie. "You're so stupid, they had to burn down the school to get you out of the fourth grade."

She laughs and swats at me. "Fourth grade was hard. I'm still not as stupid as you, though. In fact, if we had a penny for your thoughts right now, we'd all get back change!"

Dani howls, and I flip her off before narrowing my

eyes at Andie. "You're so stupid, you grabbed a bowl when I said it was chilly outside."

Andie scoffs. "But I love chili! Don't even play around when it comes to food. You're so stupid, you went to Babies R Us and asked where the babies were."

I frown because that really did happen. "I thought we were checking out a day care center. How the hell was I supposed to know it was a store?"

Reagan shakes her head at me. "You guys are so weird."

"Your mom is weird," I retort back.

Dani starts laughing so hard, she can't breathe, but it's Andie who punches my thigh. "That's your mom too, nerd!"

"Her mom *is* weird," I try with a grin.

Reagan sticks her tongue out at me. "Well, *your* mom is so weird she made you take me on your first date as a reminder for birth control!"

Andie grumbles. "A lot of good that did."

"Your mom is so weird she made you wear that denim outfit with rhinestones sewn all over it to your eighth-grade dance because she said bling is how you get a boyfriend," I retort and waggle my brows at Chase. "Whatcha think? You like Reagan's bling bling?"

"Is her vagina bedazzled?" Linc questions, sitting up, suddenly a little too interested in my sister.

"NO!" Reagan hollers. "Oh my God, you're such a punk, Roman!"

"Your mom is a punk," I tell her with a snort.

"Our mom is the most beautiful woman on the entire planet, and you fuckers just solidified my place as the favorite child," Ram tells us smugly as he wiggles his phone that's recording us.

My siblings and I all shout out at the same time, "Love you, Mom!"

We're all still laughing when my phone rings. I pull it from my pocket and see it's Diane calling through.

Shit. This isn't good.

"I need to take this," I tell Andie and stride from the room.

Once I'm in the guest bedroom, I slink into the bathroom to take the call.

"Hey."

"Hey. Sorry to call you on a Saturday," Diane says with a huff. "I really need to see you about something."

"Is there a problem?"

She sighs. "A tiny one. You can fix it, though. Just meet me tomorrow morning at the house. We'll take care of it together."

I groan and run my fingers through my hair. "Diane, you'd tell me if something was wrong right? I can't lose this."

"I know. I'll take care of you. I always do."

"Is that all?"

"For now."

"Bye, Sweeney."

"Bye, Holloway."

I pinch the bridge of my nose after I hang up and will the stress to leave my tense shoulders. Keeping things from Andie is difficult. If she finds out about this…

Shaking away that thought, I twist the knob of the door and swing it open. I'm not paying attention and

133

bump into Linc's solid chest. When our eyes meet, they lock in a fierce hate-filled glare.

"Is there a problem?" I spit out.

"Besides you being in my way," he snaps back, "no."

"Were you eavesdropping?"

"I have to take a goddamned piss. That okay with you?"

I let out a sigh of relief that he didn't overhear and push past him. I'm nearly to the door when he growls out his words.

"Hurt my sister and I'll fuck you up."

I'd said similar words to Chase earlier but had never expected to hear them back the same night.

"Yeah, and if you even think about looking at mine, I'll fuck *you* up. Looks like we're about even," I tell him with a wave of my middle finger. She may be dating Chase, but I don't like the way Linc looks at her as though she's something for him to conquer.

When I make my way back into the living room, Andie isn't there. I find her in the kitchen raiding the trays of snacks. She looks beautiful today. I can't get over how fucking sexy she looks in her damn leggings. The woman is still too tiny for maternity clothes but her normal fitted outfits have become too snug. I love how the leggings hug her fine ass and give me easy access to her pussy.

Today, she piled all her blonde hair up in a messy knot on top of her head and she's wearing hardly any makeup. Her thin burgundy sweater hangs loosely off one shoulder, baring her creamy, freckled flesh. I've become familiar with all of the freckles on her perfect body—freckles I'd never noticed when we were simply fuck buddies.

Now, I notice everything about her.

"Looking good, Holloway," I murmur as I stalk over to her. My palms find her belly as I hug her from behind. "Looking good enough to eat."

She turns her head and looks at me with an amused smirk. "You talking to yourself again? You said Holloway." Then she frowns. "Unless you were talking to Ram or Reagan. That's just sick, Roman."

I laugh and let my palms roam to her swollen breasts under her sweater. "I was talking to *future* you. But *present* you is hot too."

Her body stiffens, and for a moment, I wonder if I squeezed her sore tits too hard.

"You okay, babe?"

"I'm not ever going to be a Holloway. It's bad enough I have to be a Miller like my fucking dad for the rest of my life," she says in a clipped, harsh tone.

Releasing her tits, I twist her around. Her blue eyes are piercing—the way they get when her mind is clear and whirring with lots of dark thoughts.

"You don't want to get married one day?" *To me?*

Her chin quivers for a minute, and then she bites on her lip before shaking her head. "Look how great that turned out for my mother. Besides, I'm not like that," she gestures toward Dani and Ram, who are laughing in the living room. "I don't care about wedding dresses or bridesmaids' dresses meant to terrorize single women everywhere by making them wear hideously colored fancy table cloths with big bows in hopes of making them look lesser than the bride." She takes a deep breath after that mouthful. "I don't care about venues and people. I don't have friends—not really, besides your sister and Dani—so weddings are such a waste. Not to mention I'm impatient. I'd be a bridezilla from hell or something."

"But—"

"I don't care about flowers and vows and frilly tulle-wrapped birdseed. It's all nonsense. I don't care about cake tastings and—"

I snort. "You *do* care about cake tastings."

Her lips twitch with a smile, but then it evaporates. "Fine, I do love cake but that's beside the point. What I'm trying to say is I don't do weddings or marriage or happily ever afters. I'm not wired like Dani."

Sliding my fingers into her hair, I kiss her to shut her up. When she finally melts against me and her tongue dances with mine, I kiss her until she's putty in my hands. Then, I break away. "In case you didn't notice, I'm not with Dani. I am not attracted to Dani. I don't care about Dani, aside from the fact that she's a nice gal who will be my family one day." I nuzzle my nose against hers. "I care about you. You're the one I want. And you *do* care about happily ever afters, despite what you think, because I know you're excited about having this baby with me. What did you think? You want to be *just* fuck buddies with a baby? Screw that. I want all of you and dammit, Andie. I'll wait until you're ready but know that you *will* be a Holloway one day. I won't stop until I make that happen."

Tears well in her eyes and she slowly nods. "I just worry—"

My phone buzzes in my pocket, but I ignore it. "Worry about what?"

Her gaze hardens. "Do you need to get that? Is it Diane calling again? What did she want earlier? I know it was her calling. I saw it on your screen when you answered."

I clench my jaw and dart my gaze toward the living room to avoid her penetrating stare. "It was just business shit. Nothing to worry about."

When I meet her gaze again, her eyes are watery. "You promise?"

Technically it's not a lie…right?

"Andie," I murmur, my lips brushing against hers. "I promise you I'm going to give you everything you didn't even know you wanted. I'm going to give you what you think you don't want as well. You're just going to have to trust me."

She softens her gaze and nods. "When you get like this, I hate you." Her bottom lip wobbles, but I can see her fierce feelings for me flickering in her gaze. "I *really* hate you."

We both know she doesn't hate me.

We both know she clings to that four-letter H-word so she doesn't accidentally say a certain four-letter L-word I can't wait to hear one day.

I smirk and steal a kiss. "I know."

Chapter Eleven

Andie

Pull Over, You're Not Killing Me Today

P REGNANCY ISN'T THAT BAD ONCE YOU GET OVER the first initial hump. What those dumb know-it-all books call the first trimester. One thing was correct: the moment I bypassed the twelve-week mark, things started to change. I was no longer so tired that I was passing out at my desk and being confused with someone who had narcolepsy.

I was lucky and never got plagued with morning sickness, but it was clear I had food cravings like no other. I was dreaming about burgers and ice cream a little less now, and more focused on trying to eat balanced meals. Like a donut and an orange for my first breakfast. A cookie and some grapes for mid-morning snacks. A healthy salad with chocolate morsels sprinkled over it for lunch. I was learning balance and kicking ass at it.

Tomorrow, I'll officially be eighteen weeks pregnant, and we have our appointment to find out the sex of our little bean.

One thing that *hasn't* seemed to go away is my uncertainty. The past five weeks have been perfect. Roman has been catering to all my needs. Patient when I'm not. I've even felt accomplished at work. Roman has been so busy with clients that he finds himself asking me for suggestions on contracts and numbers. All easy stuff for me. I mean, I *did* work at a bank for a billion years.

The looks of pure pride from him make me giddy inside. I like to say that I don't need anyone's approval. I am who I am. But to get it with flying colors from Roman makes me feel good. Happy.

He's still keeping things from me, and he still swears it's nothing I should be worried about. But I'm also me and I am worried. I don't understand what could be so important that he has to hide it from me. Is he in trouble? Is he slowly knocking off all his ex-lovers before I find out about them and kill them myself? *I mean that wouldn't be a bad idea. Not!* I'm about to be a mother soon. I can't have the blood of his exes on me!

Whatever it is, he is mum about it. And as smooth as I am, I can't seem to find any answers. Not that I'm looking. Or checking his suit pockets when he's in the bathroom, or hacking into his emails, searching his deleted folders.

Nope.

Not looking.

Whatever it is, he's keeping it tight lipped.

Besides trying not to stress over Roman's secret whereabouts, I have been stressing out about today.

Because today Linc and I have lunch with my dad.

I've been putting this off for a while now, but Linc

has been up my ass to get it out of the way. As much distaste as I hold for my dad, Linc said I need to tell him about the baby.

I'm finishing up typing a contract for Roman, when my brother pops into his office. I see him and wave while Roman, who's on a conference call, growls.

Fucking boys.

"There's my favorite sister in the whole wide world." Linc smiles brightly at me, while he waves at Roman. As he walks farther into the office toward me, a stress ball goes flying, whacking Linc in the head.

"Roman!" I snap while Linc starts laughing.

"Oh, let's not mind him. Come give your brother a big hug." He lifts me off my chair and gives me the biggest, most exaggerated hug ever. "You smell just lovely today."

"Stop fucking manhandling her," Roman snaps, the phone pulled away from his ear, a hand covering the receiver.

"Both of you knock it off. I don't need this shit from either one of you today." I'd say I'm dealing with enough stress from having to face my dad without having to deal with these two kids.

"You ready?" I ask, grabbing my purse and putting on my jacket.

"You know it. Unless you need to calm down Daddy over there. I can always go back to Reagan's office and have her keep me company some more…"

A large block of Post-its goes flying. Linc ducks as it crashes into the bookshelf. I just roll my eyes. Not defending him this time. He deserved to get hit.

"Man, do you ever worry about how violent he is?" Linc asks, covering his head as we both see Roman stand, holding something in his hand.

I push Linc out of his office, and give Roman a quick wave. His eyes are dark, his brows scrunched. He hates my brother. And my *brother* is not helping ease that hate.

"You really have to do that?" I ask as we head down to the parking garage where my car is.

"I'm sorry, sis, but it's just too much fun."

I give him a good shove as we make it to my car. "It's not fun for me. So knock it off. He isn't going any-where…*I don't think*…so whatever you're doing, stop."

I unlock my car, but he tries to snatch my keys.

"Let me drive."

"No! It's my car."

"Yeah, and you drive like a grandma."

I ignore his taunts, because it's been forever since he's been in a car with me. Plus, knowing he proba-bly doesn't even have a license right now, I'm going to choose to let his poke at me slide.

We're meeting my dad at a diner outside the city. Neither of us wanted to go home. Linc said he saw his mom recently, which I think is a lie, but it's also not my business. The last time I spoke to my dad was probably Christmas. He called to wish me a nice holiday and to ask if I was coming home. I gave him the same answer I gave him the year before. I had other plans.

I didn't, though.

I spend every Christmas holed up in my apartment, alone.

I didn't want to go home and act all merry when I wasn't.

It made me miss my mom, which always led me to getting angry with my dad. He wasn't around to deal with holidays spent taking care of her when she couldn't even get out of bed. He wasn't getting my time now.

"You know, he's pretty stoked to see you," Linc says, rolling down the window to flick out a gum wrapper. Damn litterbug.

"Yeah, I'm sure he is. And don't go ordering anything big. Eat quick, then we're out. Got it?" Linc gives me a look, but I ignore it. My dad should feel lucky I'm coming at all.

"Andie, he loves you, you know. And despite him being a deadbeat to you and your mom, you always told me if you ever lost focus, to remind you. This is me reminding you. Your mom would want this."

Fucking stupid reminder.

When I choose to hate my dad, always remind me that my mom wanted peace between us. It was her last dying wish.

I wish I never made that pact with him when we were kids, before we both split.

"Hey, I'm just sticking to my part of the deal. You've always stuck to yours."

At that I laugh. My promise was to never judge him or his poor choices, actions, failures, weaknesses, and most importantly, the crimes of his past.

"Whatever, I would never judge you, even if you made me swear on it." With a smirk, he turns back to the window.

We drive in silence for a few miles before I break, asking the question all curious minds want to know.

"So what's the deal with you and Reagan? You know it can't happen right? As in, if Roman doesn't kill you first, Ram will."

I rotate my head to get a good look at him. My comment doesn't seem to faze him, judging from the creeping smile on his face.

"I'm serious, Linc, don't mess with Reagan. She's not like—"

"Like me? I know."

"That's not what I meant."

"You meant she's pure and innocent. Unlike my tainted fucked up self. No, it's true."

I feel like an asshole. Linc may have had a rough life, and made more than a handful of bad choices, but he's been nothing but an amazing brother. He might be covered in tattoos, and possibly jobless, but he's loyal and protective. He's smart in his own way, funny, and a damn good friend.

"I'm not sayin' that. I'm just saying to be careful with her. She's had bad luck with guys, and I just don't want to see her get hurt."

He turns, meeting my eyes before turning back away.

"It's not like that. She's different. Special. I would never fucking hurt her."

*"*Then how *is it* with her?"

"Different. We're friends. I can just talk to her. She listens. Understands."

I feel a little hurt that he just admitted he has someone else in his life who he opens up to. Ever since we crossed paths, it had always been me. A part of me wants to argue that that person should still be me. But then, there's that other part of me that is thankful he has someone too.

"I haven't touched her. I swear," he adds. He's staring out the window, tapping his finger on the ledge. He looks lost in thought. Lost in thoughts of Reagan, I assume. I've watched them together, and it shocks me to hear nothing has happened. Linc is not one to have *just friends*. He's a good looking guy. The one all the good girls want to say they had a wild ride with before running back home to their perfectly manicured lives.

I'd call his bluff on nothing happening with her, but now doesn't seem like the right time. Maybe he is changing and in a good way. Maybe Reagan *is* helping him.

We enter the small café and spot my dad sitting in a corner. The second he sees us, he stands. Linc goes in first and offers my dad a man hug and pat.

"Good to see you, Linc. You look well." He pulls away and brings his eyes to me. He looks nervous.

But I'm sure I do too.

"Hi there," he says, not making a move to hug me as he did Linc.

"Hey, Dad," I reply and slowly walk over to him to give him the hug he wants, despite my feelings on the matter. He looks shocked at first but wraps his arms around me, tugging me close. He smells the same. Old Spice and a hint of saw dust.

"I've missed you, kiddo."

His sweet endearment soaks in, but it quickly turns my stomach sour. All those years he was gone, making a new life with a *new* family, and never once did he reach out. He never sent a letter or expressed that he ever thought about us. About me. Missing me now just doesn't cut it for me.

I pull away.

His grimace at my withdrawal tells me that he knows he's already messed up. "Well, should we order? I'm sure you both are hungry."

We take our seats. Linc and I next to one another with my dad across from us. The waitress comes and takes our drink order. Linc orders a beer while my dad and I both stick to water. The conversation is light, and I know my dad is treading lightly.

Once the waitress is back to take our order, I start. "I'll take a side salad with Ranch dressing. Small one. The smallest you have." I close my menu and hand it to her, looking anywhere but my dad's wandering eyes.

"And for you, handsome?" the waitress asks Linc.

"Yes, I'll have the double cheeseburger, two orders of fries. Can I get a side of onion— *ouch*!" Linc yelps. He looks at me like *what the hell*, but I look at him like *what the hell*. We had a deal. Order light. Quick. He's on the fast track to ordering the whole damn menu. "Sorry, my sister has muscle spasms." The waitress smiles, while my dad now looks overly concerned. "As I was saying, those onion rings look *delicious*. And can you bring me out any type of pie or sundae you have? I'm a growing boy." He winks at her as she blushes like a hussy. I roll my eyes because he is seriously ridiculous sometimes.

She takes my dad's order last—he orders a club sandwich—then leaves us to another round of awkward silence.

"So how have you—"

"I'm pregnant." I also have fucking Tourette's it seems. *What the fuck, Andie!?* I wasn't even sure I was going to tell him, yet I spit it out the first chance the floor was open.

"You're what?"

"Pregnant." I choose not to look at my dad. I don't want to see his judgment.

"Wow. That's great. Are you…"

"What, keeping it? Yeah, Dad, I am. I don't plan on being like you and turning my back on my child."

Linc kicks me under the table, but it doesn't faze me. I've now locked eyes with my dad.

He looks pained. "Kiddo, I wasn't going to say—"

"Stop calling me kiddo. I'm not a child. And you have no idea about me as one, because you weren't around for it."

He opens his mouth to argue but shuts it. I know I'm being hateful, but I can't help it. I live with the hate and hurt every single day. And no matter how much I try, I can't forgive and I can't forget.

"Andrea, please…" he starts, but stalls to get his bearings. Linc grabs my hand under the table, because he knows me well enough lately to know the tears are threateningly close. "I can't take back my choices. I know that. But I want to try and fix them. I want to get to know you and spend time with you. I just want to try and be your dad."

He ran himself ragged trying to be my friend, parent, anything to allow me to let him in. When I came back to live with him, I shut down. I didn't speak to his new wife or sit at their family dinners. I kept to myself and counted down the days until I turned eighteen and could leave. It was Linc who helped me manage. He was just as pissed off about having a step dad and being forced to smile and share conversation over meatloaf. We just got each other.

He made it tolerable.

I guess we both did that for each other.

"I'm not asking you to be my dad. You can't make up for what you lost."

Feeling the emotions rise between us, Linc steps in. "So Andie over here locked herself into a great job, didn't ya, sister? Works as an executive assistant to the CEO of a marketing firm."

My dad's eyebrows raise. "Wow, that's wonderful. When did you leave the bank?"

With no filter, I say, "I got fired. Told my boss off. Then went to the firm because the father of this baby owns it. Told him off. And he gave me a job." In a nutshell, right?

My dad's surprised expression doesn't shock me. I probably could have sugarcoated that story.

"Wow. And the father. Are you two a couple? Planning on getting married?"

The air thickens at his question. Quite ironic question, if you ask me.

"Well, Dad, you see he probably wants to. Loves this baby and probably loves me. But you know where the problem is? I don't trust men. I don't trust them to stay in their marriage and fight. To stay and be a parent to their child. And because of that I refuse marriage. Why would I set myself up for the same life my mom endured?" The tears have begun to fall. Linc tries to grab my hand, but I push his away. He opened the door for this conversation, he is finally going to hear me roar.

"Do you know how much I fear one day I will wake up and Roman will be gone? That I'll find a letter telling me he didn't sign up for this? I'm afraid to put all my eggs in one basket, just like Mom, and love him. I'm afraid to trust in him for us to become a family. Because what if he breaks me? Do you know how it feels to always fear letting someone in because I'm too damn afraid they will just let me down like you did Mom?"

"Andrea—"

"No, you don't get to Andrea me! You left me! How did you think that would affect me? Mom? I live with *your* choices every single day! The insecurities, the loneliness, the sadness because I watched my mother, *your wife*, die of a broken heart. How do I get over that?"

My voice has risen, causing a few patrons to look our way. I take a deep breath, needing to calm down. I know it's not good for the baby for me to get upset. I take a good look at my dad and speak, "How do I forgive myself for turning away all the great things in my life because I am so damaged by your choices?"

I drop my head into my hands and cry. I've been wanting to ask those heavy questions every time something great has come into my life and I turn away from it. I want to yell and cry that I am sick of holding the burden of what he did to us. I want to be free of his wrongdoings and live my life. I want to say yes to Roman on every account. I want to be able to fully trust him. I want to open my heart and tell him all these feelings that keep me awake at night.

But I can't.

And for that, I will ruin us.

"Andrea."

"Don't." I've had enough. I knew this was a bad idea. I knew with how emotional I've been, that this lunch would turn into a disaster. I push my chair out to leave when his voice stops me.

"I live every single day with regret. And I will never be able to take back that decision."

I lift my eyes to connect with his, and I notice the unshed tears.

"I won't apologize. Because I know it means nothing. It won't fix what I did to you and your mom. I will die hating myself. And I know that means nothing to you, but I'm paying for my sins."

He brings his hand cautiously to mine, placing his large palm over my hand.

"Don't revolve your life around a decision I made. This man? He is not me. He isn't a coward. You deserve happiness, Andrea. Don't take that away from yourself. From your child. Please, continue to hate me, because I deserve it. But don't turn your heart away if this man loves you."

My vision is blurry with tears. Linc clutches my other hand for support.

"I hate you," I respond, because there is a part of me

that always will.

"And you should, kiddo."

His honesty is like a storm rushing through me. My thoughts, wants, dreams—they all start pouring out of my mouth. I struggle to keep up with each one as I sob.

"I just wanted a dad. I wanted to feel loved. I wanted *you* to love me. But you didn't. You left. I'm having this baby, and I have no parents to share it with. I miss Mom. She won't get to see her grandbaby, ever. I just want what every other person has. To have parents. I just want you to be there for me." I can hardly catch my breath.

Linc is cooing me to calm down. I don't realize it, but my dad has gotten up from his seat and kneels to the side of me.

"I am your dad. You're my blood. And aside from my cowardly mistakes, I want to be here for you every step of the way. I don't expect you to forgive me. But let me try. Let me be a part of your life. This child's life. Let me meet your boyfriend. Let me love you."

We are both crying. Most likely causing a scene. I turn to my dad, and within seconds, I am throwing myself into his arms. He hugs me tight, a parental closeness in our embrace.

"I love you, Andrea."

"I… I… I love you too, Dad."

"You okay?" Linc asks as we drive back to the office.

"Yeah. Fine. Emotionally drained, I guess, but I feel okay." That was *not* how I thought lunch would go. I never expected such words to be exchanged.

"You sure? I don't need you going back home all upset and giving your boyfriend another reason to want to kill me."

At that, I laugh. I'm sure Roman is worried about the state I will return in. I'm not normally, as he would say, calm whenever I speak of my dad.

The rest of lunch went a lot smoother. I have to admit, as deep as it got, it feels as if a huge weight has been lifted off my shoulders. I never allowed my dad to explain why he did what he did. But honestly, he never truly tried. I was so closed off when I was younger and he had no idea how to handle me, or the pain and anger that I was holding in. It all resulted in everything just getting shoved under the rug.

But today we both had a lot to say. And in some way, I felt a little bit closer to being able to forgive. I also thought about my mom up in heaven and I could see her smiling, looking down on us.

It was a blessing Linc ordered all that food because I didn't even touch my salad. I guess he's caught on to my unusual eating habits and allowed me to eat half his burger, fries, and dominate the sundae.

The rest of the conversation was light. We talked about my job, the baby. Roman.

Linc jumped in with a few details of his goings ons, but he kept it short, which had me setting a mental reminder to dig into him later about it. Something is going on with him, and he isn't sharing. Not with me, at least.

We left with a verbal commitment to make plans for Dad to come visit me before the baby is born. He seemed really eager to meet Roman, and a small part of me was excited as well. I think he would like him.

We're almost back into town when I begin to yawn.

"Oh shit, you need me to drive?"

"Nah, I'm good. We're almost there." Another deep yawn escapes.

"Dude, I've seen you go down in seconds. Sitting at your desk typing, then face planted into your keyboard. Pull over, you're not killing me today."

I laugh and slap him on the shoulder.

I go to switch lanes because the car behind me is starting to ride my ass.

"You just want to drive so you can say you did something rebellious today. Do you even have your license…"

I fade off as I notice the same car change lanes with me, still driving too close to me. I speed up a little, not wanting to go too fast. I *am* carrying precious cargo here.

"In a hurry now? You *are* going to fall asleep!" He laughs. "Seriously I can drive, it's no big—"

He gets cut off as our car jolts forward. I scream as I try to keep the car on the road after getting hit by the car driving behind us.

"What the fuck?" Linc grunts, twisting to look in the back mirror. I try and get a look at the driver, but my hands have begun shaking, and I don't want to lose control of the steering wheel.

"Andie, get in the other lane. NOW!"

I nod quickly, doing as I'm told. I look in the mirror and the car follows us.

"What the fuck is this guy doing?"

I try switching into the right lane, which puts one vehicle in between us.

"That asshole just hit us. And I think on purpose!" Linc pulls out his phone, trying to take a picture of the car's license plate. As I do my best to drive, breathe, and focus on who the fuck is driving, I finally get a good look.

Fuck.

"*Frank*," I gasp, trying to pass another car.

"Who? You know that fucking guy?" He looks from me back to the car. He's behind us again.

"Fuck, Andie pull over. Get away from this guy!"

"I'm trying!" I snap back. I try and speed up, but he is so close. Frank veers left super-fast and speeds up. "Andie…" Linc warns.

Before I have a chance to figure out his next move, he swerves his car into my lane and slams on his breaks. Without thought, I scream.

Linc grabs the steering wheel and turns it right, throwing us onto the shoulder. Thankfully, I panic and release my foot from the gas.

"Brake!" Linc yells, and I snap back into action, slamming my foot on the brake, as the car fishtails, narrowly avoiding a pile of barrels.

"Who the FUCK is Frank?" he snaps at me, trying to catch his breath.

"He's nobody."

"Fucking nobody?" he roars. "Andie, he just tried running you off the fucking road!"

"Stop yelling at me! God. He's an old employee at the bank. He's a dick, and I kinda got him fired."

Linc stares at me in disbelief. "What did you do?"

I huff, throwing my hands into my hair. "I called in a

complaint. It was nothing."

Linc leans back in his seat, his chest still heaving. "Clearly it was something."

"Listen, I know. And I will deal with this. Don't say anything to Roman."

He turns to me, eyes wide. "You're kidding me right? Some psycho just tried to run us off the road, and you want to keep this from your boyfriend?"

Yes.

Pretty much.

"Yes."

Linc shakes his head, sitting forward. "Whatever you say, sis."

He's quiet the rest of the ride, his face in his phone. He better not be texting anyone about this. I'm hoping I didn't really pee in my pants, and that it's just sweat build up.

There was no doubt. That was Frank. And he just tried to run me off the road.

We get back to Holloway and Linc jumps out, seemingly upset.

I'd ask if he's upset with me, but... I'm not gonna give him any reason to tell on me. The last thing I want is a lecture from Roman on how I can't do blah, blah, blah, blah.

We go our separate ways, me to my desk, while I know he's going to Reagan's office. I'm sitting down safely in my cozy chair when my phone dings.

Dani: What happened?! OMG Reagan came in here freaking out! Is it true? Did Frank try to run you off the road? Why didn't you answer

your phone when I called?!

Me: Sorry…my phone was on vibrate. But yeah. It's fine though. I'll take care of it.

Reagan: I'm so glad you're okay. I'm sorry, though. I may have spilled the beans to Dani.

Dani: Well Ram heard everything. He's pulling Roman out of his meeting.

Reagan: And well Ram may have been there…

Dani: Oh no. Where are you?

Reagan: And he may have told my other brother.

Dani: Oh boy! Roman just went storming out of his meeting in the boardroom! You might want to hide.

Three seconds later, the door swings open and crashes against the wall.

Oh, shit.

Chapter Twelve

Roman

Our Story Is Different.
Our Story Is Explosive.

"WHO THE FUCK IS FRANK?" I ROAR AS I storm into my office with the fury of a thousand hurricanes. I'm going to kill him. I *will* fucking kill him. But first, I'm going to wring her pretty little neck for keeping this shit from me.

My eyes find her widened blue ones as she bites on her plump bottom lip in a sexy-as-shit way that would normally have me bending her over her desk. Not today. Today I'm too fucking pissed to get distracted by her dick-sucking lips.

"Goddammit, Andie," I snap as I prowl over to her.

She jolts into action and holds up both her hands as if to calm me. There's no calming me. She's going to tell me about this fucker who just tried to kill the woman I love and our baby.

"Talk."

Her tongue darts out and licks that swollen lip. It's distracting as hell. I let out a low growl of warning.

"It's nothing," she insists, her voice shaky. "So stupid. Frank is just a stupid, harmless idiot who's mad because he got fired." But despite her words, I can see the fear glimmering in her shiny blues.

"You could have been killed," I say in a low voice. My palms find her throat, and I run my thumbs along her jaw on both sides. "Tell me everything."

When her eyes dart away and her nostrils flare, I know she's about to start lying. I've been with her long enough now that I can read all of her emotions and tells.

"Don't lie, baby," I warn, drawing her gaze back to me.

I lean into her and take a moment to revel in the way her slightly swollen stomach presses against mine. My kid is in there—a kid this Frank fuck could have taken out this afternoon.

"I made an anonymous call and made up some shit. Most of it was true…some of it couldn't be proven, but, whatever, I'm sure it was true too," she says with a huff. "He took advantage of Dani all the time and was mean to her. It pissed me off, and once she got fired, I decided to give him a taste of his own medicine. I was hungry and emotional and I just did it. Frank's a big loser. I didn't think he was capable of harassment."

I blink at her and clench my jaw.

She frowns. "I think he's been following me. Dani and I ran into him a few weeks back and he pushed me—"

"HE WHAT?!" Her whole body flinches at my tone, so I lower my voice because I don't want to freak out our unborn child. "Why are you just now telling me this?"

"And then," she continues, swallowing, careful to

157

avoid my question. "You and I saw him that one day."

"Wait," I interrupt with a growl. "That beady-eyed, tall and lanky motherfucker you used to work with?"

She nods. "In the flesh."

I knew I was getting a weird vibe from her. "Jesus," I grumble. "If I would have known, I'd have kicked his ass right then."

Her palms slide up my chest, and she links them around the back of my neck. "You're sexy when you're pissed."

My brows furl together because this is no time to joke, but it doesn't stop me from leaning in to inhale her sweet scent. "I'm more than pissed, Andie. I'm fucking furious."

She parts her lips and stands on her toes to try to distract me with a kiss. And, my God, is she good at distraction because after another second, her tongue is in my mouth. Sweet and perfect and mine. The anger swirling through me funnels its way into our kiss. I devour her. I scold her for being secretive by biting at her lip and sucking on her tongue. My fingers find her ass through her leggings, and I draw her up against me. Those sexy, long legs of hers wrap around my waist, so that when I walk her over to the wall, I can grind my now hard dick against her sweet spot.

She whimpers when I bite her lip again, and I feel like we may be breaking my lame-ass, self-imposed, *no-sex-in-the-office* policy very soon.

"Roman," she begs, her voice breathless. "I need you."

"I need you too," I groan. I hold her ass up with one hand and fumble with my belt with the other. I'm just unbuttoning my slacks when the door flies open.

"Yo, fuckface!" Linc bellows. "Dani gave me that idiot's address and *holy shit* I did *not* expect to walk in on you fucking my sister. Jesus, Andie! Gross!"

She slides to her feet, her face and neck beet red. "Oh my God! Leave, punk! If the office wall's a rockin' don't come a knockin'! Common decency!"

I quickly adjust my pants and allow his earlier words to settle in my brain. "Address? You have that dead man's address?"

Linc gives me a triumphant smirk as he waves the paper. "You want to go fuck him up with me?"

He's still grinning from ear to ear when my two siblings and Dani file in behind him.

"You're not going to fuck anyone up," Ram says with a grumble. "You two can go to the police station, like normal, responsible adults, and file a report. Kicking that twit's ass will only get you both in trouble."

Since when did Ram become Mr. Responsibility?

"But he tried to run her off the road," I argue, my fury once again rising in my chest. "He fucking shoved her."

Ram winces at that thought, and a flash of anger flickers in his eyes. But then he takes a deep breath to calm himself. "I know. I'm pissed too. Just trust me, okay?"

I nod and glance over at Andie. She's still flushed but pretty as ever. God, I'll never tire of looking at her.

"Is that all you two do, anyway? Fuck every time you're alone?" Linc questions, his massive arms crossed over his chest.

I roll my eyes. "Why are you even here? Don't you have some property to deface or something? Banks to rob? Cops to evade?"

His jaw clenches, and I can tell I picked at a wound. He counters back with a vicious bite to his words. "Why are you even with her? If all she is to you is a piece of ass, you should run along, rich boy. Do you even know what her favorite movie is? Her favorite color? Do you know what she loves to do in her free time?" His words pick at my wound too.

It's in this exact moment, with everyone's eyes on me, that I realize something.

I've been to dinner with Andie many times. We've been shopping and to parties and to bars. I know her body, every beautiful square inch. Together, we're having a baby. But I don't know much about what makes Andie, Andie. I don't know what makes her tick. Her past is something she reveals in snippets and she tends to keep pieces of herself locked away.

But you never ask her to show them to you.

You just accept that she doesn't want to talk about those things.

A sense of sick embarrassment washes through me. I've never dated my girlfriend. Ignoring everyone, I snag Andie's hand and drag her past the group crowding my doorway. "We're going to the police station to file a report," I bark out to anyone who cares. "We're not coming back today."

"I still can't believe they won't do anything," Andie gripes as she stares out the window. After we left the office earlier, we stopped by the police station. They said they'd talk to him but they really didn't have anything to go on. I did make her file a restraining order but a lot of good that will do if he harasses her again. "Where are we going, anyway?"

I reach over and grab her hand. We'd gone home, so I could change out of my work clothes, and are back on the road. While she checked her mail, I packed us some food. Now, we're headed out on a date.

"It's a surprise," I tell her with a grin and squeeze her hand.

Her smile is cute, and I crave to see more of them. As we drive, I wonder if our kid will have her smile. If she's a girl like Andie thinks, I'm in big trouble. I'll have to kill people. Boys to be precise. We'll have to get a farm where I can bury all their dead, eyeless bodies. Nobody will even look at my daughter.

Thank God we're having a boy.

We drive outside of the city as the sun sets. Mom and Dad used to take us out to a lake on one of Dad's friends' properties. A gate with a keypad, which we all know the code to, protects it. Mr. and Mrs. Johnson are always traveling around in their RV, visiting their kids, so they're never at their lake house. When I pull down the long gravel road, Andie turns to frown at me.

"Where are we going?" she tries again. "Are you taking me out to the woods to kill me?"

I laugh and bring our joined hands to my lips so I can kiss her knuckles. "If I was gonna kill you, it would have been months ago. Now, I just want to keep you." I wink at her, which earns me another one of those breathtaking smiles.

"Do you know these people?" she questions when I key in the code and drive through the opening gate.

"Yeah. Friends of my parents. Last I saw on Facebook, they're in Fort Worth visiting their youngest. We're all alone."

I drive another quarter of a mile down the winding road toward the lake. Once we roll up to it, Andie lets out a gasp. My gaze follows hers to the water's surface that seems to glitter with a thousand warm colors as the setting sun's rays bounce against it. As soon as I put it in park, she jumps out and walks toward the pier. I gather the bag of food and the blanket I brought. While she kicks off her shoes and then sits to dip her toes in, I stretch out the soft blanket in the grass before mimicking her actions. Once I'm seated next to her on the small pier and my own toes are swirling in the still-icy water, despite the warm early spring day, I turn to look at her.

Her palms are on the wooden planks behind her and her head is tilted up toward the sky. Long blonde locks of hair spill out behind her and just barely touch the pier below her. She's smiling—a smile so fucking serene— and I could simply stare at her all day.

"You're beautiful," I tell her, my voice hoarse. The words don't seem to describe just how fucking stunning she is.

She cracks an eye open and peeks at me. "So are you."

"Who knew you could be so nice?" I tease as I lean in and kiss the bare flesh on her throat.

Her giggle is sweet and innocent and so fucking perfect. "I was going to also say, 'If you're into big heads and all.'"

I roll my eyes and take a playful bite of her neck. She yelps and drops back so she's flat on the pier to escape my nibbling.

"Asshole," she grumbles.

I beam at her. "You like it."

Her smile tells me I'm right.

"Why are we here?" She shields her face from the sun with her hand to look at me. "Seems kind of random."

I lie down beside her on my elbow and run circles with my finger along her slightly swollen stomach. "I never do anything special for you. I'm sorry for that. You deserve…" I trail off and sigh. "A lot more than I give to you."

Her brows scrunch together and she gives a slight shake of her head. "Roman, this," she says pointing between us, "is more than anyone has ever given me. You've given me everything."

"I just…" I frown down at her. "Linc has a point. I don't know anything important about you."

She looks out over the lake, her gaze distant. "There isn't much to know," she argues softly.

I shake my head. "There's plenty. I want to know if you played sports in high school or if you were a cheerleader or a band nerd. I want to know what kind of music you listen to when we're not in the car together. I want to know what you'd be doing this evening if you were all alone. I feel like there are all these hidden parts of you—like little gifts—and I want to open them all like a greedy kid on Christmas morning."

She laughs. "Well, I was never good enough to be a cheerleader or a band nerd. Try all black wearing, heavy eyeliner, and blue-streaked hair. I had bracelets made out of chains, and black concert T-shirts were my go-to. You could say I was a bit of a misfit."

I'm grinning as I try to imagine my blonde-haired angel trying to be bad. I mean, the girl has a mouth on her and can be meaner than hell, but I can't picture it. "So you were a rebel. While I was out tossing footballs, you were what? Tagging buildings?"

"We're an unlikely pair," she says with a wicked gleam in her eyes.

"We're a perfect pair," I correct and kiss her on her luscious lips. "So I'm guessing you were into 90s alternative rock then?"

"Yep. Nirvana, Pearl Jam, Soundgarden. That's why I always like when Ram chooses the music. He knows the good stuff."

"What would you be doing tonight if you were all alone?" I question.

Her blue eyes—that are extra brilliant in the sunlight—look past me. Sadness draws her features into a frown. "Nothing."

I quirk an eyebrow up at her. "No hobbies?"

She chews on her bottom lip. "This is stupid."

"What? Us talking or your hobby?"

"Both."

My heart drops, and I begin to question if I'm pushing her too hard. She's so fucking difficult to read sometimes. I'm about to tell her we can talk about something else when a look of guilt washes over her features. Her bottom lip wobbles and her pretty blues become glassy with unshed tears.

"I…" she trails off and darts her gaze away from mine. "Please don't laugh at me."

I'm far from laughing. She's holding this sweet gift right in front of me but has her hands desperately trying to keep the lid on it. *Just take the lid off, baby. Let me see inside.*

"My mom and I used to scrapbook. When she was ill and couldn't do much else, I'd crawl into her bed with her, and together we'd look through old photos so that we could organize them by themes and dates. It was fun. I have my entire childhood catalogued in scrapbooks and a ton of friendship books with Dani." Her eyes skip to mine, and I can tell she's waiting for me to make fun of her.

"I'd like to see some one day," I tell her as I run my thumb across her bottom lip. Then I lean in and kiss her. "Now was that so hard?"

She lets out a nervous giggle. "It's just…it probably seems cheesy to you."

"I think you forget I have the girliest mother ever and a little sister. They did their fair share of scrapbooking growing up. Once, Reagan was mad at me, so she made a book full of every unflattering picture of me she could find. When my prom date and I showed up to take pictures at the house, Reagan sat right between us on the sofa and proceeded to show my date every single picture I hated of myself. I don't even know where that thing ended up, but if it were up to me, it'd be in the trash."

Andie sits up on her elbows. "Wait? Reagan and your mom scrapbook? Like are they serious scrappers? Do they go to any meet ups or anything?"

"Guess you'll just have to ask them." I tangle my fingers in her messy-from-the-wind hair and steal a kiss. It's not sweet at all—it's hungry for her. We kiss slow at first, and then hard. But then she's rolling me over onto my back and straddling me. My palms roam over every perfect part of her body. She rubs against my hard cock until I'm nearly coming in my pants.

"Stop," I groan.

She lifts her head and her blonde hair curtains us in. "Why?"

"Because you're going to make me come in my pants like a fucking teenager," I tell her with a grumble.

Her eyes gain the evil glint I love so much, and she starts rocking her hips against me. Slow and teasing. My fingers dig into her hips, and I urge her faster. Our lips meet again, and I want to own her body right on this hard pier. Instead, I rise to my feet, with her wrapped around my body, and stride back over to the blanket on the banks. I drop to my knees with her still in my grasp as I yank at her shirt. Once it's gone and I free her swollen breasts from her bra, I lay her down on her back.

I can't take my eyes off her perfect tits. The pink nipples are hard and at attention as a cool breeze blows across her flesh. I need to see more of her. She lifts her ass off the ground when I begin tugging her pants down. Soon, I have her completely naked and at my mercy.

"This was supposed to be a date but I can't not be inside you right now," I grunt in frustration. I'm pissed at myself for having no self-control whatsoever.

Her lips quirk up in a conspiratorial smile. "I won't tell anyone we fucked on the first date if you don't."

And just like that, all apprehension is washed away as I rip off my shirt. Seconds later, I'm naked and hovering on top of her. I like staring at her when she's like this. Blonde and angelic and a goddamned vision. My thick cock rubs back and forth against her clit, making her shiver, but I don't even attempt to enter her. I'm perfectly content watching her writhe with need.

"Roman…" she growls in warning. "Stop teasing."

"But you love it," I argue with a smirk and pinch one of her nipples with my finger and thumb.

Her body shudders and she scowls. "Just fuck me already."

I throw my head back and laugh. She's so damn cute when she gets demanding. "How else may I serve you?" I tease.

She sticks her tongue out at me. "God, I hate you." But for someone who supposedly hates me, she's grabbing for my cock with ferocious intensity in an overwhelming need to have me inside of her.

"I know," I tell her with a wink.

Her tits push forward, and she lets out a moan of pleasure when I drive all the way into her slick opening. Our mouths meet, and I kiss her sweetly while I fuck her roughly. We're two stars on a collision course for each other. There is no orbiting around one another like some sweet love story.

Our story is different.

Our story is explosive.

Our story is chaotic.

Our story is my favorite.

Chapter Thirteen

Andie

Log Jammed

I'M IN THE MOST COMFORTABLE POSITION EVER. IN MY bed, with a large warm oaf wrapped around me. And I couldn't feel more content. Well maybe minus the fact that I have to pee. And my stomach keeps pulsating, which means there sadly might be some gas in my future.

Roman's warm breath is on my neck as his hand leisurely rests on my stomach. Ever since the baby, this has been his thing. Covering my belly with his strong embrace. Like it's his way of protecting our little bean.

I snuggle into him, inhaling the scent around me. I try not to move, because I don't want to wake him. I know he's been working a lot lately, and with my needy hormones, I keep him up late at night.

I lay in his arms reminiscing about our date. That was the first time anyone has ever done something so romantic for me. It wasn't about how fancy a restaurant was or how much a date could impress me. It was... honest. Beautiful. It was the start of something I knew, down to my bones, I wanted. I wanted a forever thing with Roman. I can admit that to myself now. And with the strength of his support, I feel like I can admit that to him as well.

Roman's hand snaps me out of my thoughts, as it starts traveling down my stomach, his fingers sliding past my shorts.

"I thought you were sleeping," I whisper, my eyes fluttering closed. His fingers dip past my pelvis and begin to caress my sex.

"I was, but you get all squirmy when you're in your head. Plus, I couldn't stop thinking about this warm pussy." He inserts one finger inside me, and slowly strokes me inside and out. I relax my body into him, his chest a solid mass against my back.

"You know we can't have sex, right?" I say, biting my lip. His finger feels amazing, the slow movement bringing my body alive with need. I want to tell him he should probably stop, because we *cannot* have sex, but his mouth wraps around my earlobe, nipping at my skin.

"Are you sure about that? If I'm not mistaken, I think you want this. Your body is craving it." He picks up the pace, adding another finger to the mix. I moan, my body betraying me, as I begin to thrust my hips into his hand.

"Roman, we can't. The appointment," I moan as he pushes deeper inside me.

"What about it? We're going to find out we're having a boy, and I'm going to treat you to anything you want." He picks up his thrusts, and I'm lost in his assault. "Maybe take my girl up to Wellerton, where I hear there's a brand new stationary store. Filled with paper…" One hard thrust. "Stickers…" I am about to lose it. "And all sorts of hole punchers." At that, I explode. I grip his fingers with my walls as I orgasm.

"That's my girl," he murmurs into my ear, his tongue pressing against my neckline just before he presses his full, warm lips to my skin. Fuck, he's good. I sigh as he sucks on my flesh. He rolls me onto my back, his heavy weight covering mine. Our eyes connected, he dips down to place a soft kiss on my lips.

"Good morning."

"Good morning," I reply shyly.

He lowers his head, dragging his large frame down my body until his mouth stops on my belly. I'm about to thrust my hands into his hair and pull him back up. As much as I want another orgasm, and especially from his magical tongue, I kind of need to shower. Before I get a good grip to pull, he does something so unexpected. He presses a gentle kiss to my swelling stomach. A small gasp filters through my lips at his touching gesture.

"And good morning to you, Roman Jr."

I feel his smile on my skin, and I softly whack him on the head. "It could be a girl," I remind him as he brings himself back up, his eyes glimmering with mischief.

"You're right. It could be. But my swimmers are tough. It's a boy." I can't help but match the smile he's wearing. "So are you sure I can't show you what a good morning it could be?" he asks, dipping low, placing kiss after kiss along my jaw line.

My fingers tangle in his messy morning hair and I tug until he's looking up so I can lock my lips to his. I kiss him feverishly until my lungs give out.

"Is that a yes?" He smirks, pressing his hard dick into

my thigh. I bite my lip to stop myself from demanding he fuck me senseless.

"Not until after the appointment," I state, bringing my palm down, caressing his clean shaven cheek. I love the way his always-smooth skin feels under my fingertips. The way his face leans into my touch every time. The goose bumps that cover my skin when he looks at me as if I'm the only thing that makes his clock tick. I love the way he makes me feel like I deserve happiness.

"Thank you, Roman Holloway," I say softly as I watch his eyes blink in slight confusion.

"What are you thanking me for, sweet girl?"

"For being the best thing that has happened to me. For sticking around even when I tried furiously to push you away. For giving me a chance when I probably didn't deserve one." I try to hold in the tears. I don't want to cry. I'm so tired of this emotional roller coaster. I just want him to know that I am thankful. I know I'm not an easy person to love. I struggle to love myself. But he does it so effortlessly. I wish I could take back all the bitchy things I've done or said. He's never deserved that side of me.

My dad *is* right. Roman is *not* him. Roman is everything.

"Babe, where's this coming from?" He presses his lips to mine, offering me strength to continue.

"I just don't tell you enough how thankful I am. I'm always too consumed with complaining or bitching or crying or eating. Christ, anything but showing you that I appreciate you."

A small chuckle leaves his lips as he offers me his mouth, this time increasing the pressure. His arms wrap around my waist, and before I can object, he's flipped us so his back rests against the mattress and I'm lying on top of him.

"Thank you for telling me that. You're right. You're not one for words. But you show me in other ways."

Huh?

"I do?"

He chuckles again, tucking a lose strand of hair behind my ear. "You do. When you set the coffee maker just for me, so it's ready when I wake up. When you pick up your three muffins each morning but put one on my desk, in case I'm also hungry."

"But you always give it back to me!"

"Because I know you're hungry. And I get so full from your sweet gesture, that I am okay giving up the muffin."

Okay, so much for not getting emotional. But that was seriously the *sweetest* thing ever. "What else?"

Roman laughs. "How about, all the days you wear those skirts just for me, knowing I love seeing those sexy legs all day long." At that, I join in laughing with him. Dammit. I thought I was being slick, trying to wear those damn things.

"Okay, so you got me there." I lie down, resting my head against his chest. We're quiet for a few moments until I speak. "Will you tell me something about you?"

He squeezes me closer to him, pressing his lips to my head. "What is it that you want to know?"

"Anything. Something stupid. I shared with you my dorky secret. Tell me something about you that no one knows."

"Hmmm…" he says as he thinks. "Well, when I was a kid, I had an ant collection."

"Awwe! That's kinda cute. How old were you, like seven?"

"Actually, more like fifteen."

A choked giggle escapes my lips as I try to hide my amusement.

"I know. Laugh it up. Pretty nerdy to have an ant collection at age fifteen. But I was crazy intrigued with their behavior. Observing their habits. I actually created a colony, breaking them into intelligent groups. They would form units and create colonies within the tank. It was quite fascinating."

I try to hold in any further laughter as I allow him to tell his story.

"I tracked each unit. Made journals of their evolution. I turned my closet into a small base where I kept my tank and journals. Made a small camp out in case it got late and I needed to take a nap."

I lift my head from his chest, taking in his serious expression. He must have really liked those damn ants.

"And what happened to them? Why did you not pursue a career in ant-ology?" I smirk.

He grabs my hips, raising his head just the right amount to steal a kiss. "Because it wasn't meant to be," he states, giving me another peck.

"Why not?"

"Because Reagan killed them all. Her current *Blue's Clues* episode had taught her about fireflies. That flies eat ants. Reagan had convinced Ram to help her catch fireflies one night, and then let them all lose in my ant tank.

I didn't realize it until morning. Complete devastation."

I throw my hands over my mouth. "Oh my God! Were they all dead?" *Poor Roman.*

"Mostly. Enough that all my hard work was ruined. I cried like a baby to my mom, who said she would help me rebuild it, but the damage was done. My *ant-ology* career was over."

I offer him a sad smile, picturing a young fifteen-year-old Roman crying over his murdered ants. I bend down, offering him my lips and he graciously accepts. The kiss doesn't get out of control. Before it even has a chance to, I sense a fluttering feeling in my stomach.

I pull away.

"Did you feel that?" I ask, raising to a kneeling position on top of Roman.

"No, what happened? Is everything okay?"

"Yeah, it's just… There it is again!" I bring my hands to my stomach, the weird sensation almost tickling the insides of my belly.

"What, is it gas? If so, maybe I should give you a minute." Poor Roman has been trapped in a car with me too many times to not know the routine.

"No, shut up. It's not gas… Wait, there it is, feel." I grab his hand and place it over my belly. "Feel it?" I ask.

"No. What is it? What do you think it is?"

My eyes swell with thick tears. "Roman, it's the baby. I finally feel the baby."

"Oh my God," I groan. "He's so gonna know." I cover my face with my hands, horrified.

Roman laughs, stealing one hand and pressing a kiss to the top. "He's not going to know. And who cares. He obviously knows we have sex."

"Yeah, but the poor guy is going to stick that wand up me, and he's going to get all log jammed by all the sperm you shot up in me!"

Roman howls in laughter, dropping my hand to hold his chest. "Andie, you peed, showered, and jumped up and down. I think anything I shot up in you is out."

Ugh…no it's not. I can practically smell him still! My stupid hypersensitive senses. *I should have never given in*, I tell myself. I'm getting restless in the chair, the paper crinkling underneath me.

Roman goes to offer me a kiss, but the doctor walks in, and I swat him away. Kissing will give us away.

"Ahh, hello you two. Big day."

Romans shakes the doctor's hand while I try to not make eye contact. He walks over to his equipment, shuffling around with the monitor. With every second that passes, I become more anxious. We're about to find out the sex of our baby. In less than five minutes, this guy is going to reveal if we are having a girl or a boy. Do I want a girl? Do I want a *boy*? Does it matter? Will Roman be upset if it's a girl?

"Now I am just going to put some warm—"

"We had sex this morning!" I blurt out. *No idea why.*

Roman shakes his head at me, while the kind doctor smiles and pats me on my knee. "Good for you two. Very healthy. No harm to the baby."

I stare at him confused. "No, we had sex. He…you know…all up inside me."

Jesus.

Another head shake from Roman. Another pat on the knee from the doctor.

"Totally safe, dear. You can't get pregnant twice." He smiles again and grabs for the tube of lubrication.

"Well, I'm just saying," I huff. "In case it's foggy in there and the wand is...well... covered and you can't see anything."

"Andie." Roman tries shutting me up, but I've already said my piece.

The doctor lifts my gown, exposing my bare belly. "No worries. We'll be doing an external ultrasound today." He brings the lubrication tube to my belly. "Just a warm gel." And squeezes a glob onto my stomach. When the image appears, both our eyes are glued to the screen.

The doctor doesn't speak, moving around my stomach. An image of a little tiny human pops up and instantly Roman grabs my hand. I peek at him and the look in his eyes catches my breath.

"Right there, kids, is the heart. It's too soon to count the valves, but this baby has a nice speedy heartbeat." He maneuvers the mouse-like contraption around my belly, until placing it over another body part. "Ahh and look at that. That's the head. Size is looking good." More moving. "There are the hands.... Feet..."

He continues to move the mouse as we both stare at the beautiful little thing on the screen. Our baby. The little human growing in my belly. I use my free hand to wipe a tear off my cheek, and when I turn to see if Roman caught me being a baby, I notice the unshed tears in his eyes.

"All right. This baby is making it tough. Being a little difficult and not wanting to show us the sex…" Dr. Patterson chuckles. "Ahh…there we go. Good… Well, congratulations, Mom and Dad, you're having a…"

Chapter Fourteen

Roman

Is a Rocket Launcher Too Much?

"**I** CAN'T BELIEVE THIS," I MUTTER FOR THE thousandth time since we found out the sex yesterday afternoon as I pull into my sister's driveway.

"I know," Andie chuckles. "It's about to go down too."

She's already climbing out of the Range Rover and making her way over to the front door where Reagan and Dani are waiting. I'm still stunned out of my mind.

I need to prepare.

I need to buy a gun.

Perhaps some grenades.

A Taser could be handy too.

I hear a whistle and look through the windshield to see Ram in the yard, beaming at me like the cat that ate the fucking canary. Jesus.

"Come on, loser," he bellows and waves me inside. "Time to pay up. It's written all over your face. I won."

I flip him off through the glass before getting out of the vehicle and trotting across the grass. "What did we bet again?" I grunt.

He ruffles my hair and snorts with laughter. "That," he says with a laugh, "pretty boy."

I shove him away and walk inside. Seems the party already started without us. We were supposed to arrive at five, but I was so wrapped up in my head—and over-whelmed with the possessive need to keep what's mine safe—that I tied her sexy ass to the bed. I had my way with her, and we took a nap after. It wasn't until I jolted awake two hours after we were supposed to be here that we got it in gear to come over.

"What's got your panties in a wad?" Linc's annoying ass questions the moment I walk through the door.

I give my sister a pointed glare that says, *Why the fuck did you invite this asshole?*

She sticks her tongue out and gives me the *because-this-is-my-house-and-I-do-whatever-the-fuck-I-want* glare.

"Okay, you two," Mom chides as she gives me a hug. "Honey, you're as pale as a ghost. Your father had that same look in his eyes when we found out what our third baby was going to be."

Guns.

Definitely need to buy more guns.

"Oh shit," Linc hollers as he points to a giant poster board that's been hung over the fireplace showing all of our bets. "Roman, you're fucked, man." He snorts and I growl.

"I knew it," Chase exclaims from somewhere in the room. Jesus, did they invite everyone to watch my men-tal breakdown.

Knives.

And knife sharpeners.

Lots of knives for sure.

"Rey," Linc laughs, "I told you. Fucking told you. Do you remember what we bet?"

Reagan throws a couch pillow at him. "We don't know for sure. I could still win."

Ram comes up behind me and clamps a hand on my shoulder. "Little sis, this is not the look of a winner. This is the look of a motherfucker who's already googling in his head 'how to weld a chastity belt out of scrap metal.'"

My eyes find Andie's across the room as she chats with my mother, and she smirks. I'll tan her pretty little ass for that smirk later. She may have won this round, but I'll win once I have her pinned and tied to her bed. Not that she'll mind. Once I got over my fear of hurting her, I quite like having her at my mercy.

"What're you losing?" Dani questions as she looks up at the poster board. "Oh, boy. Does Andie know that?" She points to the square where Ram and I bet. Of course we couldn't be normal adults. Nah, this motley crew had to bet like this is a fantasy football game—not my goddamned life and future we're talking about here.

"Tense? Just imagine that first time some guy steps up on that front porch looking like me," Linc says with a chuckle. He waggles his eyebrows at me and then flexes his tattooed, muscled bicep.

Rope.

And duct tape.

Mace. I'll definitely need mace.

"I think he's in shock," Chase quips as he tugs Reagan

into his lap.

Linc's playfulness melts away but his gaze never leaves them. "Hey, Rey, can I ask you a quick question?"

Reagan pops back out of Chase's lap and follows Linc into the kitchen. When I turn to look up at the board, Dani is shaking her head. "You were pretty confident, huh?" She snorts and points at another box, a bet with my mom no less. "Scrub all of your mother's toilets for a month?"

Ram chuckles and saunters over to her. "Aww, babe, don't tease my big brother. He's already losing hair as we speak. Being a dad is making him old."

She laughs. "I don't think losing a bet and having to shave your head is the same thing as hair loss from old age. Besides, I don't see Andie letting this happen."

"Let what happen?" Andie pops in behind her friend. Then she screeches at me. "YOU BET TO SHAVE YOUR HEAD?!"

I run my fingers through my messy and soon-to-be gone hair. "I thought it was going to be a boy!"

"I TOLD YOU IT WAS A GIRL!" she yells back. "Ew! You can't have a shaved head. Linc has a shaved head! Ack!"

Linc hollers from the kitchen and yanks off his bean-ie. "I'm growing it out. Don't hate." He scrubs the short dark hair on his head before pulling his hat back on and winking at my sister.

Knives.

Guns.

Is a rocket launcher too much?

Nah…definitely going on the list.

"I thought it was going to be a boy," I mutter again, mostly to myself.

Andie grins and wraps her arms around my neck. "You were wrong, ya big oaf. All kinds of wrong. When are you gonna learn I'm the brains of this operation?"

I crack a smile and press a kiss to her nose. "You were right. I guess I'm changing diapers for a week straight when our little princess comes along."

And then fuckface Linc is right in my ear. "Until a villain comes along and swoops her right out of your arms."

"Lincoln Justin Carter!" Andie bellows and smacks her brother upside the head. "Stop antagonizing my man!"

Pliers. For ripping out teeth.

And hedge trimmers. For cutting off dirty little fingers that even think about touching my daughter.

Super glue. I'll glue all the little boys lips shut. No kissing my baby girl.

"Roman," Andie says, her palms on my cheeks. "Focus. Take the murderous scowl off your face. Everything is going to be okay."

I grit my teeth. "Homeschool. We'll homeschool her. Keep her locked in the house forever. No boys. Ever."

She giggles and presses a kiss to my lips. "You're obnoxious. God, she's going to hate you." Her blue eyes twinkle.

My lips quirk up on one side, and I wink. "I know."

"WHO'S READY FOR TEQUILA?" Dani hollers.

"I'll get the scissors!" Linc yells back.

"Touch my man's head, and I'll cut your eyeballs out

with those scissors," Andie growls at her brother.

"A bet's a bet—" Ram starts but Andie cuts him off.

"And it'll be YOUR balls I cut off next," she hisses.

I shrug my shoulders. You don't argue with this hell-cat. She always wins.

"Fine," Ram grunts in concession. "You can clean my loft then. You left it a mess when you left in such a haste—"

Andie stiffens, and I shut my brother up with a glare. She jerks her head up to look at me, a frown painting her pretty features. "*His* loft?" Then her cheeks blaze red. "Did they kick you out of your own house?"

Fucking Ram.

"No," I huff. "He's just being a shit. Did Reagan tell you she made cucumber sandwiches?"

She purses her lips but lets me change the subject. The gleam in her eyes tells me we'll be revisiting this subject later.

Fucking Ram.

Maybe I'll go buy those hedge clippers now and practice on my brother. He can't go blabbing all my secrets with no tongue.

"I was watching a thing on TV the other day. Statistics said that most girls nowadays lose their virginity between thirteen and sixteen," Linc chirps, a shit-eating grin on his face. "You're going to blink your eyes, Roman, and your little girl will be running off with some punk-ass kid with a car before she even gets her first period."

I growl and Andie hugs me tight. "Ignore my idiot brother," she murmurs against my chest. Then she hollers. "Jesus! Don't we even get a *'congratulations, it's a girl,'* for crying out loud?"

"CONGRATULATIONS! IT'S A GIRL!"

I cringe.

Girl.

We have a few months and then this innocent little thing will be in this world. She's going to rely on her big, bad daddy to keep her safe from fuckwits like the one Linc was as a child, no doubt.

I'm definitely going to need a gun.

A big fucking gun.

Linc taunts me with a pair of scissors from the love seat where he's sitting across from Andie and me. "I think you'd look good with a little off the top."

"Last warning before I stab you with those," Andie growls at him.

I'd decided to give up alcohol in solidarity with my pregnant woman but after learning we're having a fucking girl, I've lost my head a bit and have taken to drinking myself blind. Andie must sense the overwhelming terror flooding through me because she's the one who keeps fetching me a refill.

"A bet's a bet," I tell her and nibble at her arm through her shirt. She lets out a squeal and smacks me upside the head.

"Well it's a bet you just don't get to follow through on," she snips and crosses her arms over her chest. *Goddamn those tits.* If we didn't have Linc and Reagan as an audience, I'd have already yanked her shirt off and taken a bite of her creamy flesh.

"I can't believe Dani got so drunk," Reagan says as she wobbles into the living room, carrying two freshly made margaritas. She hands one to Linc and plops down clumsily next to him. He stretches his arm across the back of the loveseat behind her. And normally I'd be ripping his arm right from its socket, but I'm too fucked up to care right now.

"Dani," Andie tells her with a chuckle, "can be quite the spitfire when plastered. Just ask Ram."

I bite my woman on her arm again.

And she slaps me.

Again.

"Where's your boyfriend, anyway?" I question my sister, enjoying the way Linc sends death glares my way. "He didn't drink at all. I think he was trying to impress Mom."

Reagan shrugs her shoulders. "He was tired. I'm sure Mom was too busy babying you to notice Chase. I thought you were going to start crying," she teases me.

Linc snorts and I flip him off.

"Fuck you and fuck you!" I bellow, pointing at each of them. I use my palms to cover Andie's small belly so the baby doesn't hear this next part. "And fuck you later." I punctuate my words with another bite to her arm that suggests I'll make good on my promise to her

She laughs and squirms in my lap. "On that note, I'm going to the bathroom."

I watch her fine ass jiggle all the way down the hallway. When I return my gaze back to the only two other people here, they're having fun poking at each other.

"Scoot over," Reagan whines.

"You're the one taking up half my cushion," Linc argues with a grin. "It's like you want in my lap. Come here, Rey." He pats his thigh. "Sit in Santa's lap. You look like you've been a good girl this year."

Rolling my eyes, I rise to my feet and stumble off to find my baby momma. God, she's so fucking hot. Each day, I swear her tits get bigger. I manage to find my way to the bathroom and burst inside. She's at the sink washing her hands but jolts in surprise.

"Jesus!" she groans. "You can't just sneak up on a pregnant lady! I could have peed myself!"

"Didn't you *just* pee? Like three seconds ago?"

She flicks some water in my face. "I could pee again. All over your expensive shoes. And it would be all your fault."

I slide my fingers into her hair and kiss her hard before pulling away to give her a smug grin. "I'm learning I'm a kinky guy. Maybe I'm into pregnant ladies peeing on me."

She snorts and shoves me, at which point I stumble right into the shower curtain. Pole, curtain, hooks and me. We all crash into the tub with a noisy clatter.

"This is why drinking and Roman Holloway don't mix! You turn into a clumsy oaf!" She clutches her belly as she howls with laughter and makes no move to help me up.

"Come here," I tell her with a grin as I reach for her.

She eyes me suspiciously but gives me her hand. Gently, I tug her down into my lap. It's not comfortable, but I'll take her in my arms anywhere. Her blue eyes dart all over me, concerned despite her teasing.

"I love you," I blurt out.

All softness fades away, and she shakes her head at me. "I know. Now let's get you out of this tub and into the guest bed. I don't think we're going home tonight."

I cradle her face with my palm and smile. "I think your dumbass brother is going to have to get me out of this tub."

"You owe me a big breakfast tomorrow for this. Huge."

Thrusting my hips, I let her feel the erection she's giving me just by being her and so goddamned pretty all the time. "I hope you like sausage."

She gags and swats at me, but I catch her wrist before playfully biting it.

"I hate you," she grumbles.

I suckle the skin I just bit and wink. "I know."

"How many different types of diapers does one baby need?" Ram questions from beside me as we stare at shelves upon shelves of different sizes, brands, and types of baby diapers.

I shrug and start scanning every single bar code. "I don't know, but I should probably register for one of each just in case."

He nods his approval. "I agree. Where are the girls, anyway?"

"They went to look at bedding now that we know what we're having. Do you think they sell bars for windows here?" I question as I scan some Pull-Ups, whatever the fuck those are. The blonde toddler on the front of the package is grinning and innocent, and my anxiety levels spike. "What about guns?"

"Like squirt guns?"

"Like machine guns," I correct.

Ram chuckles. "Maybe we should go to Academy after this. I think you might need a bow and arrow set too. Spear the fuckers in the eye who decide to look at your kid wrong."

This time, I'm nodding my approval. "Definitely."

We finally finish scanning all of the diapers on the shelves when we come across the bottle aisle.

"What the fuck?" Ram complains. "There are like a thousand damn bottles. Just make Andie breastfeed and we can skip this aisle."

I grunt in agreement. We happily rush past this row and stroll into the next only to find more horror awaiting.

"What the fuckity fuck fuck fuck?" he demands and motions at the shelves lined with breast pumps and pads and nipple creams.

"Go back to the bottle aisle. Now," I bark and shove him out of the way. I happily scan the bottles because those are less complicated than tit shit.

I'm just finishing scanning every bottle brush the store has to offer when I hear Dani and Andie's giggles. When they round the corner, I stop to stare at my woman. Today she's wearing a pink T-shirt that fits her just a bit snugly and shows off the slight swell of her stomach. Fierce pride fills my chest. My baby girl is in there. I've yet to feel her kick, but Andie has been positively elated each time she does.

"Sexy guys in a baby store," Dani says dramatically and clutches her chest. "I think my ovaries just combusted!"

I snort and shove Ram her way. "Only one sexy guy around here and I'm taken."

Andie laughs and waltzes over to me before throwing her arms around my neck. I kiss her a little too long for the bottle aisle. If we're not careful, some people passing by will get a demonstration of exactly how babies are made.

"I want to show you the bedding I picked out," Andie says in a gleeful tone when we finally break apart. The excitement in her eyes has me beaming back at her.

"Let's go, beautiful."

With our hands threaded together, we make our way across the store, stopping along the way to scan a random item or two. Andie even lets me scan a pink football onesie. When we make it over to the area with the cribs, she points inside. "Isn't it sooooo pretty?"

I reach in and stroke the soft chenille fabric. "Soft too. I like it."

"Me too," she chirps. "Now help me get the bag off that shelf over there."

Pulling out my phone, I take a picture of it before shaking my head at her. "Not today."

She stops and turns around to look at me. "What? Why not?"

"Because."

Her smile is gone and she frowns. "Roman, I want it before they run out. They only have one set left."

"Not today," I tell her and start to tug her toward me.

She twists out of my grip. "What's your problem? You're being weird and vague. Just buy me the damn bedding or I'll buy it myself."

"Jesus Christ, Andie," I gripe. "For once in your damn life can you just listen to me?"

Her full lips part open in shock as if I've slapped her. Fat tears well in her eyes, which makes me feel like even more of an asshole.

"Babe—"

"No," she hisses in a scathing tone. "You've made yourself perfectly clear. I'm being a spoiled brat." Her arms cross over her chest and she stalks over to a glider to sit down. She starts tapping away on her phone—probably to Reagan to rat me out—and I let out a huff.

"I need to make a call," I growl as I hand her my scanner. "Wrap this up. I have a headache."

I'm sure I'm being an ass but I really need to make this call *apparently*.

Chapter Fifteen

Andie

I Should Have Known

"AND SO THEN RAM TOLD ME I COULD HAVE whichever cake I wanted, but he would prefer it not be taffy flavored. I mean, I love taffy, but to flavor our wedding cake with it? I'm not *that*... hey are you even listening to me?"

I'm staring out the car window, lost in thought. To be honest I haven't heard a thing she's said since she picked me up. Linc busted through my door late last night, needing a favor, which was to borrow my car. He failed to mention that he wouldn't have it back in time for me to go to work.

"Andie, you okay?"

"Huh? Yeah, fine." I go back to staring out at nothing.

"Are you sure? You've been like this for the last few days now. Did something happen? Are you and Roman okay?"

"Nope. We're peachy as ever," I reply, because I really don't know how to answer that question. Ever since his mood change at the baby store, things have been off.

He's his normal Roman self, feeding me with attention, love, and orgasms. But he hasn't mentally been there. This past week, he's been going off-site more than normal, and when he returns, he looks almost…it pains me to admit it but, disheveled. His normally crisp shirts look wrinkled, and once, he was sporting a different tie. I asked him about it, but he said he spilled soup on it at a lunch meeting. He swore to me with kisses and sweet endearments that I was overthinking things, but even factoring in my pregnancy hormones, something still wasn't sitting right with me.

"Have you noticed Roman acting strange lately?" I turn to ask Dani. Maybe she's noticed something when Roman's been at the apartment. Or during her visits to the office.

"I don't think so. Besides being a little freaked out about having a girl." She giggles. I lamely smile, because as cute as it's been watching Roman freak out, it's not that. I can feel it.

"How's he been at the apartment? Does he talk to you guys? Did he say anything last night?" He has to have slipped and said something. He confides in his brother. And since Dani and him are attached at the hip, she had to have heard something.

Dani looks caught off guard. "Well, I would tell you, but he's not really there anymore. I can't remember the last time he stopped by."

The pain in my chest tightens to an unhealthy degree. He told me he couldn't spend the night because he was hanging out with Ram and would just crash at their loft.

"Fuck," I mumble, biting on my lower lip.

He lied to me. He's been lying to me.

"Honey, why are you crying? Did I say something wrong? I assumed Roman had been at your place." She reaches over the center console and grips my hand. "Hey, whatever it is, I'm sure it's fine. Roman loves you."

"Maybe not enough," I reply, jerking my gaze over the passing scenery.

I shouldn't have turned my back to the signs. The other day, Roman told me he had to go to his place for a few hours but would meet me at mine around dinner. When he finally showed up, he looked tired and chose to order in, instead of us going out.

The secret phone calls haven't stopped.

The out-of-nowhere meetings he flees to.

I should have known.

We pull up to Holloway Advertising and my mind is drowning in doubt. I want to be the naïve girl who says that everything is okay and rests assured that my man is not hiding something big from me, but I can't, no matter how hard I dig, I just can't bury the doubt.

He *is* doing something.

I just don't know how I'm going to find out.

I climb out of the car and shut the door, leaning into the open window. "Hey, thanks for the ride. Are you coming up?"

"No, I have to get to work too. There's new inventory coming in today, so I want to get there early before Mary does. She's a real towel villain and tries to mess with my section. She clearly has no idea what she's doing either."

That comment earns a smile from me. Poor Dani is

having a turf war with another employee. No one messes with her towels.

"All right. Well, thanks again. Lunch this week?"

"And dinner. It's a date…and Andie? Cheer up. It's going to be okay. *More* than okay."

I offer her another short smile and head into work.

Because I'm not sure it is. *Oh, Andie, what are you going to do?* Do I just come out and ask him? He can deny it and just change the subject or try to distract me with his mouth and his hands. Do I flip out? Give him my mean side, until he cracks and admits he's cheating on me? I slump in the elevator, feeling at a loss. I don't want to be that person anymore. The off-the-handle bitch. I promised myself and this little girl I was going to be better. I need to keep that promise for her.

If he is doing something, then so be it. I will have this baby and raise her with all the love in the world.

I walk into the office, and Roman isn't there yet. Disappointment topped with sadness strike as I stare at his empty chair. I love watching him all day, the dominant business man at work. I could tell you exactly how his eyebrows crinkle when someone disagrees with him or the way one side of his mouth perks into a grin, when he knows he's about to lock a deal. The tapping of his large fingertips on his mahogany desk is reserved for high-profile clients who are discussing a bidding war. And the best part? When his eyes catch mine gazing at him and the smiles that breach his face, melting my heart.

Today I look at an empty chair.

Maybe he has a good excuse. Don't jump to conclusions.

Yeah, right. I said that when he came over earlier this week with paint on him, and he told me he was at a site visit. But he's not a construction worker—he's in advertising and marketing.

I toss my purse on my desk and remove my jacket. I settle into my spot and start up my computer. I go through my normal morning routine, which is to check Roman's daily calendar for meetings. He doesn't have one scheduled for this morning.

I'm replying back to some emails when Roman finally walks through the door.

"Hello there, beautiful." He strolls in, dominating the space with his easy confidence and charm. Before removing his suit coat, he walks over to me, bending down and offers me his mouth. I tell myself to not give in and smack the shit out of him the second he gets close, but instead, I allow him to kiss me.

I think the pregnancy has broken my fierce side.

"How are my two girls feeling this morning?" he asks lifting his hand to cover my belly. I fight not to break down.

He wouldn't do this to me. To us. There has to be a mistake.

"Fine…we're fine." I fight to hide my emotions, but Roman knows me too well.

"You don't sound fine. What's wrong?" He's removing his jacket, his eyes on alert.

"Nothing. Just, I missed you last night. How's Ram doing?"

Please don't lie to me. Please don't lie to me.

"Good. A lot of bullshit talk about work. The

wedding planning. You know…" He bends down placing another quick peck to my lips and heads to his desk.

I turn away so he can't see the torment in my eyes. Pretending I'm sorting through my file cabinet, I brush away the tears that have begun to fall. I'm such a fool. I trusted him. Gave myself fully to him. I've fallen so hard in love with this man, and he betrayed me.

"Fucker," I bite, kicking the file cabinet.

"Baby, you okay?"

Shit. "Oh yeah. Sorry. Drawer got stuck."

Calm down, Andie.

I need to pull my shit together. I wasn't raised to let anyone walk all over me. I certainly won't let a man start now. I take a few deep breaths and turn, beginning to slam my fingers on my keyboard. If he won't fess up, then I'll just have to find a way to catch him in the act.

It's mid-morning and neither one of us have spoken. Roman has been on a conference call since he sat down, and if I attempt to say anything I'll either end up crying or ripping his eyes out. I spent my morning searching online for a new job. I'm probably going to need it after I go postal on my boss. I know I can argue that he cannot fire me, but I won't be able to work so close to him after this. After he finally admits what he's been up to.

I try to recall any female clients I've seen him with in the office. Is it the pretty brunette from Allister Publishing? The tiny little redhead from BC Insurance? Oh my God, is it Suzy, Reagan's whore of a secretary? I don't know why I do it to myself, but I think about all the ways they are better than me. They're probably nicer. Prettier. Skinnier. Not a raging, pregnant bitch, like me. I look down at my outfit, which consists of stupid black leggings and a cream tunic. My hair is in a ponytail because I have zero energy to do anything with it lately, and my makeup is, well nonexistent.

"I've completely let myself go," I cry, lowering my head and banging my forehead onto my keyboard. I jump in my seat when I feel two large hands on my shoulders. I whip my head up, realizing Roman is kneeling to the side of me.

"Baby, what's wrong?"

I look at him, at his phone, then back at him.

"What are you doing? Aren't you on a call?"

"I told them I had an emergency. You're more important." His gaze is genuine. His eyes show concern and love. He lifts his hand to cup my cheek, and I rest my head in his palm, inhaling his scent.

"Is something wrong? You know I hate seeing you sad."

Then why are you causing so much of it?

"You would tell me if I wasn't attractive to you anymore, right? Am I attractive to you?"

He glides his fingers to the back of my head, bringing our foreheads together. "I think you are more beautiful right now than the first day I met you."

"Then why have you been ly—"

"HR must have a field day with you two."

We both turn to Linc, who's standing in the doorway, jingling my car keys. Breaking the moment, Roman stands, adjusting his tie.

197

"Do you ever go away?" he growls, walking back to his desk.

"Nope. And now that I'm about to have a little niece, I'm going to be around all the time. Gotta protect her from all those bad…"

An orange goes flying at Linc's head. It misses its intended target and crashes into the bookshelf as my brother makes his way to me and hands me my keys. "Thanks again. I even filled her up. Well…I put three bucks in."

Roman notices the exchange, confused. "Why does he have your car?"

"He borrowed it. Now he's returning it," I state, annoyed.

"How did you get to work? Why didn't you call me?"

Taking in a deep breath for strength, I reply. "I did. It went straight to voicemail."

"Babe, I'm sorry…"

"Mr. Holloway?"

What is it with the interruptions today?! We all turn to Suzy, who struts into Roman's office wearing an ugly green skirt, one that is too short for an office setting, and a cropped top that a hooker would wear.

"What is it, Suzy?" Roman snaps, not hiding the annoyance in his voice.

"You received a message on Ms. Holloway's line. They said it was urgent." She walks over to Roman, handing him a folded piece of paper. Roman stalls before snatching it out of her hand and reading it.

I can't help but stare at him, observing his every eye flicker, brow crunch, any mannerism that will help me figure out what is on that piece of paper. He reads it quickly, crumbles it in his hand and tosses it into his trash.

"That is all. You can leave now," he snaps, and Suzy jumps at his tone, quickly pivoting and exiting his office.

What the hell is on that piece of paper?

He looks anxious.

He hasn't attempted to make eye contact with me since, and worry settles deep inside my chest. It just further confirms my fears.

"Well since I'm here, sis, wanna go to lunch? Half off wings at Bender's."

"I actually have plans with Roman—"

"Baby, I hate to cancel but I have to run an errand. Why don't you go with…*him*." He motions towards Linc in an absent manner. "I'll make it up to you later."

Before I can answer, he stands and snatches up his suit coat. Throwing it over his shoulders, he hustles over to me and bends down to press a quick kiss to the top of my head. He walks past Linc, who regards him with a confused look, and turns as we both watch him leave his office.

"What the hell was that all about?" my brother asks, his hands on his hips as he regards me in confusion.

I'm having trouble replying.

One, two, three… I count to ten trying to rein in my emotions.

"I think Roman is cheating on me."

His eyebrows raise as shock spreads across Linc's face. "No shit. How do you know?"

God, where do I start? "I just do. He's been lying. Hiding things from me. He told me he slept at his place last night, but when I talked to Dani, she said he was never there." I cover my face with my hands and start crying. Linc is on me instantly, wrapping me up in his strong, brotherly hug.

"That fucking asshole," he growls. "I'll kill him."

I pull away, wiping my face. "No, don't do anything."

"Andie, no one fucks with my sister. He's a dead man. I knew he was fucking you over."

My brows scrunch together and my lip curls up in disgust. "What do you mean you *knew*?"

His eyes flicker with guilt. *Fuck.* What is he going to tell me?

"I'm sorry," he groans. "I should have told you sooner, but I didn't want to get involved. You looked happy."

Oh God.

My stomach starts turning, and I'm worried I may get sick all over my desk.

"Tell me, Lincoln. Now."

"When we were at Rey's awhile back. He took a call. I didn't hear about what, but when he hung up, he said, 'Bye, sweetie.'"

My stomach clenches. I *am* going to be sick.

"Are you sure?"

"Sorry, sis, but that's what I heard."

That lying son of a bitch. That party was months ago. He's been playing me since the beginning. I take a block of Post-its and whip them toward Roman's desk. I nail a frame on his desk and the glass shatters when it falls and crashes onto the floor.

As good as that felt, it didn't even scratch the itch of anger now building inside me. I pick up my stapler and whip it at his desk. When it strikes his open laptop, I exhale a gust of air.

Okay, so my fierceness is still one hundred percent intact.

"Damn girl," Linc says with a whistle. "You just dented the shit out of his computer."

And I'm not even close to being done. I'm going to dent everything he owns, including his pretty-boy face.

I do what I know will hurt most. I go for his special-edition copy of *Christine* by Stephen King that now wears a creased cover from my last meltdown, and I start ripping out the pages. I crumble each into a wad and throw them at his desk. Each one pinging one item or another. I actually make one into the garbage can.

Garbage can….

The note.

I drop the book, earning a small yelp from Linc since it landed on his toe, and storm over to Roman's garbage can. I dig through it furiously until I find what I'm looking for.

"Got it." I snatch the crumbled piece of paper out of the trash and open it, smoothing the wrinkles out. "What the fuck?"

"What is it?" Linc joins me and leans over my shoulder as we both read the note. It's written in Suzy's super neat handwriting complete with an address because she's a suck up like that. For once, I have something to thank that twat for.

423 Apricot Lane.
I only have a short window for you.
-D

"What the fuck does that mean?" Linc inquires.

Meanwhile, I'm seeing every shade of red God created.

"It means we are going to catch Mr. Asshole Holloway in the act. Let's go."

We googled the address and it's actually one in town. A house in the suburbs. The location is familiar, because it's in the new upscale development that everyone has been yapping about around town. So he's cheating on me with a rich whore.

Asshole.

My brother smacks his gum and drums my steering wheel with his fingers. "So just so I'm prepared, are we killing him? Or just breaking bones?"

That is still undecided. I don't want to have this baby in jail, so maybe just broken bones at this point will have to suffice.

"Okay, so your silence is kinda creeping me out," he says with a nervous chuckle. "I love you, but you may want to calm down before going all crazy in there."

Too late for that.

I shoot off a text to Dani, letting her know I'm going to need her hardcore really soon. After her and Ram, she owes me.

Me: I'm about to kill Roman. I wanted to let you know so you can be ready for me. I'm gonna need my best friend.

Dani: Oh, God. Why!? What happened? Please don't kill anyone.

Me: He's cheating on me. I confirmed it. He's with her now. I can't believe he did this to me.

A few seconds pass before she replies.

Dani: Listen…Ram says to chill out. Where are you? Please don't do anything crazy. Think about the baby.

Me: I *am* thinking about my baby by getting rid of her deadbeat father. I'm heading to an address in the Willow Oaks subdivision.

Dani: Don't! I'm calling you.

Her call comes through, but I hit the end button just as Reagan messages me.

Reagan: Linc told me what you two are doing. What's the address?

"Seriously? You had to tell Reagan?" I snap at him. I know it will get around the family circle in no time, but he's my brother. He could have waited.

"Sorry," he tells me, holding up a hand in defense. "She asked what I was doing, and I simply said I was going with you to kill her brother for cheating on you."

"Ugh!" I growl at him and go back to rapidly typing a reply text.

Me: 423 Apricot Lane. I'm sorry I have to kill your brother. You can find his remains there.

I toss my phone into my purse. I'm not in the mood to hear any more. There's no talking reason into me at this point. We pull into the neighborhood, and it's beautiful. Crisp houses line the brand-new sidewalks. I spot a few people walking dogs or going on their daily runs.

"Jesus, I feel like I'm on an episode of *Leave it to Beaver*," Linc groans, slamming on the breaks to avoid hitting a soccer ball a kid kicked into the street.

"Well, it's about to turn into *Nightmare on Elm Street*," I snap, staring at the perfectly cut grass lines.

He laughs at my unintended humor and grabs his phone out of his pocket, reading a text while diving. "Reagan says to not go in the house. To wait."

"This isn't *Reagan's* problem. Seriously. What is it with you two?" I bite back.

He doesn't reply just puts his hands up in surrender.

"There! Right there. That's Roman's Range Rover." Of course a shiny red Beamer is next to his. I hope she is rich enough to help cover all the plastic surgery he's going to need when I claw his face and rip off his balls.

Linc pulls up into the driveway, and I'm opening the door and jumping out before he's fully in park.

"Andie, wait! She said to wait!"

Fuck that.

I run up to the front door and throw the damn thing open. It slams so hard, I think the doorknob causes a dent in the wall.

Good.

"Where are you, YOU BIG OAF CHEATING ASSHOLE!"

Chapter Sixteen

Roman

I Lied to You. I'm an Asshole.

FUCK.

Fuck.

Fuuuuuuuuuuuuck.

I'm caught. Red fucking handed. And she's insanely pissed.

"Let me explain," I start but she throws her purse at me. Her purse! "Ow!"

"YOU ASSHOLE!" she screeches, her fury rolling off of her in waves. "I TRUSTED YOU!"

"Honey, calm down," Diane says, her tone soft. But it's all wrong. Wrong timing. Wrong person. Wrong damn thing to do right now.

Andie's death glare skips from me to Diane. "You," she growls as she charges forward "YOU HOMEWRECKING BITCH!"

I snag Andie by the waist before she pummels Diane's face in. The last thing I need is to pay for Diane's newest nose to be repaired. "Calm the fuck down and listen!"

My woman goes wild in my arms and snatches my hair—hair that I now wish was shaved. She yanks until I release her.

"I HATE YOU!" she screams at me.

"I know," I start, "but it's not what you think."

She picks up a stack of brand new coasters from the coffee table and starts slinging them at me like Frisbees. They're glass and they hit the brick fireplace behind me smashing one, two, three, four. Then, she throws the holder at me too. I manage to duck the coasters but the holder clips me in the shoulder.

"Andie," Linc bellows from the doorway. "You need to stop—"

She grabs her hair and releases a choked sob, her only show of crushing emotion, before she goes back on the rampage. Next, the lamp I just unwrapped from Pier 1 gets swept onto the hardwood floors. Glass shatters and the light bulb pops.

"Listen—"

"Nooooo!"

"Oh fuck!" Ram's voice joins the fray, but I don't have time for this shit. I need to calm my woman down before she hurts herself or our baby.

"Listen, babe—"

"You listen to me," she roars, pointing a long finger at me. "I am not your babe anymore! You will never be allowed anywhere near me or my child ever again! Keep your whores far away from me!" She screeches as she looks for something else to destroy. The only other available thing is Diane, who seems to be once again on Andie's radar because she launches herself at her.

I step on the coffee table and leap in front of her just as she rears her fist at my realtor. For a pregnant lady, Andie packs one helluva punch. She clocks my jaw, and I swear she about knocks it off its hinges. Before she can land anymore hits, I grab her in a bear hug that pins her arms.

"Listen to me, goddammit!" I snarl against her hair. Her body is tense as fuck but the steam is rushing from her. She sags in my arms as a gut-wrenching sob overtakes her.

"How could you? You broke me!" she cries.

Guilt tears through me. I should have just told her everything from the get-go. We could have avoided all of this. Her getting upset can't be good for our little girl. I need to calm her the fuck down.

"Babe—"

"No! I'm not your babe—"

We scuffle some more, but I manage to clamp my hand over her mouth.

"Diane Sweeney is my realtor," I hiss into her ear. "We're not fucking. Jesus Christ, Andie!"

Hot tears soak my fingers and my heart clenches in my chest. "Baby," I murmur against her ear. "I love you. I love only you. I'll only ever love you."

She's sniffling hard, and I steal a quick glance at the doorway. Linc and Ram wisely stay out of the way. I can hear Diane murmuring something behind me, but my focus is on Andie. Always Andie.

"This was supposed to be a surprise," I whisper and kiss her hair. "I wanted to give you a home. It's taken a long time to acquire this property and get it decorated. I just wanted to fucking surprise you, woman."

She stiffens in my arms, but I don't dare release her mouth. Not until I've said my piece.

"Diane is a friend of mine. She's happily married to a buddy I went to college with. They have three cute little kids. This is her job, selling houses. But helping me decorate the damn thing was because she's my friend and wanted to help. I'm not cheating on you, crazy. I'm fucking nuts over you and just want to give you the entire goddamned world."

Finally, I release her mouth and my grip on her. Her head falls forward as her shoulders quiver with silent tears.

"Say something, babe…"

I give Ram a pointed look that says, *Get everyone the fuck out of here.* Thankfully my brother can read me and gives me a clipped nod. Soon, the door slams shut and we're alone.

I walk around to face Andie and cup her soaked cheeks with my palms. I tilt her red face up to look at mine. Devastation. Embarrassment. Relief. Her eyes are a stormy sea of emotion. I just want to fix her. To never see that look of utter despair in her eyes again.

"Please forgive me," I try, my voice hoarse. I can't bear to see her looking so broken. It fucking guts me. "Please."

"T-There's nothing to forgive," she chatters out. "I f-flew off the handle again."

"I lied to you. I'm an asshole," I argue. "I just wanted to give you something beautiful. I wanted to start a life with you."

Tears roll down her cheeks like a steady stream through a forest. I don't dare stop them. She's beautiful and perfect—even when she's messy and destroyed. I'll love her any way I can get her. Even like this. Even worse than this.

"I just thought…" she trails off and chokes on a sob.

"Shhh," I murmur and press a kiss to her red nose. Then, I kiss her soaked cheeks. Kiss after kiss, I try to soothe her pain. Pain I caused by being a secretive dick. "Shhh."

When my lips brush against hers, she lets out a sigh. It's a cross between happy and relieved. I devour her sweet lips and make promises with my tongue. Andie is a teary, snotty mess, and all I want to do is kiss away every bit of it. I want to kiss her until she laughs. Kiss her until her blue eyes sparkle with delight. I crave to kiss her until she's tearing off her clothes and begging me to make love to her.

It takes a good fifteen minutes of kissing and hugging and touching in silence before she seems to calm down. When her hiccups subside and her tears are swiped away, I pull away to regard this gorgeous woman. *My* woman.

"Do you want a tour of our house now?" I question with a small smile.

Her lips quirk. "I feel so stupid,"

"I'm the stupid one," I tell her with a sigh. "Trust me. You're anything but stupid. I just want you to be happy. Dani has all but moved into the loft, and we spend all of our time together in your apartment. Our daughter didn't really have a home. I want the three of us to be a

209

family. To plant some roots. So I bought a house."

She stands on her toes and kisses me. "Thank you."

I stroke her hair and give her a lopsided grin. "Don't thank me yet. You haven't seen the shower."

With our fingers threaded together, I guide her away from the piles of shattered glass and through the kitchen. She is amazed at the brand-spanking-new appliances and lets out a squeal upon discovering the fridge is already filled. I'd spent last night doing some last-minute shopping and decorating. I had planned to show her the house this weekend, but she found out a little earlier than planned.

"Roman," she murmurs as her fingers run along the chair molding in the hallway. "This is too much."

I chuckle. "I will never be able to give you everything I want to. But I sure as hell won't stop trying."

She squeezes my hand as we step into the laundry room. "Oh my God! No more trips to the building laundromat!"

Her giggles are sexy as fuck as she pretends to hump the cherry red dryer. "I think I just came!"

I hook my arm around her waist and haul her to me. "Not yet, baby. But soon." Our mouths meet for a heated kiss, and then we're back on our tour. I save the nursery and our room for last. When she walks into the newly painted nursery, she lets out a choked sound before rushing over to the crib. She picks up the soft chenille blanket and hugs it to her chest.

"I'm such a bitch," she whispers, regarding me with tears in her eyes.

I frown and stalk over to her. My arms wrap around

her from behind, and I kiss the top of her head. "You didn't know. I was an asshole. Especially over the bedding. Apparently my surprise came as a detriment to our relationship. I'm sorry, Andie."

She shrugs it off. "Forget about it. We're both stupid. That's why we make a perfect match. Now show me to the bedroom."

Her naked body looks good in my bed. Well, our bed. After our tour, I brought her in here and spent hours making love to her. I think after the third orgasm, all sadness and despondency were chased away for good. I'll be damned if I ever let them come back. Her eyes are closed and lips parted. She's so fucking pretty when she sleeps. Those fiery emotions she wears on her face so well are dormant when she's passed out. I can stare at all of her soft features without fear of a playful punch to the gut. I can take my time with her.

My eyes fall to her chest. Goddamn those tits. I don't know what I did to deserve them, but God apparently really fucking likes me because he makes them better and better each day as she grows with our child. My mouth waters to suck on her nipples until she cries out, but instead, I slide my palm over her stomach, which has really started to expand lately. I fucking love her belly being swollen with my daughter. I'm just stroking her stomach when I feel a weird sensation. Like maybe I bumped an organ or something. My back stiffens and I freeze my hand.

A nudge.

So tiny that if she were awake and talking, I'd have missed it.

My heart threatens to beat right out of my chest.

"Is that you, baby girl?" I murmur and lean closer to Andie's stomach. "Is that my—holy fuck it is!"

The nudge disappears when Andie's entire body shudders with laughter. "You scared her," she tells me, her voice soft and sleepy.

I press my lips to the last place I felt our daughter. "You're not scared, are you? Daddy's here. I'll protect you." It feels really damn weird to talk to a baby inside a stomach, but when I feel another tiny nudge against my fingers, I turn into a goddamned chatterbox. "I'm going to buy you a pony and a Barbie car and a million toys. We'll go to Disney World and Branson because your soon-to-be auntie loves that place. Mommy and Daddy are going to give you whatever you want. You're going to be spoiled as fuck, princess."

Andie slaps my head. "Roman!"

"Sorry, baby girl," I coo against her skin. "Daddy didn't mean to say the F-word." I kiss Andie's stomach. "I love you." Then, I look up at Andie's shimmering blue eyes. "And I love you too."

She ruffles my hair and beams at me. "I know."

"I can't believe we missed a whole day at work," Andie says as she flips her grilled cheese sandwich in the pan over her new stove. I'd been proud as fucking punch when she gushed over every single item in the kitchen. I worked hard to give her cool shit, so it makes me happy that she notices it all.

"Benefits of owning the company," I tell her before biting into the sandwich she made me. When I'd said to her, "Go make me a sandwich, woman," earlier, I'd been joking. But, she seemed excited to want to cook in her new home. I didn't even get to show her the double-headed shower because she had food on the brain.

"I'm going to need to get my clothes from the apartment after we eat lunch. There's no way I'm spending another night there. Not when we have this. I can't wait to show Dani," she chirps as she transfers her sandwich to a plate.

"I'll stay here and clean up this mess, but once you get back, maybe we'll invite everyone over to celebrate or go someplace nice for dinner," I suggest.

"I kind of want to cook some more in our new house. I love it here," she tells me in a breathless voice that reminds me of a little girl who just got the best present ever.

She joins me at the table and her feet tangle with mine underneath. I love when Andie is all smiles. I've never seen her look so fucking happy and serene in our entire relationship.

"You're beautiful," I blurt out.

She looks up at me from under her dark eyelashes and her cheeks redden. "So are you. Even if your head is a little big." Her eyes twinkle with mischief. I suddenly have the overwhelming hope that our daughter looks exactly like her. Every single feature.

"I hope Madonna doesn't have a big head like me," I tell her and chomp into my sandwich. "For your sake, of course."

She snorts and almost chokes on her bite. "What the hell, Roman?!"

I frown at her. "What? I do have a big head, and I don't even want to imagine what my own mother went through during childbirth—"

"MADONNA?!"

"Kind of has a ring to it and—"

"No."

"Taylor?"

"As in Swift? No."

"Cookie?"

"WHAT THE FUCK?! COOKIE IS NOT A NAME!"

"My grandma's name was Cookie."

"Don't lie to me."

"Ask Mom!"

"Oh. My. God. I'm texting Dani this shit."

"Cookie is cute—"

"Cookies are delicious! Not something you name your baby!"

"Fran?"

"The Nanny?!"

"Well, she was pretty. Ram and I used to have a crush on her and—"

"NO!"

"Latifah?"

"What?"

"She'll be a little princess and then grow up to be a queen—"

"You're just fucking with me now."

Our eyes meet and we both start laughing.

"What names do you like?" I question and reach for her hand.

She bites on her lip and looks away. "I don't know."

"Don't lie to me. I can see right through them. I told you all my awful suggestions. Anything in comparison would be a step up," I joke.

"I like a name, but if you don't like it—"

"Tell me."

"Molly."

A beat of silence.

"But Roman, if you don't like it—"

"I love it. I'd be honored if our daughter had your mom's name," I tell her, my voice serious.

The tears begin to flow down her beautiful cheeks, so I tug at her arm until she's sitting in my lap. I wrap my arm around her so that I can rub her stomach.

"Molly? You hungry in there?"

I get another little nudge that makes me fucking delighted as hell.

"So that's that, huh?" she questions with a sniffle.

"That's that."

Her fingers thread with mine over her stomach. "Sometimes I really, really, really don't hate you."

I chuckle. "I know."

Chapter Seventeen

Andie

I'm Sorry, Molly

I CAN'T STOP KISSING HIM.

Each time I tell him that I'm really leaving this time, I go back for more.

"Screw your clothes. I love you naked and all to myself."

I giggle again, going in for one last kiss. I swear. "No, I would prefer our friends and family not see me pregnant and naked."

He grabs my hips, bringing me up against his hard body. "Heck with them. Let's reschedule. I want you all to myself."

More giggling when I use my palms to push off his chest. "No. I want everyone over to celebrate. Plus, I want to cook every single thing in that fridge. I want to grab my mom's cookbook, too." He allows me the distance, even though I can see the large strain in his pants.

"That is just going to have to wait till later," I tell him with a smirk, pointing at his hard-on. "You can give me the private tour of the shower. Promise."

Roman growls and comes at me but I squeal and avoid his arms as I go running to my car.

"I'll be back in no time! Thirty minutes. Start counting now." I wave and jump in my car.

Who would have thought this is how my day would have ended? I pull out of *my* driveway and head to my apartment. I wave and smile like an idiot to a couple walking down the street. "Hey Bill, Cindy, great evening," I joke to my closed window. I laugh at myself, thinking that I now live in an episode of *Leave it to Beaver* with my handsome baby daddy. And I cannot be any more thrilled.

I turn up the radio, and my favorite Taylor Swift song blares through my speakers. I'm singing at the top of my lungs, the biggest smile on my face, while I think about today. There's no doubt that Roman's friend Diane thinks I'm a lunatic. My cheeks burn crimson with how I acted in front of her. She didn't stick around to allow me to apologize, so an *I'm sorry for trying to take your head off with my brand new lamp* care package is definitely in order.

My mind is racing, going back and forth over everything that just quickly transpired. All my thoughts are trying to settle, but it all still seems too surreal. The baby's room. The pink bedding I wanted so bad is now laid out beautifully in the chestnut wood crib we picked out together. Even when I looked around, I noticed some of the stuffed animals that had been stored in my apartment were now lying around the baby's room. I wonder when he was able to smuggle those out without me noticing. But then again, a lot of the baby stuff that was laying around my apartment was in the new house.

Roman thankfully explained and squashed every single worry I had the past couple of months. The secret lunch meetings early on were showings. His late nights were him working hard to get the house ready for us.

The paint makes sense now since our daughter's room is the same color as the paint speckles in question.

The times where he looked disheveled were when he was building the crib and dresser. He eased my main worry which was when he didn't come over last night. He'd wanted to work on filling up the kitchen with food and new gadgets, as well as, making sure some last minute decorating was done on our house.

Our house.

We have a home where we are going to start our family.

The rush of pure happiness fills my entire being. I have never felt so filled with love, joy, hope. Roman gives me all of that. He loves me something fierce, and I vow that I am never going to doubt that again.

That is one thing I swear to myself. If I have doubts, about anything, we're going to talk it out. Because what we have is real. I know that now, and I will never ever again take what I have for granted.

Because I am, without a doubt, in love with Roman James Holloway.

I lower my head to talk to our daughter. "Do you hear that, little Molly? I love your daddy. So, so much." I cradle my belly, holding a confident smile on my face. She must agree, because she takes the perfect moment to move.

I still cannot get used to that. Being able to feel her inside me. It's a feeling that I may never know how to explain.

The books say it will get even more intense. I cannot wait.

My cheeks begin to burn more with the thought of how we just christened the house. I will never grow tired of the way Roman brings me to the most powerful orgasms. His words, the way he knows my body better than I do… And whatever we don't know about each other, we have the rest of our lives to figure it out.

I gasp at the thought.

I just said the rest of our lives.

I want to get married.

I want to get married!

A single tear drops from my lids. "I'm not broken anymore," I whisper to Molly, knowing that I want to be Mrs. Roman Holloway one day.

I take a left on Conrad Street and see my building in view. I swear the sunset has never looked so beautiful before. The bluest clouds mixing with rays of orange and red.

"Isn't that a lovely sunset, Mrs. Holloway? Why yes it is." I laugh to myself. "Mrs. Holloway, would you and your family like to join us neighbors for a barbecue? Why sure, Bill and Cindy, we would love that!" I am in a fit of giggles now, pulling into my apartment complex.

"Mrs. Holloway, since you're the boss's wife, can we fire Suzy, that whore-mouthed skank? Why yes…yes, you can."

I think I'm going to love being married, I think to

myself as I pat my belly. "What do you think, Molly Holloway? Should we tell Daddy the great news?" I climb out of my car, grab for my purse, and head up the stairs.

I know the perfect way to break the good news, too. Knowing what a large sexual appetite Roman has, I picked up something kinky to wear while Dani and I were lingerie shopping for her honeymoon. It might be a wee bit snug now, but it doesn't matter. I know he's just going to tear the damn thing off me, anyway.

I am bouncing up the stairs to my apartment. I see Mrs. Pitts, the cat lady who lives across from me, and this time, instead of giving her the *get-a-deodorizer-or-stop-adopting-so-many-fucking-cats* look, I smile and wave.

Wow, the new me is really a *new* me.

I push my key into the lock and skip into my place. I toss my purse on the entryway table and head straight to my room. Just gonna grab a few things and—

"What in the hell are you so happy about?"

I jump three feet in the air at the intruding voice. When I turn, I almost trip over my own feet when I see Frank standing inside my door.

"How the fuck did you get in here? Get out!" I snap, hoping the instant terror doesn't show in my voice.

"Ahh," he grumbles. "Not such a tough girl now, are you?" He takes a few menacing steps toward me, and I retreat just as many backward. My entire body is beginning to shake, and I stumble over the carpet.

"Seriously get out, Frank, or I'm calling the cops." I bring my hands to my back pockets to realize I don't have a way to call anyone. My phone is in my purse. Shit!

Stupid leggings.

"With what? The phone that's over here in your purse? Doubtful." He steps closer, and I look to my left and then to my right for something to grab.

"Well…my boyfriend is waiting for me downstairs, and he'll be on his way up if I take too long. He's going to kick your fucking ass, so you better run." God, why didn't I let Roman drive me home, when he insisted on doing so?

"I know you're alone, Andie. Don't try and bullshit me. It's just you and me."

"Wh—what do you want, Frank?"

"I want my job back," he snarls, his nostrils flaring with anger. "But *that's* not going to happen. I want the two harassment charges to be dropped, but *that's* not going to happen. I want you to pay for what you did. And the way I see it, that's the *only* one that *is* going to happen." He comes at me, and I dive to the right. I attempt to jump over my couch, but he grabs my hair and tugs me back. I scream at the pain of my hair being ripped from my scalp. He doesn't ease up as he pulls harder before he tosses me to the ground.

"Frank, listen. I'm sorry. But I had nothing to do with—"

"YOU'RE FUCKING LYING!" he yells and launches at me, grabbing at my shirt, dragging my body back to my feet. I'm trying to break free of his hold, but his rage is making him way stronger than me.

"Frank, please, I'm pregnant," I beg, my voice quivering. God, the baby. Don't let him hurt the baby.

"Well, isn't that just sweet to hear. What are you

expecting, a congratulations from me?" His eyes are wild with hate. I'm trying not to panic, but it's impossible.

"Frank, please…"

"You ruined my life," he spits, pushing me so forcefully that I trip and slam against the wall. My head goes crashing into the hard surface, causing stars to form behind my lids. He pounces on me, but I bolt to the left, trying to run for the door.

I'm not quick enough, and he grabs at my hair once again. I scream, the pain doubling this time as he pulls back, whipping my body around like a rag doll. I'm thrown back to the ground, my arms protecting my stomach as I fall on my side. A stinging pain jolts up my spine, causing my eyes to water.

"You fucking bitch. Get up." He stalks over to me and then he rears his foot back ready to kick me. I quickly curl into the fetal position before he has a chance to reach his intended target.

My stomach.

Pain explodes down on my backside where I take the brunt of the kick, and I howl out in pain.

"P-Please, I'm s-sorry, I'll tell them I lied, I swear it!" I cry, but it does no good. I risk looking up at him and wish I didn't.

My eyes meet the barrel of a gun.

"I said get the fuck up."

I'm crying heavily now, and it takes me a moment to get fully to my feet. I try and speak—to plead with him—but his gun comes smashing across my face. The blow knocks me backward, and almost immediately, I feel the wetness dripping down my face.

"I always thought you were a fucking bitch. You know that? A tramp who was all talk, probably never put out and just talked her shit, like she was some tough girl. Well, it doesn't look like you're so tough right now, does it?"

I don't answer him, which makes him more agitated.

"I asked you a QUESTION! ANSWER ME!" he screams, slamming the gun back across my cheek. I'm trying to speak, but I'm shaking so bad, and the dizziness is causing a delay in my thought process.

"F-Frank, p-p-put the gun d-down. If you j-just give m-m-me my phone, I'll call right n-now and tell them I lied," I chatter in fear through my tears. "I swear. I c-can f-fix this." There is a small glimmer of hope when I see him take a second to process my suggestion. Please give me my phone. Please…

"You just think I'm some dumb asshole, don't you?"

"No," I whisper in argument. "F-Frank, I don't. P-Please…"

"YOU DO!" He lifts up his gun, and I take that moment to run. I know I can make it to the door and open it and scream for help. "FUCKING GET BACK HERE!" His roar echoes so loud that I can feel the floor rattle. I'm so close when he tackles me. The sound of a gunshot fills the room as we go down. We land on top of a table, my face crashing into the corner. I feel something slice into me, and the guttural sounds of pain erupt from me.

"You bitch! Look what you've done!" I hear Frank's voice, but it's far away. I managed to shield my stomach once again from the fall, but when I pull my hands away, I see blood. Lots of blood.

My baby.

Please not the baby.

I'm so sorry, Molly.

I flip through the next page of the scrapbook my mom made of me as a baby. "And how long did it take you to make this?" The detail is insane. Nothing my attention span could handle.

"Oh, not long. Once you get into it, it's really enjoyable. Trust me. When you have kids, you'll make one for your little girl or boy."

I look at my mom and roll my eyes. "No, thanks. I don't plan on having kids."

She looks at me tenderly, knowing the aftermath of her mishaps have had a huge effect on me.

"Baby, yes you will. You might see things a little cloudy now, but one day, you will find love. And you will have a child and it will be the most beautiful thing you can ever imagine."

"Kinda like how you found love?" I ask dryly. "No, thanks."

She brushes my hair behind my shoulders and begins braiding it as I shuffle through more decorative pages of myself as a child.

"Honey, love comes in all shapes and sizes. Sometimes it's messy and sometimes it can be the most rewarding thing imaginable. As is having a child of your own. You were a miracle to me, kiddo. And you always will be my heart. One day, when you have one of your own, which you will, you will understand."

I turn back to my mom, giving her my best teenage eye roll. "Whatever you say, weirdo."

She offers me her motherly wink and finishes braiding my hair. "I love you, Andie. Always remember that."

"I love you too, Mom."

Chapter Eighteen

Roman

I Should Have Been There to Protect Her

"MOLLY," I SAY ALOUD, TESTING THE NAME again on my tongue. A stupid grin is permanently affixed on my face. We're having a little girl. Molly. My smile falls when I look up at the clock. It's been forty-five minutes, and Andie still hasn't returned.

Me: Stop trying to pack up the entire apartment, beautiful. We'll get it done this weekend. Hurry back. I miss you.

Ignoring the unease settling in the pit of my belly, I focus on straightening the house. I've already cleaned up all the glass and stolen a lamp from the guest room to put in the living room until I can replace the broken one. Another fifteen minutes come and go.

Me: Babe. Call me.

I don't wait even five minutes before I dial her number.

"This is Andie," she chirps on her voicemail. "You

know what to do."

"Call me when you get this. I'm trying not to go caveman on you, but if you don't call me back in five minutes, I'm hunting you down, woman." I sigh and run my fingers through my hair. "Seriously, though…I need you to call me back. I love you."

I can imagine her smirking and saying, "I know," back to me as I hang up the phone. I'm still pacing in the living room when my phone starts ringing.

"Jesus, Andie," I grunt out as I answer. "You scared me when you didn't answer—"

"R-Roman." The voice on the other end is so choked with tears, it takes me a second to realize it's Dani and not Andie.

"What's wrong? Is Ram okay?"

"R-Ram's fine…" A pained noise comes from her throat. No. Jesus, no. "It's Andie."

Ice trickles through my veins, and I become hyper-aware of every passing second.

Tick.

Tick.

Tick.

Don't say it, Dani.

Whatever it is that's about to come out of your mouth, don't fucking say it.

"No." My voice is a whisper but it's also a goddamned command.

"H-He…I know it was him…"

"Who?" I hiss out. "Dani, who?"

"Frank."

Tick.

Tick.

Tick.

"What about Frank?"

"H-He must have f-f-followed her inside the apartment and—" A wail echoes on the other end and it chills me to the bone. "I'm her emergency c-contact. Th-They took her to the hospital and—"

I snag my keys and bolt out the door. "Is she alive?"

"They wouldn't tell me much," she chokes out. "Oh God! I can't lose my best friend!"

Molten fury bubbles up within me. That fucking Frank bastard hurt my woman. If I wasn't so worried about her and Molly, I would hunt down that sick psycho and slit his throat from ear to ear.

"Call Ram. Get him to take you to the hospital. Text me if you get any information," I bark out, fighting furiously to keep my rage at bay. I can't go flying off the handle on a murder mission. Andie needs me. "And call her brother too."

I hang up and climb into the Range Rover. Our new house is on the outskirts of town in a suburb, so I'll have to haul ass to make it to the hospital in a timely manner. With a screech, I peel out of our driveway and nearly take out an old couple walking their dog. The old man scowls at me. Well fuck him too. Andie needs me, goddammit.

My chest aches as though someone has tried to carve my heart out with a rusty spoon. I can't lose her or the baby. We're a family. A motherfucking family.

"FUUUUCK!" I roar and slam my fist on the steering wheel.

Had I just manned the fuck up and drove her to the

apartment, I could have protected her. I was so stupid drunk on love for her and Molly that I completely forgot about Frank.

I should have been there to protect her.

My phone starts ringing, and I mash the Bluetooth button on my steering wheel.

"What?" I bark.

"Oh, sweetie," Mom cries out. "Is she okay?"

Tears burn at my eyes, and I furiously rub at them to keep from crying. I will not cry. I will be strong for my family. "Momma…" A tear tries to escape, but I smudge it away. "I don't know."

"I'll meet you at the hospital. Dani called me absolutely hysterical. Try to stay calm until we know what's happened," Mom tells me.

I punch my steering wheel and bellow, "I know what happened! I didn't keep her and our baby safe!"

"Shhh," Mom coos. "Honey, this is not your fault. Please calm down. You need to drive safe, son."

But I can't calm down. The seconds are ticking away faster now, *tick, tick, tick,* and I'm going fucking crazy. I won't even begin to relax until Andie is in my arms and she's safe. Mom continues to talk in hushed tones like she used to do when we were upset as children. It doesn't fucking work anymore. My heart is being torn from my chest with every second that passes

"I'm here. Gotta go," I snap and hang up.

When I pull into the hospital parking lot, I barely put it in park in a spot before I'm sprinting toward the building. I run in through the emergency room entrance and storm over to the attendant.

"May I help you, sir?"

"Andrea Miller. Pregnant. Just brought in here. I need to see her!" I practically yell at the poor woman with eyes wide as saucers.

"Sir," she tries, holding a palm up to me, "I need you to calm down—"

"WHY IS EVERYONE TELLING ME TO CALM THE FUCK DOWN?!" I roar at her and kick the pillar beside the desk. "I CAN'T CALM THE FUCK DOWN BECAUSE I DON'T KNOW IF SHE IS OKAY OR NOT!"

The girl, clearly new and unable to handle my tone, bursts into tears as she picks up the phone with a shaky hand. Normally, I'd feel bad about making some chick cry but right now as her lip wobbles and she questions someone on the line, I don't feel sorry for her. There is no room in my heart for anything but Andie and Molly.

Please, dear God, let them be okay.

"Sir, it appears that she is here, but the doctors are assessing her now. I'm sorry but that's all the information I have right now—"

I stalk past her when someone exits the locked double doors and shove through them on a hunt for Andie. The woman hollers from behind me before finally I hear her yell, "Security!"

This puts a pep in my step, and I run like I used to back in college. When I had the ball and all those big fuckers were after me. I only had one goal: get the ball to the finish line. And now, as I dart past angry nurses and confused doctors, I still have one goal: get to my family. I see a flash of a black uniform from the corner of my eye, so I take off in the other direction.

"Andie!" I yell as I run past each room. "Andie!"

When she doesn't answer me back, I stall and let out a choked sound. *Please be okay. Please be fucking okay.*

Two strong hands grab my biceps from behind. "You are not allowed to be back here. Let's go," the man grumbles.

I jerk out of his grip and stalk back in the direction I came from. "I can walk without your help, asshole."

He escorts me back out to the waiting room where the red-faced attendant refuses to make eye contact with me. The security officer points to a metal chair. "Sit there and don't move. When there's information, you'll be informed immediately."

Defeat overwhelms me, and I crumple into the chair. *Andie, baby, please be okay.*

"What do we know?" Linc demands as soon as he sees me upon entering the waiting area. "Where's my sister?"

I scrub my face with my palm and let out a ragged sigh. I've been here at least another forty-five minutes. "I don't know. No word yet."

An older guy trots in after him with a grim look on his face. "You Roman?"

The guy looks familiar but I can't place his face. "Yeah."

"Roger Miller," he says with a tip of his head. "Andrea's father."

I'm taken aback for just a moment until two uniformed officers stroll over. "Are you Andrea Miller's family?"

I bounce out of my chair and stride over to them. Linc and Roger file in beside me. "Is she okay? This stupid hospital won't tell us anything!"

The female officer pales slightly and frowns. "Frank Gillson has been apprehended and taken into police custody for the assault and battery of Andrea Miller. He's also being charged with breaking and entering, assault with a deadly weapon, and attempted murder. An eyewitness found him behind the building in a hysterical, suicidal state. They were able to retrieve his gun and restrain him until we arrived. His statement alone is enough to prosecute him, but we'd like to ask you all a few questions as well."

Someone is growling like a goddamned mountain lion.

Roger touches my shoulder. "Calm down, son."

The growls are coming from me.

"That motherfucker," I snarl. "I'm going to kill him."

"Duuude," Linc grumbles. "Not a cool thing to say in front of two cops." He shakes his head.

"He's just shaken up," Roger offers in my defense to the cops. "What is the report on what happened?"

Again the female's face turns ghostly white. "I won't sugar-coat it. The scene was graphic. There was a lot of blood loss from both the victim and the assailant. While the assailant's wounds seem to be superficial, the victim left the scene unconscious."

I stumble back as the room spins. "B-But she's okay, right?"

The female cop forces a smile. "As far as we know, she left the scene in stable condition, but you'll have to get more information on her status from the doctors. I'm sorry."

"The baby?" I question.

She winces. "I don't know."

My mother bursts through the door and makes a beeline for me. As soon as she wraps her arms around me, I feel myself starting to break. I can't do this. I can't wait around for zero goddamned answers.

"Momma," I whisper, the waiting room blurring around me from unshed tears.

She helps me to my chair while Linc and Roger continue talking to the officers. I let my mother fuss over me. I'm told Dani is in quite a state, and that Ram was trying to get her to compose herself before they came inside. Everything she says seems to go in one ear and out the other. I feel as though my body is beginning to numb one cell at a time.

"She's going to be okay," she tells me and kisses my forehead, which reminds me of when I was a kid.

"I love her," I choke out. "I fucking love her."

She sniffles. "I know, baby. I know."

"Are you the family of Andrea Miller?" A tired looking doctor questions from the doorway.

I bolt from my seat and storm over to him. "Is she okay? What about the baby?" I demand.

"Are you a relative?"

"I'm her goddamned boyfriend!" I bellow.

Irritation washes over his features.

"I'm her father. You can tell us what happened,"

Roger tells him firmly and once again clutches my shoulder in a supportive manner. It reminds me of my dad, and for a split second, I almost smile. But then I remember I'm in my worst fucking nightmare and growl instead.

"I'm Dr. Chisolm. Andrea is a lucky woman," he says as he scratches his jaw. "I'll be honest. Things looked pretty bleak when she arrived. She was covered in multiple contusions, was unresponsive, and was bleeding heavily from her face."

I shudder and my knees buckle. Roger grabs my bicep to keep me from collapsing.

"And…" I choke out.

"But after we got her in there and really started assessing her, most of her injuries were superficial. We were able to stitch up most of them fairly easily. It was her nose that required the most attention. I'm fairly certain, though, that she'll be able to heal normally from the break without plastic surgery, but only time will tell. She has some swelling and it looks a lot worse than it is right now. Don't be alarmed when you see her," he tells us.

"So she's okay?" I clarify. "And our baby?"

"We assessed the baby and everything is fine. However, we're going to need to observe her overnight to make sure there wasn't any distress to the fetus. We'll know more in the morning."

"I need to see her—"

"Only immediate family can go back—"

"Son," Roger tells me in a firm tone, "I will go to her. We'll make sure you get back to see her, and I'll keep you apprised of her state just as soon as I'm able to."

The doctor nods at her father. "Come with me."

I stand there like a fucking idiot. I'm not her family according to the worst hospital on the planet. She's carrying my daughter inside her, and I'm not fucking family. As soon as I get her out of here and in my arms, I'll change that pretty damn quick. Another day will not go by where she isn't considered my family, both legally and by the heart.

Twenty-four hours turned into thirty-six, but thank God Andie approved me to be on her family members list once she was conscious so I could go in to see her. That first day when I walked into her room, I thought I was going to throw the fuck up.

My beautiful Andie.

Mother of my child.

Sweet love of my life.

She was lying in the bed with bandages covering her nose, sleeping soundly. They'd given her a nasal cannula to help her with her breathing since her nose was damaged, but she was alive. I swear, the second I saw her, I went blind with rage. Had that fucker not been in police custody, I would have stopped at nothing to stab him to fucking death. If I was a thug who knew how to get people killed in jail, I'd do that too.

But I'm just Roman.

And all I can do is be strong for her.

Which is why, three days later, I'm half asleep in the chair pushed up against her bed with her tiny hand in mine. She's been sleeping heavily—which they tell me is her body's way of healing and is good for the baby. My crystal clear blue-eyed girl would come to for a brief hazy moment, cry, and then pass back out. It was fucking heartbreaking. And Dani…dear God. Every time she shows up to check on Andie, she ends up collapsing in Ram's arms, crying hysterically.

My nerves are frayed and I'm freaked the fuck out. But I refuse to leave her side or waver. I will not cry or show weakness. This woman is mine and she needs me to be strong enough for all three of us.

Her hand twitches in mine, and I blink away my fog. I watch her eyelids flutter. Each time, I hope will be the time she fully wakes up and recognizes me. They've long since pulled the nasal cannula but she still breathes noisily. Dr. Chisolm says that's to be expected as her nose is still incredibly swollen.

Blue eyes blink open and focus on me. Her brows scrunch together as she regards me, but then she winces in pain.

"Owwwww," she complains in a nasally voice that doesn't sound at all like her.

"Shhhh," I whisper as I stand. I lean over her and kiss her bruised forehead. That fucker really did a number on her face.

"My dose hurts," she tells me. "Why do I dound like I'm topped up?"

I stroke her still semi-bloody matted hair from her forehead. "You're all bandaged up, beautiful." I kiss her again and give her hand a squeeze. "My God, it's so good to see your pretty eyes."

She attempts a smile but then winces again. Her blue

eyes become liquid lakes as tears well in them. "Da baby?"

I fight off my own tears. Don't cry. Don't fucking cry.

"Molly is safe," I assure her.

Relief flickers in her eyes, and she tentatively pats her stomach with her free hand. "Roban?"

"Yes, baby?"

She releases my hand to stroke my face. "I lub you." Her thumb swipes away a tear that escaped. "I was so scared I wouldn't get to tell you, but it's true. I lub you so buch."

I cover her hand with mine. "I know." Then, I wink at her. "And the moment we get out of here, I'm marrying you because I love you so much it fucking hurts, and I'll be damned if I let another doctor tell me we're not family. We were family the moment I knocked over your best friend and you kicked me in the shin in front of that bar. We just didn't know yet."

Tears roll down her temples. "Yes. I will barry you, ya big oaf."

I smirk. "It wasn't a question, beautiful. It was a motherfucking statement. You're mine and that's all there is to say about it."

This earns me a smile that lights up her entire broken face. "I lub you…eben when you're being a big-headed cabeman."

"I love you too." I grunt and slap my chest. "Me Tarzan. You, Jane."

She shakes her head at me, but I see the Andie I know so well twinkling in her eyes. "Jane's a cute middle nabe."

"Molly Jane Holloway. I love it."

"Andrea Holloway. I lub dat too."

Chapter Nineteen

Andie

Bring It On, Mr. Holloway

Two months later…

"I LOOK HUGE."

My soon-to-be mother-in-law clicks her tongue. "You look beautiful."

"I look like a fat cow. Like literally. A white fat cow. You might as well draw spots on me," I complain as I smooth out the pretty material covering my thighs.

Reagan and Dani laugh, while Virginia continues to play with my hair. "Honey, I told you. You look absolutely beautiful. So shush with all this crazy talk."

I grunt as I gently tug on the hem of my dress. "I don't, so stop telling me I look beautiful. I look hideous and this dress is way too tight. Who even picked this out?!"

"You did," Dani and Reagan both reply in unison.

I turn to give them both the evil stare down before bringing my eyes back to the mirror in front of me.

"Honey, you look fine," Virginia says, meeting my

gaze in the mirror.

"I look fat! I will forever remember my wedding day as the time I was a fat sausage stuffed into its too tight casing. Fat. Huge! Roman's probably gonna run when he sees me."

Reagan and Dani start laughing again, and I'm half tempted to throw myself at them.

"Stop laughing or I'm going to hurt you both."

"Aww," Dani says with amusement. "We're not laughing at you, we're laughing with you. You just make such a cute pregnant bride. You don't have to put up a front with us. We know you love the dress. It's okay to admit it."

I'm going to kill Dani. Ratting me out. She caught me in my dress last night practically twirling around in it. I don't hate it. I actually love it. It's a white simple knee-length dress, with a heart shaped neckline, which Roman requested so he can see my tits. Pig. The sleeves are covered in beading and crystal, which makes the simple dress, simply dazzle.

It's perfect.

I just wish I wasn't seven months pregnant on my wedding day.

And tired.

And did I mention super pregnant?

Molly has been incredibly active lately and keeping me up at night. She's definitely going to have a big head like her daddy because it's taking up room where my bladder should be, hence having me up three to five times a night. Good thing our fancy bathroom has heated floors so my toes don't get cold on my frequent trips.

The house is coming together nicely. Roman and I have spent every single weekend working on stuff, decorating and planning for Molly. He does all the heavy lifting. Well, *all* the lifting since he will barely allow me to take the milk out of the fridge.

Together, we finished decorating Molly's room. Roman, the sexy handyman he is, built a shelf to store my mom's baby books, so I can show our little girl what an amazing grandmother she had. And just when I thought Roman couldn't be any more perfect, he one-upped himself with one last surprise. A room that had been previously locked on the second floor is now my scrapbook room. While I was recovering, which meant lots of sleeping, Roman was keeping himself busy, building me that room. It's equipped with everything ever made for a scrapbooking queen. Of course I cried like a baby when I saw it. I cried because it reminded me of my mom. I cried because it made me miss her and wish she were here to see it. I cried because I didn't know how I got so lucky to have found someone so amazing.

Roman is my heart.

My life.

He is the father of my child and my soon-to-be husband.

He is what my mom told me about all those years ago.

And I am able to admit that I finally understand.

It wasn't easy to get past the accident with Frank. The nightmares still plague me. When I wake up screaming or in tears, Roman holds me until I settle. I worry I am stressing out the baby, which causes me to cry more.

But the doctor said it's normal.

Often, the guilt consumes me. Had I not been so angry about how awful he used to always treat Dani, I wouldn't have ever provoked him in the first place. I didn't know he'd turn full-on psycho and hunt me down. I never expected Frank Gillson to go from pissy geek to crazy stalker, hell bent on murdering a pregnant woman. And although it was out of my control when he kicked my ass, I could have not sent him hurtling over the edge to begin with. I've whispered these regrets to Roman in the safety of the dark night on numerous occasions, and he always kisses it away, offering me soothing words. It'll take a long time to get past it all.

During the times when I feel close to a panic attack, or the memories won't fade, I grab for one of Roman's many music machines and talk to Molly. I sing to her, even though I sound like a dying cat. I tell her stories of my mom and some of our greatest times. I tell her all about her auntie Dani and her strange obsession with Christmas. I warn her that no matter how much she loves or despises taffy, she is going to have to eat it to make her aunt happy.

I tell her how lucky she is for having such a wonderful grandmother, and how Virginia is going to spoil her rotten. If it's possible for her to spoil her any more than we plan on doing.

I'm learning to be okay on my own again. During the first couple of weeks, Roman wouldn't let me out of his sight, which I was perfectly okay with. I would jump at my own shadow, throwing myself into a complete panic attack.

However, I knew I needed to overcome the fear. I wouldn't let Frank win. I allowed Roman to arm me with Mace and a Taser. He put every single tracker available on my phone and almost convinced me to put a video camera in a necklace. Key note *almost*. I needed to stand on my own two feet. And if I didn't start soon, I never would.

Frank was convicted of attempted murder, breaking and entering, the whole shebang. Too bad for him, when the idiot tackled me, the gun went off and he shot his own damn self in the shoulder. Based on the police report, my apartment resembled a blood bath, but thankfully, it wasn't all from me. The sickness in my stomach never leaves when I think of how much worse it could have been.

Roman refused to let me go back there. He had my entire apartment packed up, cleaned, and paid my landlord for the remainder of my lease.

It took some time to be able to look at myself in the mirror. That asshole did a number on my nose. I wouldn't consider myself a vain person, but when your nose is a size bigger with two black eyes, it tends to freak you out a bit. I won't lie when I say that a few times, catching myself in a mirror while going to the bathroom, I screamed thinking it was someone else, sending Roman barreling into the bathroom naked and half asleep, like a warrior ready to kill anyone in my path.

Thankfully, the swelling and bruising are gone, and I'm looking more like my old self. I've inherited some nasal issues, which haven't been so pretty. Roman tries to mess with me and tell me that I've started snoring. After

Molly is born, I'll probably have to consider surgery to remove the swollen tissue.

Roman kept his word about making us a family, and once I was released, he put a ring on my finger. Knowing I wasn't about all the bells and whistles of a wedding, he kept it simple. Well he kept the *wedding band* simple. He played dumb when he slipped a gigantic diamond on my finger. We both laughed when the band refused to slide past my swollen knuckle, and after we made the sweetest love ever known to man, he took me shopping for a simple white gold chain so I could still kinda sorta wear my engagement ring.

I didn't want a big wedding, and Roman was okay with that. He said he didn't need one, as long as he had me.

I was thankful he was in agreement, because I couldn't even fathom going through all the torture of cakes, venues, tons of flowers, and gaudy bridesmaids' dresses. I mean, don't get me wrong, I love being a part of all Dani's planning, but it takes a special kind of person to plan a wedding. Since I'm not her, I will enjoy being on the outside of that crazy nonsense.

Roman and I lay in bed, matching each other for who could come up with the simplest wedding plans. We went from Vegas drive-thru to a backyard barbeque. Pizza night with a priest. We even mentioned having someone we know get ordained, so we didn't even have to hire a minister!

We finally agreed on a simple court wedding. We were thankful for Dani and the over-the-top Christmas festival she has planned because it got Virginia off our backs about doing the same. She said we were giving her a grandbaby so she would allow us a pass.

Of course just family was invited, which consisted of my dad and Lana, Virginia, Linc, Reagan, Dani, and Ram. The perfect amount of people. I wouldn't want it any other way. Roman put a stop to having Chase at the courthouse, claiming it wasn't a work party, but he was able to meet us afterward at Bender's.

As I stand here reminiscing on how I got to this day, I can't help but feel humbled. I lived a life filled with disappointment and anger. I hated my dad for causing me to think so badly of men and love. I was willing to give up the possibility of love, marriage, and building a family because I was so afraid that it would ruin me. But with the help of the man I am about to marry, I realized that true love conquers.

Life has taught me to forgive.

I have finally forgiven my dad. I have so much happiness in my life that I needed to make room for all the love I was letting in. I needed to let the anger go. My dad cried when I told him I forgave him. Of course then I cried like a baby.

The hardest part was taking the trip with him to the cemetery to visit my mom. He broke down and all the pain he was harboring poured from his mouth as he begged for her forgiveness.

My mom was such a selfless person, that she forgave him long before she died. And I know she is looking down on me with her heart full. Her dying wish finally came true.

"You ready?" Dani's soft voice breaks into my

thoughts. I wipe the tear from my cheek as I adjust the dress one last time.

"Yeah. I just… I just can't believe I'm getting married today." It's still super bizarre to hear that come out of my mouth.

"And I cannot wait for you to become a Holloway. My baby boy out there is one lucky man. He's been searching for someone like you his whole life," Virginia hums from behind me. I turn and wrap my arms tightly around her neck.

"Thank you," I whisper into her ear.

I hear her sniffle, but I ignore it and continue to hold her tight.

"No, thank you, dear. You do know that once you two are married, he's your problem. When that boy gets sick, boyyyeeeee, he's a handful. Good luck to you, child." She giggles and when I pull away to ask her to explain, and fast, the door opens, and all three girls jump in front of me.

"Calm down. It's just me." Ram sticks his head into the private room we've been holed up in while they dressed and primped me. "I hope you ladies are ready, because the groom is about to go all caveman and drag his bride-to-be out of here if she doesn't hurry up."

We all start to laugh while Ram blows his fiancée a kiss and shuts the door.

"All right ladies," I tell them with a confident grin. "It's go time."

As we exit the small room, I notice Roman instantly.

His large frame is pacing the hallway, until he sees me. He stops in his tracks, taking me in. A tightness in my chest forms at how handsome he looks, dressed in a simple black suit. He doesn't wait a second longer and storms over to me, bringing his large hands up to cup my cheeks.

"Dammit, you look gorgeous."

"I look fat," I pout, wrapping my arms around his waist.

"You are everything I have ever wanted, Andrea Miller. If you were anything different, I wouldn't want you." He bends to press a kiss on my mouth.

"So if I were skinny then you wouldn't want me?" I mumble underneath his lips.

"I want you so bad, that this quick court wedding was the best idea you've ever had. The best idea *I've* ever had was getting our own limo to Bender's, because I'm going to need to fuck my wife before I share her with everyone."

Wife.

I love the sound of that.

"Yeah, so you guys do that *after* the vows," Linc pipes in, and I feel Roman's hand whip to the side, in hopes of punching my brother. I giggle and pull away. "Stop trying to hurt my brother."

"But he's an asshole."

"And you're violent," Linc retorts. "Maybe my sister should seek protection for—"

Linc doubles over as Reagan sucker punches him in the gut.

Everyone erupts into a fit of laughter as Reagan pats

my brother, telling him it's going to be okay.

"Excuse me, but are you the Holloways?" a lady questions. "You're up next."

We nod to the woman and Roman grabs my hand.

"You ready to become Mrs. Holloway?"

I look my soon-to-be husband in the eyes and reply with love, honesty, and devotion.

"Bring it on, Mr. Holloway."

Chapter Twenty

Roman

Two Become Three

A couple months later…

"**D**on't move," I growl as I yank her ankle to me.

"You're such a bossy asshole!"

I grab the flogger and slap her thigh. "Do I need to tape your mouth shut too?"

She glares at me as her pale flesh, where I slapped her, turns bright pink. Despite her faux act to seem pissed, I know better. My wife's cunt is dripping with desire.

"You started this," I tell her as I finish knotting the rope around her ankle. *"Oh, Roman, I want you to tie me up like that stud from the Sixty-Nine Shades of Red movie."*

"Fifty Shades of Grey." She snorts. "And I do not talk like that."

"Oh, Roman, spank me and fuck me and do bad things to me," I say in a high-pitched tone, pretending to be her.

"You're a dick."

"Correction, you want my dick."

"Correction, I want you to stop dicking around and fuck me before I have this baby already," she gripes and wriggles against the restraints.

I smirk as I tease the flogger along her gigantic stomach. "Molly isn't due for another week and a half. You're all mine until then." I give her pussy a little tap with the flogger, causing her to shudder.

"You can't keep teasing me, ya big oaf," she whines. "It's not good for the baby if I'm in distress."

Frowning, I slide off the mattress and stand at the end of the bed, staring at her. "Am I hurting you?"

She squirms. "You're hurting me by not making me come!"

My cock jolts at her words. We're both stark naked and ready to play. I just want to tease her a bit first before I gift her my dick.

"Beg me," I demand with a growl as I tickle the bottom of her foot.

"DO NOT TICKLE ME, YOU CUNTSUCKING PRICK!"

I tickle her even more because she's at my mercy, and she starts laughing so hard, I find myself chuckling with her. When I'm sure she's laughed herself to tears, I climb up beside her. She curses me until I shut her pretty mouth up with mine. I kiss my wife hard as my palm roams over the swells of her huge breasts—*goddamn those tits*—and stomach.

"Roman," she breathes against my mouth.

"Shhhh…"

"Roman…"

My finger finds her clit, and I massage her slowly at

first but then quickly pick up the pace. She groans against my mouth, so I suck on her tongue as I drive her closer to the edge of bliss.

"Roman!"

"That's it, baby," I murmur.

She fights against the restraints as she cries out. "JESUS CHRIST!"

I slide my fingers lower and discover she's soaked. Like, really fucking soaked. I jolt up and grin down at her. "I made you squirt!" I am a sex god. I always knew this, but now it's been verified.

"No, you big dummy!" she whines. "I think my water just broke!"

The stupid smile is wiped right off my face. "What?"

"Owwww," she hisses. "Motherfucking fuckity fuck, I think that was a contraction. Get me out of this now!" Her body fights against the ropes.

I stare at her stunned. No way. We still have a week and a half. I made her squirt, dammit!

"So help me, if you don't get me off this bed in the next thirty seconds, I'm castrating you, Roman Holl—owwwwwwwwwwww!"

Her pained moan jerks me out of my stupor, and I jolt to action. My hard-on is long gone as I start frantically trying to untie the ropes at her wrists.

"Get your big dick out of my face," she grumbles.

"I'm freaking the fuck out here, babe," I snap back. "Maybe you could suck me off and then I could concentrate!"

She howls. "How about I just bite it off, because so help me if you bring that thing anywhere near me right now I swear to God, I will owwwwwwww!"

"Fuck!" I yell as I manage to free her wrist. My dick flops around like it's a goddamned cheerleader cheering us on as I race to the next restraint. This one comes loose quicker. I help her up into a sitting position and give her a chaste kiss. "We're having a baby."

Her fury melts away and she beams at me. "We are. God, I love you." Then she clutches her belly and cries out. "GOD, I FUCKING HATE YOU! Why did you do this to me?" She starts to sob, and I'm really fucking panicked now.

I hate that I'm a damn pro at knots after months of practice because suddenly I can hardly get the ropes loose. Thankfully, I free an ankle and then move to the next.

"Everything is going to be okay," I assure her and give her a quick supportive glance.

Wrong move. She's glaring death daggers at me. "Fuck you and your sperm," she hisses.

Swallowing, I throw myself into the task of freeing her. Finally, I manage to get her untied. Another slice of pain cuts through her and she screams.

"Fuck!" I shout. "We need to get you to the hospital!"

"Why does it hurt so bad?" she cries. "I HATE YOU!"

I help her to her feet and guide her to the bathroom. "I know, baby. I hate me too. Fuck!"

I quickly clean up her mess and help her into a dress. Then, I toss on some clothes before ushering her out the door.

"What now?" she questions, clutching her belly. Terror dances in her eyes. I know that terror matches my own. We're about to be parents and neither of us knows what the hell we're doing.

"Two become three." I kiss her sweet lips. "Let's go do this."

She nods rapidly. "Yeah," she agrees. "Let's go do this."

Growing up, I wanted a lot of things. Some materialistic, some not. And being the competitive jock that I am, I got what I wanted. I worked hard and earned it.

Never in a million years could I have dreamed of ever wanting this.

A family.

My gorgeous wife and fucking beautiful baby girl.

And yet, I have it. I didn't have to work hard or earn it. It was just given to me. Just like that. I'm stupefied. Maybe all those times I used to help Grandma Cookie clean her gutters, God looked down upon me and thought, "*Yeah, kid, I have a reward coming your way because cleaning gutters for an old lady certainly sucks.*" Or, maybe Dad's up there, calling the shots. He always was a bossy ol' thing. Mom says I'm just like him, and that makes me proud.

I hope Molly is just like Andie.

Funny and smart.

Adorable as hell.

I cringe. Maybe she could stand to look a little more like my ugly mug. Then maybe the boys will stay away.

Fuck, who am I kidding. She's the prettiest damn little girl on the planet—those fuckers will be crawling into my yard like it's the zombie apocalypse and she's fresh meat.

Guns.

Thank God for guns.

"What are you smirking about?" Andie questions from the bed.

I press a kiss to the softest skin I've ever touched and tear my gaze unwillingly from our daughter to regard her. "Thinking about how I'm going to murder anyone who ever looks at her wrong. You know," I say with a chuckle. "Dad stuff."

Her blue eyes twinkle despite the fatigue in them. "Dad stuff looks good on you. You're definitely a DILF."

I beam at her. "Don't worry, babe. I'm going to let you ride this cock until we have at least ten more of these."

She scoffs. "Slow down, killer. I am not having eleven babies."

Looking down at my angel, I sigh. "She's so pretty, though. Don't you want to fill up our house with more like her?"

"Not eleven!"

"Eight then?"

"Jesus, Roman, I'm not Octomom!"

"Maybe we'll have quintuplets next time..."

"Don't you dare put that curse on me!"

"Mom was a twin."

"No, she wasn't."

"Yes, she was!"

"Call her right this instant and we'll end this."

"She's on her way sooo…"

"Dear God…multiples run in your family?"

"Grandma was a twin as well."

"Now you're just fucking with me."

"If we have twins, let's name one Cookie after Grandma."

"Roman…"

"Ginger!"

"Roman…"

"As in gingersnap…like the cookie…"

"Roman…"

"Or Snick!"

"Roman…"

"Like snicker doodle. Get it?"

"Roman…"

"Snooky? Like that Jersey chick?"

"Roman…"

"Maybe—"

"Shut your pie hole, oaf!"

I snort, but then Molly flinches, so I keep my sniggering to a minimum as not to scare my angel. "Fine, you can name the next baby. But I definitely want more little princesses, like this one."

Andie giggles and it's sweet music to my ears. "We'll talk about it later."

"Later, as in six weeks from now when I'm pumping my seed into you against the shower wall the moment the doctor gives us the okay to fuck again. That's how babies are made, in case you didn't know," I tease but then grow serious.

"God, Andie, I love her."

Our eyes meet and my wife's shine with tears. "I know."

Epilogue

Reagan

Thick As Thieves, Right?

"RUN!" I SQUEAL AS I BOOK IT ACROSS MY FRONT yard to get to safety and dryness. When I bought my perfect bungalow house, I loved it so much. The fact that the garage was detached wouldn't be a deal breaker for me, or so I told myself. Add in a monsoon, and I'm starting to second-guess this purchase.

"You run like a girl," Linc yells over the loud thunder and slamming of rain against the concrete. He races past me with his backpack bouncing on his shoulder. I stick my hand out and he snatches my keys.

"Well, I *am* a girl, so…" I point out as I almost slip, just before my front stoop. Thank God he's quick because he has my door open in no time and we're both throwing ourselves into the dryness of my front room.

"Holy shit!" he grumbles. "It's like a monsoon out there." He drops his backpack to the floor, pulls off his soaked jacket, and removes his beanie before shaking out his hair.

"Stop!" I shriek, as I attempt to peel my wet jacket

off. "You're getting my walls wet! What are you, a dog?"

A twinkle of mischief in his dark eyes is the only warning I get.

"Linc, don't you dare."

His grin is wolfish. "Oh, but I thought you *loved* dogs?"

"Yeah, small cute little dogs. Not big goofy ones." I start to laugh and hold my hands up to guard his next move, which I know is coming any second now.

"Oh, so…you probably wouldn't enjoy this then?" He charges at me, dipping his head down and shaking his hair, splattering water all over me.

"Linc!" I squeal and close my eyes to block any of it from getting in my eyes.

"*Woof! Woof!*" he taunts, and I smack him in the shoulder.

"Knock it off, bad doggie." I'm giggling like an idiot. I swear Linc acts more like a child sometimes than the mid-twenty-year-old he really is.

"Seriously! You're making it worse—"

Just then a loud crash of lightning and thunder booms, startling me. I scream and practically jump into his arms. "Dammit! That was so loud. Scared the crap out of me. Do you think it hit my house?"

As Linc cradles me in his arms, he fights not to laugh.

At my expense, of course.

"What? I don't like storms. They scare me."

"The fearless Reagan Holloway has a weak spot," he says with a wicked smirk. "Interesting."

I go to smack him again, but he tosses me over his

shoulder. The man is solid muscle, and I don't stand a chance of escaping.

"Linc! We're dripping water everywhere!"

"And that's why I'm carrying your ass to your bathroom so we stop creating a mini pool at your front door."

He's dropping me on my two feet in my bathroom in no time. I swipe my sopping hair out of my face. He's super close to me, which always allows me to get a good look into his guarded eyes.

A man with a secret. It's what I've thought since the first time we met.

"Okay, so change, get dry, and then let's drink." He pats the top of my head as he always does, and walks out, shutting the door behind him. I laugh at his typical playfulness and turn to grab a towel and change out of my wet clothes.

I'm trying to peel my wet jeans down my legs when I feel my phone vibrate in my back pocket. I pull it out to see Chase's face appear across my screen.

"Hi, babe!" I'm looking forward to him coming over tonight. After hearing way too much information about Andie and her strange fetishes, I shamelessly took the book she practically threatened I read. I told myself I would give it a few chapters, then lie and tell her I read the whole thing, but I found myself up at three in the morning engrossed in the darn book.

Now, with the curiosity of a damn cat, I've been waiting for tonight to try and swindle Chase into trying some new moves in bed.

"Hey, Pet," he greets. "How was your brother and the baby?"

"Sooo cute! I just want to eat her." Roman and his adorable family just came home from the hospital, and we got to swoon all over little Molly. She has to be the tiniest little princess I have ever held. While she slept in my arms, I browsed through Amazon and bought her a billion bows and little tutu dresses. "Sorry we missed you over there. But we all made plans to have dinner next week. You can see how cute she is then." I rest my phone between my ear and shoulder and attempt another shot at pulling my pants off. I swear, I may have to cut these things off me.

"Sounds great. So about tonight. I'm sorry, but I have to cancel. With the Master's being at Cedar Hilltop this year, I am having to put in a lot of time making sure everything is just right. Right now, we're sorting out a VIP list. I *am* the chairman of the board," he says, pride in his voice. "That means I have a huge responsibility to the country club. Tiger Woods is coming, so it has to be perfect. I'm sorry, Pet, but I just won't make it out."

"Really? That sucks. I mean, about not seeing you. That's super cool about Tiger, though. I just…I haven't seen you much lately," I pout, bending down and attempting to rip one pant leg off.

"Can we rain check for tomorrow? I'll take you to dinner. We can go see that war movie that just released."

I love our dates, but they always seem to revolve around *his* interests and hobbies. I sigh into the phone, trying to hop on one leg. The damn fabric is now stuck around my ankle.

"Yeah, I guess. I'm disappointed but tomorrow sounds fun too." Disappointed is an understatement.

That book really got me all worked up, and I was really counting on letting go of some major built-up stress tonight.

"I know, Pet. I promise I'll make it up to you. Sleep well," he says, a smile in his voice. "I'll drop by your office tomorrow morning and bring you donuts."

"Okay." I hang up and toss my phone into the sink. I doubt sleeping will be anywhere close to being on my mind, since all I had plans to do was stay up all night. I grunt and tug harder at my ankle.

"Come on you stupid jeans!" I snap. I lose my footing and try to grab for the shower curtain to hold me up. I fail and fall into the tub, ripping the brand-new curtain off the rod. The last person to rip my shower curtain was my brother and Linc had to come to the rescue. I'm sensing a clumsy-ass Holloway theme here.

As I lay in my tub, defeated, the door to the bathroom bursts open, and Linc, now shirtless, stands in the small space, staring down at me. He's my best friend, but right now he doesn't look so friendly with muscles bulging and eyes wild with concern. The intensity rippling from him causes me to shiver.

"You okay?" His bulky and colorfully tattooed arms cross over his chest as he peers down at me with an unreadable expression on his face. "What are you doing in the tub, Rey?"

I grunt, blowing a piece of frizzy semi-dried hair out of my face. "Trying to get my jeans off. But the task seems to be impossible. Any chance you have a pair of scissors handy?"

His eyes seem to darken for a brief moment, but

then he flashes me the infamous Linc smile. All perfect teeth and playfulness and boyish charm.

"No scissors," he says with a chuckle. "But how about I pull and we can teamwork you out of those pants."

I lift a brow and snort. "You are *not* going to help me out of my pants, Linc."

He simply shrugs his shoulders. "Why not? It's not like I haven't seen you in your underwear before."

Ugh… It was that one time. In my defense, I was super drunk and had thrown up on my pants. Thank God Linc was there to help clean me up.

His eyes glimmer, seemingly screaming ulterior motives. "I promise I won't look. Anyway, we're friends. I barely find you attractive," he says with a smirk. "Let alone wanting to see you in your granny panties again."

My mouth drops as I gape in horror. "I do *not* wear granny panties!"

His laughter fills the small space as he puts his hands up in surrender. "Whatever. I'll close my eyes. You're wasting precious drinking time, and unless we're drinking in your tub, let's get this show on the road."

I stare at him, weighing my options. I really do like these jeans, when they're dry and not painted on my legs. I'd hate to have to cut them into pieces. And Linc *has* seen me in my underwear. But they weren't granny panties. They were boy shorts for the record. I let out a sigh of resignation. We are just friends. We've been practically inseparable since he came to town, so it wouldn't be the worst thing if he saw my underwear. Which might be white, boring panties, like he assumes.

But its laundry day, dammit!

I grunt because after being blown off and sexually frustrated, I also need a drink. "Fine," I concede and ignore the shit-eating grin it earns me. "Pull."

I stick my leg out and he happily obliges by grabbing my ankle and beginning to tug. "Damn, girl. How did you get these things on in the first place?" he asks upon realizing the pants are going nowhere.

"It's because they're wet," I argue. "Denim turns into suction when wet."

Another tug and no help. "You sure it's not from all the sandwiches you ate at your brother's house?" he asks, and quickly prepares to catch my other foot before I kick in him in his crotch.

"No, it's *not* because I ate food. And those were cucumber sandwiches. They're practically fat free."

He laughs again, giving me the *okay* look, as he bends down. Startling me, he gets super close to my laundry day goods, and I about slap his hands away when I realize he's reaching for the top of my jeans.

"Okay. Hold on tight. I'm going to tug real hard." He grabs for the material, and with one swift pull, slides them off my leg. I would say it was a success. That is, until the jeans get stuck around my ankle. This causes him to tug harder. And me, fearing dislocation of my foot, I wiggle along with each pull. Too bad for Linc, he doesn't prepare his stance, and the second the material lets go, he goes stumbling backward and crashes somewhere in the hallway.

"Are you sure you don't want any ice for your head?" I

ask for the third time, trying not to laugh. He claims he's fine, but hitting his head on the wall as he went down couldn't have felt all that great.

"Head of steel," he assures me as he taps his noggin. "All good."

We're both dressed in warm clothes now, and sitting next to one another on my couch watching TV. Linc managed to find a full bottle of Fireball in the back of my liquor cabinet and we're watching reruns of *Game of Thrones*, casually matching each other shot for shot.

"So what time do I have to take off?" he questions as he stretches his arm along the back of the sofa behind me. "When's your owner coming over?"

I smack him in the chest before bending over to grab the bottle. "Shut up," I grumble. "He's not my owner." I fill up our shot glasses again and then hand him one.

"Rey," he mutters, a slight hint of disgust in his voice. "He calls you Pet." He regards me with an annoyed stare. I have about three seconds of seriousness in me before my smile breeches and we both begin to laugh.

"God, I know," I say with a curl of my upper lip. "Isn't it just horrible?" And it is. I mean, I know Chase is being sweet giving me a *pet* name, but I cringe just thinking about the day he calls me that in front of one of my older brothers. He's been wise enough not throw it out while in front of either one of them so far.

"Super fucking horrible," he agrees.

We clink glasses and the warm liquid soon makes its way down my throat. I should probably stop drinking any minute now. The guy on the television show is quickly forming into two.

"Why the fuck do you let him call you that shit, anyway? Makes me want to pummel his ass every time…" He growls, and I stare at him thoughtfully. "What?" he demands, a defensive tone in his voice. "You're my favorite friend in this world, and I don't like the way he treats you sometimes. As if *he's* the motherfucking catch. Plastic boy has it so wrong."

I offer him a thankful smile. I pat his thigh and let out a huge sigh as I lean my head against the back of the couch where his arm is still stretched across the back. "I don't know. I guess I should tell him I hate it," I agree.

When I turn to face him, he's staring at me with his brows scrunched together. "So tell him tonight when he shows up."

I bite on my bottom lip. "Friends right? No judgment?"

"Thick as thieves." He raises his hand pretending to hold an imaginary sword.

I give him an eye roll, but his usual *I-can-do-no-wrong* smile wins me over.

"Fine. Well, for starters, he's not coming over. He blew me off." I swear, for a second his eyes look pleased, but then he masks it with a sad smile.

"Sorry, Rey."

"Oh, its fine. I just… I was just hoping we would…" I stall because I'm not sure this is something I should be sharing with Linc. Friends or not, it's still pretty personal.

But on another note, I'm pretty drunk, and so is he, so there's a chance neither of us will remember this talk tomorrow, anyway.

"Okay, don't laugh."

"Promise."

"No judgment either!"

"Friends don't judge friends."

I stare him down one last time before I take the plunge.

"I was hoping tonight we were going to take it a step further…in the bedroom."

Linc's eyebrows shoot up in surprise at my words.

"Ugh. Wow…" I trail off in a half whisper. "That's embarrassing. I should have kept that to myself. You don't want to hear this." I sit up and reach for the Fireball. After refilling our glasses, we both clink and knock another one back. The slow burn making its way down my throat is enough to keep any other stupid words from spurting out.

"Hey," he says, his voice soft and warm. "If you can't share things with your favorite friend, then who can you share them with?" He smashes the sweet moment to smithereens when he waggles his eyebrows at me, causing me to snort. This boy is such a clown sometimes.

At least he makes you laugh, unlike Mr. Serious.

I shake away the abrupt and inappropriate thought. "We *are* thick as thieves." I laugh at his previous comment. "Okay, so screw it. I wanted to get kinky in the bedroom. There. I said it. Chase isn't really an outside-the-box kind of guy. He knows how to pleasure me, but it's like Sex Basics 101." I glance at Linc but his smile is long gone. "What? Are you judging me?" He probably thinks I'm some sort of sicko now.

"No, sorry…" He clears his throat and scrubs his palm along his scruffy cheek. "Go on."

Feeling more confident, I sit up and tuck my legs underneath me as I turn to face him. "It's just... I want more passion. I want to try new things, like spanking and maybe hair pulling. I want to know how it feels to have such hot sex that you fear blacking out from such intense pleasure." I look at Linc to see if he understands where I'm coming from. I bet he does. He looks like a man who knows how to toss a girl around. I've never seen him with one, but it's probably because I'm ruining his game by always being nearby. "Anyway, I was hoping to...you know...test it out with him tonight."

Linc is unusually quiet. I probably just made things weird. For a moment, I get caught up staring into his deep, enigmatic eyes, watching his jaw tighten.

"I'm sorry," I murmur and unlock my gaze from his to stare down at my lap. "That was probably *way* too much information for you. How about you tell me about some chick to even out the awkwardness?"

He doesn't say anything at first.

I'm assuming he's just as drunk as I am, and slow on the receiving end, until he lifts his hand as if to touch me. Our eyes meet again, and a storm brews in his gaze. He seems to think twice about touching me because he drops his hand back in his lap.

"Rey," he mutters and then clears his throat. "When Chase kisses you, how does it make you feel?"

I'm caught off guard by his question and frown. "I'm not really sure what you mean."

"Exactly what I'm asking. How do you feel when plastic boy kisses you?"

I stop to think. I try to picture the last time Chase

and I were locked in a passionate kiss. I can't say any extraordinary word comes to mind. All of our kisses are brief and simple.

"I don't know, nice?" I reply, hesitation in my voice. "It feels nice." And the kisses *are* nice, I suppose.

His eyes darken, and I feel like I gave him the wrong answer.

"Thick as thieves, right?" he questions, his voice husky. I'm not sure what our friendship has to do with this. "You'll forgive me if I ever do something stupid?"

"Yes," I tell him with a smile. "You always do stupid things. But we're thick as thieves. Always."

I'm not given time to prepare before Linc's palms are gripping my face and his lips are on mine. My eyes bulge out of my head at his sudden move. I'm about to tug away from him when his tongue pushes past my lips, parting them and inviting himself in to explore.

My mind is beginning to race. The warmth from the liquor is starting to boil in my belly. The temperature in the room spikes, and all I can focus on is the way his soft wet lips brush against mine. The way his tongue tastes of liquor and *him*.

Embarrassment ripples through me when a moan filters up my throat, and I find myself leaning into his kiss. His touch is still gentle but the pressure of his lips has increased. I'm suddenly lost, wrapping my hands around his neck matching him, my tongue dancing around his. A strange buzzing starts in my chest and shoots all the way down to my toes.

This is crazy.

Insane.

I'm kissing my best friend.

But…

I need more.

I bring my hands up into his nearly black hair, which has recently grown longer. I'm craving more of his mouth and lean in for more when he abruptly pulls away. I blink away the dizziness of our kiss and meet his eyes. We're both breathing heavily and his lips are wet and somehow fuller looking than normal. I can't help but lick my own, which draws his eyes down to them.

He runs his thumb along my bottom lip and his voice is low. "That's how you should be kissed." His eyes lift to mine and all playfulness is gone as he regards me with a fierce stare that makes my entire body tingle. "If that ain't what he's giving you, then you ain't getting what you deserve."

To be continued…
Thieves 2 Lovers
Coming soon!

Dear Reader,

We hope you enjoyed our little book and thank you for taking the time to post a review. *Thieves 2 Lovers* will come out before you know it and we're pumped to write all about Reagan and Linc—those two have a story we can't wait to tell!

If you were wondering, K Webster wrote Roman and J.D. Hollyfield wrote Andie. Hollyfield can write some feisty, hilarious females and Webster has a knack for growly, bossy males. Together, it's magic. HA!

If you want to have more fun with us, come find us in our active reader groups on FB. We like popping into each other's groups and harassing each other from time to time (okay every day)! See ya there!

K & J

Acknowledgements
K WEBSTER

A huge thank you to my amazing friend J.D. Hollyfield. You're my hero. You cheer me up when I'm down and make me laugh when I truly need it. And sometimes you entertain me when you try to talk me off my ledge but I jump off anyway because we all know there's no controlling me ha! I do what I want. I'm so glad we started this journey together. You get me (except when I start talking about murder and mayhem) but for the most part you get me. I cunt wait to see what else we concoct, friend!

Thank you to my husband, Matt. I love you more than words can describe. Your support means the world.

I want to thank the people who read this beta book early and gave us incredible support. Elizabeth Clinton, Jessica, Viteri, Ella Stewart, Amanda Soderlund, Amy Bosica, Shannon Martin, Brooklyn Miller, Robin Martin, and Amy Simms. (I hope I didn't forget anyone.) You guys always provide AMAZING feedback. You all give me helpful ideas to make my stories better and give me incredible encouragement. I appreciate all of your comments and suggestions. Love you ladies!

Also, a big thank you to Vanessa Renee Place for proofreading our story after editing. You truly are an amazing person and I can't thank you enough!! Love ya, friend!

A big thank you to my author friends who have given me your friendship and your support. You have no idea how much that means to me.

Thank you to all of my blogger friends both big and small that go above and beyond to always share my stuff. You all rock! #AllBlogsMatter

I'm especially thankful for my Krazy for K Webster's Books reader group. You ladies are wonderful with your support and friendship. Each and every single one of you is amazingly supportive and caring. #Cucumbers4Life

I am totally thankful for my author group, the COPA gals, for being there when I need to take a load off and whine. Y'all rock!

Vanessa Bridges and Jessica D. from Prema Editing, thanks so much for editing our book!

Thank you Stacey Blake for working through a time crunch and always being so flexible. I love you! I love you! I love you!

A big thanks to my PR gal, Nicole Blanchard. You are fabulous at what you do and keep me on track! And also thank you to The Hype PR gals for sharing the love!

Lastly but certainly not least of all, thank you to all of the wonderful readers out there that are willing to hear my story and enjoy my characters like I do. It means the world to me!

Acknowledgements
J.D. HOLLYFIELD

Thank you first to my bomb ass husband. Who always puts me before himself. I know it takes a lot to deal with a writer. So thank you for all those times you've questioned my sanity at two in the morning, and just turned and walked away. Since they haven't invented a word strong enough for how much I love you so we will stick with the four letter word for now.

To K Webster. Thanks for being the peanut butter to my jelly. Even though I think you are absolutely crazy, I still find you to be one of the most amazing humans in this industry. Thanks for such a fun, wild ride. Thank you for being awesome and funny and scary all in one. This friendship has been one big laugh after another. You are talented and kind and one giving human. My heart feels funny just knowing I have such an amazing friend in my life and I cunt believe how lucky I am. I'm thankful for you. And always remember, "We're so cute."

Thank you to my editor Vanessa Bridges and her team at PREMA for their efforts in this story. Thank you to my amazing Beta team, and all the ladies who offered their eyes on this project. Amy Wiater, Jennifer Hanson, and anyone else I missed who took the time to jump on my story and work together to make it what it is today. I appreciate you all!

Thank you to All by Design for the amazing cover! You nailed it. As you nail everything else. (Not everyone. Whole nother conversation…)

Thank you to my awesome reader group, Club JD. All your constant support for what I do warms my heart. I appreciate all the time you take in helping my stories come to life within this community.

A big hug and wine clink to Stacey at Champagne Formats for always making my books look so pretty.

And most importantly every single reader and blogger! THANK YOU for all that you do. For supporting me, reading my stories, spreading the word. It's because of you that I get to continue in this business. And for that I am forever grateful.

Cheers. This big glass of wine is for you.

About
K WEBSTER

K Webster is the author of dozens of romance books in many different genres including contemporary romance, historical romance, paranormal romance, dark romance, romantic suspense, and erotic romance. When not spending time with her husband of nearly fourteen years and two adorable children, she's active on social media connecting with her readers.

Her other passions besides writing include reading and graphic design. K can always be found in front of her computer chasing her next idea and taking action. She looks forward to the day when she will see one of her titles on the big screen.

Join K Webster's newsletter to receive a couple of updates a month on new releases and exclusive content. To join, all you need to do is go here (www.authorkwebster.com).

Facebook: www.facebook.com/authorkwebster

Blog: authorkwebster.wordpress.com

Twitter: twitter.com/KristiWebster

Email: kristi@authorkwebster.com

Goodreads:
www.goodreads.com/user/show/10439773-k-webster

Instagram: instagram.com/kristiwebster

Books by
K WEBSTER

The Breaking the Rules Series:
Broken (Book 1)
Wrong (Book 2)
Scarred (Book 3)
Mistake (Book 4)
Crushed (Book 5 – a novella)

The Vegas Aces Series:
Rock Country (Book 1)
Rock Heart (Book 2)
Rock Bottom (Book 3)

The Becoming Her Series:
Becoming Lady Thomas (Book 1)
Becoming Countess Dumont (Book 2)
Becoming Mrs. Benedict (Book 3)

Alpha & Omega Duet:
Alpha & Omega
Omega & Love

War & Peace Duet
This is War, Baby
This is Love, Baby
This Isn't Over, Baby
This Isn't You, Baby

Taboo Series
Bad Bad Bad
The Brat and the Bully

Standalone Novels

Apartment 2B
Love and Law
Moth to a Flame
Erased
The Road Back to Us
Give Me Yesterday
Running Free
Dirty Ugly Toy (Dark Romance)
Zeke's Eden
Sweet Jayne
Untimely You
Mad Sea
Pretty Stolen Dolls
Pretty Lost Dolls
Whispers and the Roars
Schooled by a Senior
Surviving Harley
Blue Hill Blood by Elizabeth Gray

About
J.D. HOLLYFIELD

Creative designer, mother, wife, writer, part time superhero…

J.D. Hollyfield is a creative designer by day and superhero by night. When she is not trying to save the world one happy ending at a time, she enjoys the snuggles of her husband, son and three doxies. With her love for romance, and head full of book boyfriends, she was inspired to test her creative abilities and bring her own story to life.

J.D. Hollyfield lives in the Midwest, and is currently at work on blowing the minds of readers, with the additions of her new books and series, along with her charm, humor and HEA's.

Read MORE of J.D. Hollyfield

My So Called Life:
Life Next Door
Life in a Rut, Love not Included
Life as we Know it
Faking It
Unlocking Adeline
Sinful Instincts
Passing Peter Parker

CONNECT WITH J.D. Hollyfield

Website: authorjdhollyfield.com

Facebook: www.facebook.com/authorjdhollyfield

Twitter: twitter.com/jdhollyfield

Newsletter: http://eepurl.com/Wf7gv

Pinterest: www.pinterest.com/jholla311/

Instagram: instagram.com/jdhollyfield

55103588R00157

Made in the USA
Columbia, SC
14 April 2019